Jane turned faint with apprehension when the telephone call came for her to go at once to Mr. Windle's office. She hurried wildly up the stairs, not delaying even to wait for the elevator. What could Mr. Windle want of her except to find some fault with her work, or to dismiss her perhaps? And what would she do if she lost her job? This time of year jobs were almost impossible to find.

Her hand trembled so that she could scarcely open the door.

"Are you Miss Jane Scarlett?" he asked, and his keen eyes seemed to search her face.

Jane took a deep breath and nodded. She couldn't summon her voice to speak.

"Well, Miss Scarlett, just step into this side room," he said. "A friend of mine wishes to ask you a few questions."

Jane turned wild eyes to the strange young man and gripped her slender fingers together to quiet their trembling.

Tyndale House books by Grace Livingston Hill.
Check with your area bookstore for these best-sellers.

COLLECTOR'S CHOICE SERIES

LIVING BOOKS ®

CLASSICS SERIES

HOMING

LIVING BOOKS ®
Tyndale House Publishers, Inc.
Wheaton, Illinois

This Tyndale House book
by Grace Livingston Hill
contains the complete text
of the original hardcover edition.
NOT ONE WORD
HAS BEEN OMITTED.

Living Books is a registered trademark of Tyndale
House Publishers, Inc.

Printing history
J. B. Lippincott edition published 1938
Tyndale House edition/1992

Cover artwork copyright © 1991 by Steven H. Stroud
Library of Congress Catalog Card Number 91-68505
ISBN 0-8423-1494-6

Printed in the United States of America

99 98 97 96 95 94 93 92
8   7   6   5   4   3   2   1

THE day had been intensely hot. There didn't seem to be a breath of air stirring anywhere. Even in the great wide store that was supposed to be "air-conditioned" the sultriness of the fervid August day had penetrated.

Jane Scarlett had been working hard all day. Of the two girls who usually helped her at the button and clasp counter, one had been taken sick that noon and gone home, and the other had gone to a picnic. That was Nellie Forsythe. She was pretty and popular with the heads of the department and would get away with it without losing a cent from her pay. Jane shut her lips hard and fanned herself with her handkerchief, after carefully mopping her face. Not many times today had she been able to get enough respite from work to do even that much. It seemed as if there had always been somebody at the counter wanting to look over the whole stock. Not that she had had so many sales, for people weren't buying buttons and clasps in August, unless they saw a particular lovely bargain.

The fourth girl who usually served at that counter was on vacation. She would return in three more days,

that is if she didn't have to take a few more days'
sick-leave to get over her holiday.

Vacation!

Jane's lip curled. Well, *she* was supposed to have a
vacation, too, but she wasn't going to take it. She didn't
have to, of course, if she was willing to give it up and
go on working. One got a little more money if one
worked during vacation time, and she needed the
money. She had practically told Mr. Clark, the head of
the department, that she wouldn't balk at staying if he
needed her. Why should she go on a vacation anyway?
She had no place to go. Of course one could go any
place at all just for a rest, but why bother if there wasn't
any place you really wanted to go? If you had to go
among strangers? Also, she hadn't any vacation clothes.
She was making last year's things do, because she really
needed a warm coat for winter. Though today in the
heat a warm coat seemed less desirable than a summer
organdie.

Well, August was almost over, and then the winter's
work would begin. Perhaps if she worked all summer
she might get a promotion or something, and that
would be nice. She drew a deep breath and gave a tired
fagged look around, and then sighted a girl with a
button in her hand coming straight toward her. And just
at that very minute came the bugle for closing time! It
would work out that way, a girl with a button to match
at the last minute, on a day like this! Of course she must
stay and wait on the girl even if she didn't buy half a
button. That was the rule. She must be polite to late
people. She couldn't put on a distant reproving air and
say "I'm sorry, madam, it's closing time!" and slam the
last drawer back into place as if she had been insulted.
They gave lectures to the girls now and again on an
attitude like that, and she knew just what happened to

girls who persisted in such behavior in spite of the instruction. Of course some of them could get away with it by lying, or acting innocent and smiling judiciously. But she scorned an attitude like that.

The girl with the button hastened her steps and arrived definitely at the button counter now, smiling ingratiatingly toward Jane. The bugle gave the last clear note for closing, but Jane shadowed forth a weary smile, with a hope in her heart that the request might be for something she didn't have.

"I wonder if you can match this button?" said the customer pleasantly.

Jane accepted the button and saw at a glance that she had it. Just a common black gutta-percha button.

"Yes, we have it," said Jane swinging briskly around and reaching with accustomed fingers to the little drawer where such buttons were kept.

"Oh, I'm so glad!" said the other girl with a relieved sigh. "I came in town just on purpose for those buttons, and then I almost forgot them! I'll take a dozen. And if you have a smaller size, about right for sleeves, you can give me a dozen of those, too."

In silence Jane hunted out the smaller size and showed them to her customer, and then with her sharp little scissors cut in half the card that held two dozen.

"It's terribly hot, isn't it?" said the customer.

Jane summoned a semblance of a smile and agreed. Her swift fingers were putting the buttons into a bag and accepting the right change, while her mind leaped forward to her freedom.

"I'm ashamed to have kept you a minute longer than closing time," said the customer as she accepted her package. "I suppose you are just dying to get to your home and put on the coolest thing you own."

Jane smiled then.

"Oh, that's all right," she said. And then, following a sudden impulse she added:

"You see, I haven't any home! I never have had. And I guess after all this store is cooler than the little third-story-back room where I board."

"Oh! I'm sorry!" said the other girl. And then added earnestly: "Come on down with me to the shore. I'd love to have you. We have a cottage right close to the beach and there's a big cool guest room overlooking the ocean. I know mother would welcome you. Will you come?"

Jane felt something unaccustomed like a sudden rush of tears near the surface, and a little blaze of glory came into her pale face.

"Oh, thank you! I couldn't! But it was dear of you to suggest it. Just the memory of your asking me will quite cool me off for the evening."

"Well, I wish you could come. I'd like to get to know you. When I get back to the city I'll look you up. Maybe we can plan something nice together. I'm really grateful to you for being so nice when I kept you after hours. May I know your name?"

"Oh! Why, it's Scarlett. Jane Scarlett!"

"What a lovely name. I won't forget that. Good-bye. I'll be seeing you again sometime in the fall."

Jane watched her as she walked away, a lovely graceful girl in expensive clothes, with a beautiful summer home by the sea, and probably a lovelier one back in the city. But why had she answered her that way? Blurting out to her that she had no home, and never had had one? What a silly thing to do! Sob stuff, that was what it was. The kind of thing she just loathed. She had been guilty of that! She was aghast at herself.

Abruptly she turned and put the card of buttons back in its drawer, slammed it shut, drew down the gingham covers over the whole section and went on her way, hurrying her steps to make up for the loss of time.

And Audrey Havenner, the girl with the parcel of buttons, took a taxi to the station and boarded the bridge train to the shore. In due time she arrived at the lovely place beside the sea and got herself into charming filmy garments for evening.

"Did you have a very uncomfortable time in the city, dear, this hot day? I understand the mercury fairly soared in town."

Her mother said this conversationally at the dinner table after the meal was well under way.

"This certainly wasn't a very good day to select for shopping," remarked her father with a lifting of his eyebrows. "I wouldn't have gone in town if I hadn't had to."

"Nor I," said Kent her older brother emphatically. "You women never do know when you're well off."

"It wasn't so bad," said Audrey cheerily. "The stores are air-conditioned, you know."

"Yes? Well, for all that, I'd have stayed in a cool place by the sea if I'd had my choice."

"So would I," said Audrey amiably, "but you see I didn't have my choice. I went in town to see a friend who is in the hospital and is deadly lonely, and incidentally I did the shopping for the family. By the way, dad, I got your coat buttons that you are always talking about. I almost forgot them too, and went back at the last minute. Came near losing my train in the act. And mother, I nearly brought a guest out with me."

"Why didn't you, dear? Who was it?"

"Nobody I ever saw before. She waited on me for coat buttons after the bugle blew and was as sweet as she could be."

"They have to be or they'd get fired!" said Bruce the fourteen-year-old brother importantly.

"Oh, but this was a different kind of sweetness, brother," said Audrey lightly. "This was really courtesy."

"Heavens! Courtesy in a button salesgirl!" exclaimed Evalina Harrison, a self-invited second cousin who had been with them all summer. "Is that the kind of guests you pick out to land on us? I'm glad you restrained your impulses. This cottage is already overcrowded."

"Why, I didn't restrain my impulses," said Audrey. "She did it for me. I did invite her. You see I realized I had kept her overtime, and I apologized and told her I knew she was just dying to get home and get into the coolest thing she had and rest. She looked terribly warm, and utterly tired out. But she just smiled and said that was all right. She hadn't any home and never had had. And then of course I really tried hard to make her come. I told her mother would have given her a lovely welcome. But she wouldn't come."

"Heavens, Audrey!" said Evalina. "Haven't you any discretion? And don't you know her at all? I don't think that was being very kind to the rest of us. She might have been an awful nuisance. You really ought to think of your brothers, Audrey. A girl like that would be very likely to get notions in her head about Kent, think he was in love with her and all that!"

"Yes, Audrey," put in Kent solemnly, "you really ought to protect my tender impressionable youth!"

Audrey laughed.

"But really, Audrey, I mean it. A sister should be careful about strange girls. You don't even know her name, do you?" persisted the cousin.

"Oh, yes, I do!" said Audrey with a comical twinkle in her eye. "She has a lovely name. I asked her what it was and she told me. I told her I wanted to get acquainted with her sometime when I got back to town."

"Audrey!" said her cousin. "That's just like you! Have you no discretion at all? Cousin Mary, I hope you'll forbid an acquaintance like that. A mere button-saleswoman! The perfect idea!"

"What was her name, Aud? Kent is all ears to hear it!" grinned the fourteen-year-old wickedly, his eyes on the elderly cousin.

"Her name is Jane Scarlett!" said Audrey with a twinkle at her young brother.

"Jane Scarlett?" said Kent looking up in amazement and dropping his fork on his plate with a sharp clash. "You don't mean it!"

Audrey looked up with a startled expression.

"Why? Do you know her, Kent?" A shade of half fear crossed her face, lest after all her cousin would really think there was some ground for her insinuations.

"Great Scott!" said Kent excitedly. "Jane Scarlett! No, I don't know her, but I've been hearing her name almost all day long. She's been more talked of in our law office than any other one person today. Great Caesar's ghost! Jane Scarlett. If I could really locate her I'd get the attention of the office turned to my humble self, I guess! She's very much wanted, and nobody knows where to find her. But then, I don't suppose she's the right one."

"Yes," said Cousin Evalina, "I *thought* so! Some criminal, I suppose! What's she done? Killed somebody?"

"No!" said Kent crossly. "Nothing like that! Just a matter of when she was born and a few dates. You wouldn't understand."

"H'm!" said Evalina offendedly. "She's probably trying to break a will or something. I told you, Audrey, that you should never make up to strangers. You can't tell what they'll turn out to be!"

Kent opened his lips with a glare toward Evalina and then closed them firmly and drew one corner of his mouth down in quiet amusement.

"You're wrong again, Cousin Evalina, but I'm not telling any more about it. This isn't my business, it belongs to the office, and I've no right to go around discussing it. Which store was that, Audrey? Stevens and Drake?"

"No, Windle and Harrower."

"You *see!*" said Cousin Evalina. "The mischief is done. Now if anything happens it will be *your* fault, Audrey!"

The brother and sister twinkled their eyes at one another.

"My sins be upon my own head!" said Audrey comically.

Then there was a momentary cessation of the conversation as the dessert was brought in, and as callers came in for the evening the subject was not again taken up. The young people hoped their cousin had forgotten.

But Evalina never forgot. She came into Audrey's room late that evening while she was preparing to retire, and told long gruesome stories of young men who had made unfortunate marriages that might have been avoided, until finally Audrey was driven to get into bed, and her pleasant regular breathing soon proclaimed that she was asleep, so that Evalina was forced to turn out the light and retire to her own room.

Audrey was up quite early the next morning and walked with her brother to his train.

"Kent! What is this you are going to do to the girl I

discovered yesterday? Because I won't stand for anything happening to her. She's fine! And I shan't tell you where she is if—"

"You've already told me!" he laughed. "Have you forgotten?"

"Kent! I protest! You shan't do anything to her. You shan't get her in any jams. I saw the dark tired circles under her eyes and if you give her any added troubles I'll feel that it was all my fault. Why can't you just ignore what I told last night? Forget it! You haven't any right at all to take advantage of my confidences. I was just talking for the benefit of my family, and it's disloyal to take what I said and make trouble for someone I like who did me a real favor. I tell you truly, Kent, if you go and hunt up that girl and put your old law firm on her track I'll telephone her before you get there and tell her to make tracks for Nowhere and hide till I give her the high sign. I really will. I mean it, brother!"

"Say look here, kid, what do you think I am?" laughed the brother. "A sleuth? Or a gangster? I'm not even a detective. I wasn't hunting for this girl myself, but I knew the whole office force was put to it to find her whereabouts, and it's such a peculiar name I couldn't help but notice. Of course I shouldn't have *said* a word, not before the highly respectable cousin anyway. But you needn't worry about that girl. If she's the right one, which I very much doubt, because they are searching for her up in New England at a school, nothing will happen to her except what is perfectly all right. I don't know just what it is, but you needn't think I'm going to hurt your protégée. They'll only ask her a few simple questions, what her father's name was, and where she was born—things like that."

"It'll scare her to death!"

"Not at all. They'll tell her it's for some statistics the

law firm is getting out, and if she is the child of the wrong father they'll beg her pardon and buy a few buttons and take their way out of your old store, and nobody any the wiser."

"Are you being square with me?"

"I sure am. Now, will you be good? And for Pete's sake don't tell a word of what I said to the cousin with the gimlet eyes. Let her marry me off to a few heathen maidens or whatever she likes, but just laugh."

Audrey gave her brother a long level look.

"All right, brother, when you look like that I know I can trust you. I just wanted you to know that this girl is an all right girl, and I won't have her pestered."

Her brother grinned wisely.

"All right, kiddo. You win," he said gravely, "but it beats me how you found all that out in ten minutes while you bought coat buttons. I know you have pretty good hunches about people and they usually come out right, but I just want you to be sane, and realize that you couldn't be trusted in a casual glance like that to sift out a possible criminal. Some of them are pretty slick, you know."

"Yes, I know. But this girl is a real lady."

Her brother studied her for a moment and then he said:

"Oh, yeah?"

"Well, wait till you see her yourself—*if you do,*" said Audrey sharply.

"Yes—*if* I do!"

2

MOST of the other girls with whom Jane occasionally walked part way had already gone, and when she came out of the store after selling Audrey the coat buttons, her own footsteps lagged as she reached the hot pavement. What was the point in her hastening to her stifling little third-story-back bedroom? It would be unbearable there now, and hard enough to bear after dark. It was too hot to light her tiny flame of an oil stove and attempt any cooking. Even a cooked cereal would heat up the place so she couldn't sleep afterward, and to heat a can of soup would fill the room with the smell of onions. Besides, she didn't want anything to eat. She wished she didn't have to eat. It was too hot to eat. But of course she must eat. Well, probably ice cream would be the best. Ice cream and a cracker. Maybe not even a cracker. She had crackers in her room she could eat later if she got hungry. Perhaps she would just get some ice cream now, and then go around by the little park and sit there on a bench. Perhaps there would be a breath of air and she could get cool. Anyway it would be pleasant to walk past the trees and shrubs and hear the fountain splashing, for it wasn't likely she could get an empty bench at this time of the day.

So Jane turned her steps toward the place where she could get the best ice cream for the smallest money, and after she had eaten it slowly, she wandered out toward the park. But to her disappointment she found her worst fears justified. Every bench in the whole place was occupied by tired discouraged-looking people. Some of them were dirty people, with indiscriminate garments, coatless and hatless, men in shirt sleeves, women in dresses of a bygone day, with straggling hair, a few more smartly dressed but with such a look of utter hopelessness upon them that Jane could not bear to look at them. Not one of them looked as if he had a home, or a family who cared, much less a home by the sea like the girl who had come to buy buttons. That old woman over there with the run-down shoes, and eyes that looked as if they had wept till there were no more tears, what would she say if she were invited to spend the night in a pretty room in a cottage by the sea? Suppose she had such a cottage and could go up to that poor old creature and ask her to come and spend the night with her? Or that young thing over there with the tattered dirty green frock and the three whining children, one of them a babe in arms? Didn't she have a husband? Where was he? Why didn't he take care of her? Well, perhaps he was out of work! Oh, this was a hard world!

She walked briskly on past them all, feeling that in spite of her homeless lot and her little hot third-story-back room, she still had something to be thankful for. And she definitely didn't want to sit down there in the park with that tired discouraged mess of people and class herself with them. Not unless she could do something to relieve them. Doubtless they all had some kind of habitation even if it wasn't worthy of the name home, and they were just out here to try to get cool the way she was. There! There was one who had some sense. Another little mother with two children. She had a clean dress on. To be sure the sleeves were cut off above the elbow, and the neck turned down for coolness, but even the children were clean. They were sitting on the grass against a sheltering clump of shrubbery, one child kicking its bare feet lazily and chewing on a crust of bread, the other sound asleep by an empty bottle. Jane Scarlett wished she might find a sheltering bush and lie down and kick her feet too, she was so tired, and it did seem a little cooler here among the green things. The sun had definitely gone down now, and there was perhaps a trifle of breeze coming up from the river way. Or was it just the sound of the splashing fountain that made her think so? Well, she had better get back to her room. She had some stockings to wash. That would cool her off for a few minutes perhaps, and if she could just get to sleep it would soon be morning. Morning was always a little relief, even in hot weather. And besides she had that invitation to spend the night at the seashore to think about. If she went about it in the right way she could really imagine herself as perhaps accepting it sometime.

As she walked on up the street of closed offices with dim lights in the distant depths, her thoughts went back in her life, and she tried to imagine what it would have been if she had ever had a real home where she belonged.

Then she saw a familiar figure approaching. Who was it? Somebody she ought to know? Why did he stir an unpleasant memory? Oh yes, the new floor-walker in the next department. Stockings! His jurisdiction was just across the main aisle from the buttons. He had only been with the store a couple of days but she couldn't help seeing him often, although she had never had words with him. Just yesterday she had seen him in intimate conversation with Nellie Forsythe. She had inadvertently caught a snatch of a sentence and it disgusted her. He was good looking, with hair that must be a permanent wave, and long golden eyelashes. But she didn't like his mouth. It didn't seem trustworthy. Jane wasn't a girl who lost her head over young men. There had been a mother in her life who had spent time warning her mite of a girl who was presently going to be left alone.

However, it didn't matter what his mouth was like. She didn't know him and wasn't likely to, though every other girl in his section was wild over him and made it quite apparent. He wouldn't ever have time to notice her of course. Not that she cared.

Then suddenly the young man turned his head, looked her full in the face and stopped.

"Oh, I say, aren't you somebody I'm supposed to know?" he asked engagingly.

Jane gave him a level look and answered coolly:

"I'm afraid not." Her tone was distant.

"Oh, but you're from Windle and Harrower's, aren't you? I'm sure I've seen you in the store. You're not from perfumes and sachet, are you?"

"No," said Jane matter-of-factly, "only buttons. I'm on the other side of the middle aisle. You wouldn't have met me." There was no encouragement in her voice.

"Oh, but I've noticed you. Yes, I have. Buttons of course! I've watched you on the side. I've noticed how well you do your work, and how people seem to like you. Noticed your smile, you know. You're a good saleswoman. And buttons aren't easy, either. It takes patience to be a good button salesperson. You had a late customer tonight, didn't you? I noticed you were charming to her. It takes a real lady to be patient and smile the way you did to a late comer on a hot night like this. But she didn't keep you all this time surely!"

"Oh, no. She kept me only a minute or two. I stopped on my way to get some dinner."

"Dinner? Oh, that's too bad. I was going to ask you to have some dinner with me. Well, how about a movie then? I'm not keen on dinner myself tonight. It's too hot to eat. But you and I must get together and get acquainted."

Jane lifted an independent young chin.

"Thank you," she said, "I'm busy tonight. I have work to do."

"Goodness! Work on a night like this? Have a heart, lady! Don't you know this is the time for relaxation? Well, then, how about tomorrow night?"

"Thank you, no," said Jane coolly.

"Now, Beautiful, that's no way to behave. What have you got against me?"

"Nothing whatever," said Jane crisply. "I am not in the least acquainted with you, you know."

"Oh, is that it? High hat? Well, next time I'll try and bring my credentials with me. But how about having at least a cool little drink with me somewhere? I might be able to find a mutual friend if we had the time."

"Excuse me," said Jane, "I'm in a hurry," and she smiled distantly and marched on, her proud little lifting of her chin, and her dignified carriage, covering a sudden tendency to tremble.

So he thought he could pick her up as casually as he did those other girls in the store. Well, he would find she was not so easily picked. Of course it wasn't that he was exactly a stranger. He was employed in the same store with herself, and she had happened to hear his name called by cash girls and saleswomen in his department: "Mr. Gaylord! Oh, Mr. Gaylord! Will you sign this schedule for the customer please!" He was just not the type of person she cared to companion with in any way. A young man who had his hair marcelled and talked to a girl that way the first time he ever spoke to her! It would have been different perhaps if she were in his department and had been formally under his management. It would even have been different if he had been in the store for some time and had been formally seeing her in their regular business gatherings. But she definitely didn't like him anyway. She had seen him stroking Isabel Emory's hand fondly just before the girl with the button came.

She hurried on trying to put him entirely out of her mind, but there was a distinct uneasiness concerning him. His bold gay eyes darting into her quiet life disturbed her strangely, as if there were some undefined alarm connected with him, and that was absurd of course. He had nothing whatever to do with her, and never would have if she maintained her aloofness, as of course she would.

With a sigh she entered the dingy boarding house where she resided. The atmosphere was of numberless dreary meals lingering at the door to meet her, the aroma of greasy fried potatoes, of ancient fried fish, of unappetizing meats, and onions, of pork, and spoiled fat that had burned. It smote her in the face on the breath of the heavy heat of the day, and made her suddenly dead tired and heartsick.

She climbed to the third floor to her gloomy room where the evening sun was scorching in at the single window, pricking through the worn old green window shade, burning every breath of the air out and intensifying the dusty breathlessness of the apartment till it almost seemed unbearable.

Jane shut the door despairingly because the smell of the burning fat was even worse up here than down in the hall. Taking off her hat she flung herself down across her bed and let hot discouraged tears pour out of her tight-shut eyes.

Suddenly it came to her what a fool she was. Here she had been offered a chance to go down to the shore and spend a night in a lovely cool guest room by the sea, and also she had been asked to dinner by a personable young man; she could have had an appetizing meal in gay company, she could have attended a movie in a room that would have been air-conditioned and cool, and she had declined them all! But she still had her self-respect! Why bother about smells and breathlessness? She had this quiet place and her self-respect, even if the air wasn't good. Someday perhaps she might be able to afford a better spot. Till then she had better be content.

She lay a few minutes getting the ache out of her tired feet, and then she got up and washed her face in the tepid water that had stood all day in her water pitcher. It was good to get her face wet, and her wrists and arms, and summer didn't last forever. There would be bitter cold in the winter, with no fire whatever in her room and the necessity of opening the hall door to take the intense chill from the air.

There was cabbage coming up the hallway now, and fried apples, but she knew just how they would look, little gnarly apples, with specks in them. She was not going down to dinner at all tonight. The ice cream she had eaten was enough. She couldn't bear the thought of the dinner that would be served in that house.

She took her water pitcher and went down one flight to the bathroom to fill it, and then got out some soap flakes and washed a pair of stockings and some underwear. After that she was so tired she lay down and went to sleep. The drying clothes broke the dry heat of the August night and made a little moisture in the room, and by and by she had a dream. She dreamed that she had gone to the shore with that lovely customer, and was lying in a beautiful soft bed with a great cool breeze blowing over her, and the smell of the sea in the air. But after a time she suddenly woke up again and the room was terribly hot and breathless, the ham and cabbage were lurking on the edges of the ceiling, and a fire siren was blowing with all its might.

Jane lay there panting with the heat and thinking how hard things were in her life. It was harder now than she ever remembered it before.

She had been a very little girl when her father died. They were living at the time in a tiny apartment in a western city. Jane could remember the many stairs they had to climb, because her mother always had to stop and rest between landings. It seemed that she had always been climbing stairs.

Dimly she remembered the two rooms where she and her mother lived next, and her mother took in sewing. Her mother wasn't well. She coughed a great deal and had a pain in her side, but she was always there when Jane came home from kindergarten, and then from grammar school. And nights when they went to bed early to save light her mother would talk to her, and give her many precepts and principles, wrapped in engaging stories, which she told her were to be remembered for life. And Jane had asked questions and gained a pretty good idea of life and the way it should be lived.

But she never remembered any time when the place they had to live in was so unbearably hot as this little room of hers. Perhaps she ought to give up saving for a nice winter coat and change her room for a cooler one.

Perhaps—well perhaps she should have accepted that invitation to the shore for the night and got really cooled off and rested for once. No! She never could have done that of course. They were strangers, and she was only a poor girl whom they would have felt sorry for and despised. Probably the girl's mother would have been cross if she had brought her home, too. Of course she could not have gone with a stranger!

Well,—perhaps—was there any possibility she ought to have put her pride in her pocket and gone with that manager of the stocking department? Got a good dinner and had a little laugh and a restful time, and perhaps been able to sleep afterward? That was what other girls did, unless they had homes, pleasant comfortable homes, where there was some way to get cool in such intolerable heat.

No, she couldn't do that! Not if she died of starvation and heat would she go with a man who had a permanent wave, and held hands with all the pretty girls in the store, not even if she knew him. She couldn't respect a man like that.

Had her mother been right in giving her such high standards of taste and principle?

Yes, of course! There was no question about that.

After a time she got up and looked out her window. There wasn't much satisfaction in looking. She could only see a limited number of red brick walls and tin roofs and chimneys, with a high red distant glow as if the fire must have been a very bad one.

She touched her meager wash hanging across a string from the bureau to the post of the bed and found everything dry. That was a comfort anyway. She could wear fresh garments in the morning. One was always cooler after a bath, even if it was only a sponge bath, if one could put on fresh garments.

So she crept back to her hard hot bed, and finally fell asleep again, but woke in the morning only half refreshed. She could smell the breakfast fumes rolling up from the open kitchen window. Codfish on a morning like this! Blistering hot! And it was spoiled codfish too, it smelled that way! They had had it that way once before. The landlady always bought enough for two days of anything like that. Well, she would ask for a hard boiled egg. She would not take codfish!

If this heat lasted she must find a better place to board. It was unbearable to think of staying here any longer.

Then her little alarm clock whizzed out a warning and Jane got sadly up and went at the work of dressing.

Another hot day ahead of her, hard work, and nothing to relieve the monotony! Of course there was young Gaylord, the stocking manager. She might smile at him if she were that kind of girl, and perhaps he would ask her again to go out to dinner and somewhere for the evening. She was so utterly sick of the monotony of life in this awful little hot hole of a room, with no cheerful contacts anywhere except such as one could find among her department store customers.

Well, of course that was all nonsense! She wasn't going back on the principles her mother had taught her. She was going to go steadily on trying to do as nearly right as possible. And perhaps some day God would give her a break!

That sounded rather irreverent too. Mother wouldn't have liked her to talk like that. Mother always wanted her to go to church. But she had gotten out of the habit when mother was so terribly sick.

Then there had been the time after mother died, when great aunt Sybil, a widow who lived in Connecticut and had two summer places, one at the mountains and one at the shore, had sent for her and looked her over for a few weeks, finally fitting her out with some indiscriminate garments belonging to her two daughters who needed more fashionable wardrobes, and sent her off to a queer stupid school in the country where you worked for your board and learned very little. But great aunt Sybil had married again, and had shunted Jane off by getting her a place to do kitchen work on a farm where they kept summer boarders. The two daughters had meantime married and passed out of the picture. Then when fall came and the summer boarders had departed, the farmer and his wife bought a trailer, and left for Florida. Jane, obviously de trop, took matters in her own hands and hiked by slow stages to this city where she finally got a job in a department store where now at last she had a small foothold, faithfully doing her best, and working up from cash girl to notions, and from notions to buttons.

But this morning with the heat over everything, and the smell of the unappetizing breakfast coming up the stairs, Jane groaned within herself. Of course she was glad she had made some progress, but oh how long at this rate would it be before she ever had a decent place to call home? Would she ever have a home, a real home? Probably not. Other girls expected to get homes by marrying, but Jane felt she would never be willing to marry the kind of man who might ask her. She wasn't at all pretty, she told herself, as she gave a disapproving look in her mirror and slicked her hair coolly back. It was only pretty girls who attracted nice refined men who could provide comfortable homes. Homes where on a morning like this one could go calmly down to breakfast expecting to find cool melon set in ice, or thin glasses of orange juice, delicate hot biscuits, cereal with real cream, and coffee that was a joy to drink.

With a sigh Jane fastened the buttons of her thinnest shirtwaist dress and went downstairs to begin another hot day.

3

KENT Havenner walked into the office that morning and went straight to the senior member of the firm.

"Well, I've found a Jane Scarlett for you. Whether she's the right Jane or not I don't know, but she's a Scarlett, anyway. At least she says she is."

"You don't say!" said the senior lawyer who was J. Waltham Sanderson and quite well known and respected in the world. "Now how in the world did you go about it to find one after all our combing of the country failed?"

"Well, you see I didn't go about doing it at all. It wasn't my business of course. But I heard the name mentioned so many times in connection with that case that I couldn't get it out of my head, and when I heard my sister mention it quite casually last night it clicked of course."

"Your sister! Why, Havenner, does your sister know the girl?"

"Well, no, she's not a personal acquaintance at all, but she bought some buttons of her late yesterday afternoon at Windle and Harrower's."

"Why, that's most extraordinary! Had she known her before?"

"No, I think not. The girl looked tired and hot and my sister is always picking up friends in the most unexpected places. You see, she took a notion to the girl's looks or something and she asked her name. Or perhaps she was afraid she might have to return the buttons. Anyhow she asked her name, and it was so unusual that she told us about it when she got home."

"Well, that's most extraordinary!" said Mr. Sanderson. "Of course she may not be the right one as you say, but even at that it is encouraging to have found a Scarlett, for she or her family may be able to put us in touch with some other branch of the family. Scarlett, after all, is a most unusual name. And then again she *may* be a daughter or a niece of the Jane Scarlett for whom we are searching. Have you told Mr. Edsel?"

"No, I just got in," said Kent.

"Well, he ought to know at once. Edsel!" he called lifting his voice a trifle, as a man about forty-five entered the outer office. Mr. Edsel came in and stood beside the desk, a tall stern man with keen eyes, and hair silvering at the edges.

"Havenner here tells me he has found a Jane Scarlett," announced the senior lawyer.

The keen eyes searched Kent Havenner's face.

"Sure she's the right one?" he asked.

"Not at all," said Kent. "I haven't even seen her yet, only heard there is one."

"Well, I won't have time to do any investigating today. Not till I get back from Chicago. Why don't we let Havenner handle this himself?" he asked, looking at Sanderson. "I think he could find out what we want to know as well as I could."

"I was just going to suggest that," said Mr. Sanderson.

"You really can't delay that Chicago matter even a train, and I think it is quite important that we find out at once whether this person is the right one, else she may vanish from our sight while we delay."

"That's all right with me," said Edsel. "I'll give you all the papers, Havenner, and I wish you good luck. If you find it is a false lead it won't be the first one we've had. I never supposed any color as bright as Scarlett could be so hard to find in broad daylight." He said it with a twinkle in his eyes. "I'll get you the data, Havenner, and if you can discover anything on this case nobody will be gladder than I."

So, a few minutes later, Kent Havenner, armed with the necessary credentials, and a paper containing questions that must be answered, started out to find Jane Scarlett.

He went to Mr. Windle first. He knew him personally, and moreover the name of the famous law firm which he represented would have given him a hearing anywhere in the city.

Mindful of his promise to his sister he was most careful about what he said:

"Mr. Windle, I'm not going to take your time. I know you're busy at this hour of the day. I've just come to you for permission to see one of your employees for about five minutes. I think she may be able to give us a few dates and names that will help us in our search for somebody. I won't keep her but a very few minutes. We just want to make a contact with her."

"Delighted to serve you in any way we can, Mr. Havenner. What is her name?"

"Scarlett. Jane Scarlett. I have been told that she is at the button counter. I could have gone there and searched of course, but I wanted your permission to speak to her during working hours. And we do not know her address so we cannot go to her elsewhere."

Mr. Windle turned to his secretary.

"See if we have a Jane Scarlett at the button counter, and ask them to send her up here. You know, Mr. Havenner, some of our salespeople are on vacation now at this slack season. I hope she is here."

"I was told that someone saw her there yesterday. But Mr. Windle, don't let us trouble you here. I can go down and speak to her at the counter. It's only a few simple questions I want to put to her."

"That's quite all right, Mr. Havenner. You can see her as long as you wish right in the next room there, and it won't upset our routine here in the least. Just step in there and be seated and I'll send her in if she's in the store today."

A moment later Jane Scarlett, white to the lips with fear, presented herself at the chief's office.

She had turned faint with apprehension when the telephone call came for her to go at once to Mr. Windle's office, and she had waited upon the customer she was attending with frenzied haste, left the sale in the hands of Nellie Forsythe who was languid and apathetic after her picnic, and hurried wildly up the stairs, not delaying even to wait for the elevator.

What could Mr. Windle want of her except to find some fault with her work, or to dismiss her perhaps? And what would she do if she lost her job? This time of year jobs were almost impossible to find.

Her hand trembled so that she could scarcely open the door.

But Mr. Windle was very affable. Could a man look like that if her were going to fire a girl, she wondered?

"Are you Miss Jane Scarlett?" he asked, and his keen eyes seemed to search her face.

Jane took a deep breath and nodded. She couldn't summon her voice to speak.

"Well, Miss Scarlett, just step into this side room," he said. "A friend of mine wishes to ask you a few questions. He won't keep you long."

Jane turned wild eyes toward the strange young man and gripped her slender fingers together to quiet their trembling. Her lips were trembling too. She wondered if others could see that.

"Mr. Havenner, Miss Scarlett. He is of the law firm of Sanderson and Edsel."

Mr. Windle bowed and left them, partly closing the door behind him, but if he had just set up a machine gun before her for the young man's use he could not have frightened her any worse. A lawyer! What had she done that they should set a lawyer on her? Her quick mind reviewed all possibilities and her heart sank. Perhaps something valuable had been stolen and they suspected her. If they did what could she do? There wasn't a single person in this part of the country whom she could call upon to take her part or even give her advice. Even that poor little pauperized school where she had worked for her board, and where they might have given her a character, was not in session. She wouldn't know where to reach one of the teachers, or the dreary old principal.

"Oh God!" her heart cried wildly, and then she realized that she hadn't been keeping in very close touch with her mother's God and how could she expect Him to help her? So she stood there trembling.

But the young man was speaking courteously.

"Won't you sit down, Miss Scarlett," he said, and his eyes studied the girl before him in a veiled surprise. There was something fine in her face just as Audrey had said.

Jane gave him a startled look and sat down on the edge of a chair close at hand, her hands clasped nervously and her eyes alertly watching the stranger.

Kent Havenner smiled.

"You don't need to be disturbed," he said kindly, "I'm only here to get your help in the matter of a few statistics. At least I'm hoping you'll be able to help."

Jane's mind darted about again through the unknown. Was someone else in trouble, and they were wanting to check up through her? But her anxiety was by no means relieved.

The young man was calmly taking out a notebook and pencil.

"Your name, please, full name, and residence?"

Jane answered in a quiet voice, that had in it such evidence of breeding that the young man lifted his eyes with a brief glance to her face, and there came to his own voice a touch of almost deference. He was recognizing that it was this quality in the girl that had attracted his usually particular sister.

As he wrote down her quiet answer he paused at the street address she had given, and looked up again before he set it down.

"Is this your home address," he asked, "or only where you are staying?"

Jane Scarlett answered quite impersonally in a disinterested colorless voice.

"It is a boarding house," she said.

"Then you are not living with your own people, your family?"

She gave him a swift searching glance, as if to wonder why he asked that question, as if almost to resent his trying to pry into her personal affairs. There was almost haughtiness in her reply.

"I have no family. They are all dead."

A kind of shame came into Kent Havenner's face.

"Oh, I beg your pardon! I'm sorry!" he said, and then wondered why he had felt that way. She was just a working girl, yet she seemed to have the power to make him feel himself an intruder in her affairs.

She gave him a level look and then her gaze turned toward the open window.

"This routine business of statistics leads into annoying questions sometimes, I'm afraid," he apologized. "But now would you be so good as to give me the names of your father and mother?"

Jane's voice was steady as she answered:

"My father was John Ravenal Scarlett, and my mother was Miriam Warrener."

"Would you happen to remember dates, or approximate dates of their births, marriage and deaths, and where they were living?"

Her brow was instantly thoughtful, and slowly, with careful pronouncement she gave the answers.

"Thank you," said the questioner, "that helps. And your grandfather Scarlett. Do you remember his name?"

"Josiah Scarlett," said Jane easily. "He lived to be ninety-two. I can just remember him when I was a child. He must have been born about—" she hesitated and then gave a year. "I'm sorry I can't be accurate about it."

"Oh, that is near enough," said Kent Havenner, his pen jotting down the items in his notebook. "Now, was your father an only child or were there other brothers and sisters?"

"There was a sister Jessica who died when she was a child, and a younger brother Harold who left home and went abroad somewhere after my father was married. He lived abroad for several years, but after my father died my mother read one day in a paper that he had returned to this country."

"You don't know where he lived when he came back?"

"No," said Jane. "We never heard."

"Then you were not in touch with him? You couldn't give a clue as to where we might hope to communicate with him?"

"No," said Jane. "I do not even know if he is living. I only know he did not go back to the old home. It might have been sold. I do not know. And anyhow my mother said he would not be likely to live in a plain country place. He liked gaiety."

"Your mother never tried to get in touch with him?"

"Oh, no," said the girl, her chin lifting with just that shade of haughtiness again. "My mother was proud. And she had never known him very well. She went back to the west where she had grown up. I'm afraid that's about all I can tell you of the Scarletts. I've sort of drifted off by myself since mother died."

He gave her another keen approving glance and smiled, and in spite of her she liked his smile.

"You've given me quite a lot of help," he said pleasantly. "If I need anything more I'll come back. There isn't any other cousin or relative that might give me information about that Harold Scarlett, is there?"

Jane thoughtfully shook her head.

"I don't think so. There's a great aunt, Sybil Anthony, the child of grandfather's second wife but he had a quarrel with her. Still, she always seems to be able to find out things. She's married again. She is Mrs. Anthony. I can give you her address."

"Suppose you do," said the young man. "Write it here in my notebook."

Jane wrote in a clear hand, and the young man

watched her while she did it, studying the sweet profile, the lean line of cheek and lip and chin, the dark circles under the big tired eyes. If ever a girl looked as if she needed someone to care for her this one did. Why, she would be beautiful if she weren't so pale and tired looking. He hoped Audrey would not forget her threat to bring the girl out to the shore and show her a good time. He had a feeling that he was under obligation to her for having put her through this questionnaire, and yet of course that was absurd.

She handed the book back with the address. "That's where she was when last I knew," she said, and lifted her eyes for an instant to his, wondering why he dimly reminded her of someone who had left a pleasant memory.

"Well, I thank you," he said rising. "You've made my work easy."

She allowed herself a faint little impersonal smile.

"I'm glad if it helped," she said perfunctorily, and wondered why she had a feeling that this was a pleasant little interval. This man was a gentleman, and it rested one to come into touch with real gentlemen.

"And now," said Kent, "may I call on you again for help if other questions develop?"

She lifted startled eyes.

"Why, of course," she said simply, and turned away back to her button counter again, a vague alarm stirring in the back of her mind.

4

THE floor manager of her section had arrived at the button counter with an irate woman calling loudly for salesperson number fifty-one, just as Jane came back. The glint in the floor manager's eye warned Jane that he was due to misunderstand her if he possibly could. "Miss Scarlett, did you sell this lady this set of clasps yesterday?" he asked fixing a severe glance upon her and showing by his manner that the lady in question was a most important person and not to be angered or annoyed in any way.

Jane gave a quick look at the woman and recognized her as a trying customer who had insisted upon seeing every clasp in the place before making her choice. She glanced at the clasps and saw that one was broken clear in two. Now, what was this woman trying to do? Those clasps had all been perfect when they left her hand yesterday morning.

"Yes, Mr. Clark, I sold the lady the clasps," admitted Jane quietly.

"Well, how do you account for this broken one in

the lot? Mrs. LeClaire tells me that when she took the clasps out of the box this one fell apart."

Jane lifted honest eyes to her floor manager's face.

"Those clasps were all perfect when they left my inspection, Mr. Clark," said Jane honestly.

"Oh, yes, of course I knew she would say that!" exclaimed the lady. "The truth of the matter was she was impatient to go on talking with one of the other saleswomen, impatient because I took so long to decide. You see this wasn't at all the style of clasp I was looking for. I wanted something far better, more smart looking you know, but this girl insisted she didn't have anything better, and kept persuading me that these were the very latest. To tell you the truth I had a feeling all the time that she was simply too lazy to look for something else and wanted to get rid of me. And she certainly must have known this clasp was broken."

Jane was white with anger but her lips were untrembling.

"Have you forgotten, madam, that I laid the clasps out for you in a row on your piece of goods so that you could see how they would look? Don't you remember that they were all perfect then?"

Jane's eyes were very dark and they looked straight into the eyes of the other angry woman.

"You're mistaken," said the customer. "You only laid two of the clasps out. The rest were in the box."

Jane met the other angry eyes an instant and then she lifted her gaze to the floor manager's.

"I had them all out, Mr. Clark. You can ask Miss Forsythe if I didn't. She came and looked at them and admired them on the material."

"Yes, that's right," said Nellie Forsythe softly, nodding to Mr. Clark. "I counted them."

"Oh yes, those two would stick up for each other!" sneered the customer. "I never saw it to fail."

"Besides, the wrapper would have gone over each one carefully, Mr. Clark," reminded Jane.

Mr. Clark gathered up the sales slip and clasps and went back of the counter to consult with the wrapper, and Jane slipped into her place behind the counter and went to work, waiting on another customer, uncomfortably conscious of the snort of disapproval and the sneering expression that the woman of the clasps cast upon her. What was the matter with this new day? Everything was the matter! And it was going to be another scorcher, too! Oh, everything was wrong!

The floor manager came out from behind the wrapper's counter apologetically, and led the irate clasp lady aside for an earnest talk, his face suave but firm. Jane could catch a word now and then.

"They are lying of course, both those girls!" said the clasp woman furiously. "They ought to be dismissed, both of them!"

Jane lifted cold tired eyes and gave one glance at the woman. What hell on earth one misguided mistaken woman could make for a poor salesgirl. She didn't care for herself. She could pay for the clasp, though she knew the woman herself must have broken it, but she couldn't stand the thought that the little wrapper would have to bear the expense. The wrapper had a sick mother and a baby brother with a curvature of the spine, and her tiny salary was sometimes all that came into the household from week to week. Hilda shouldn't have to bear it anyway. She shut her lips in a firm determined line. She would go to Mr. Clark after this pest of a woman was gone and tell him all about how hateful the woman had been, insisting that there must be something different hidden away that they didn't want to bother to show her. She would offer to take the blame rather than have Hilda have to bear it. Poor Hilda. She could see the fear in her eyes, and a furtive tear, as she passed the little alcove where Hilda wrapped packages all day long.

The other girls at the counter cast pitying glances at Jane's grim countenance.

"You should worry!" said Nellie Forsythe as she brushed by her to get the drawer of white pearl buttons. "Don't let that old Clark get your goat! He's only trying to toady to that high flier. Isn't she the limit! I've seen her kind before. She just wants to make trouble. She's no lady! I'll bet she broke it herself and didn't want to pay for it. Some of those millionaires are just too stingy to live. I'd like to see 'em poor themselves for a little while."

Jane cast a fleeting pale smile toward her unexpected champion and went on her busy way through the morning.

At noon she sought out the floor manager.

"Mr. Clark," she said a little breathlessly, "I came about that broken clasp. I didn't break it and neither did Hilda, but if anybody's got to stand for it I will, not Hilda. She can't! She's got a sick mother and little brother to support and she's half starved herself."

"Somebody broke that clasp, Miss Scarlett," said the cold hard tones of Clark. He was new in the department and trying to show what good discipline he could establish. "Somebody has to pay for it."

"Yes," said Jane with that almost imperceptible lifting of her chin that gave her a patrician look, "somebody evidently broke it, but it was not broken when I gave the package to Mrs. LeClaire. I know that for I stood beside Hilda while she inspected each one. The lady was in a rush as she always is and I waited to take it right to her. And I know those clasps were every one perfect when they left this house. But Hilda shan't stand the blame, anyway. She's crying her heart out this minute and won't be fit to work tomorrow if this goes on. And she can't afford to stay at home!"

The cold hard eyes of the floor manager studied her sharply and the tight line of his lips relaxed a trifle.

"Very well, Miss Scarlett, I'll speak to Mr. Windle about it. You understand that Mrs. LeClaire is a very important customer. But of course somebody has to pay for that clasp."

Jane gave Mr. Clark a despairing look and bowed, trying to choke back her rising indignation.

"Very well, Mr. Clark. In that case I'll pay for it!"

She turned away quickly lest the telltale tears would appear in her eyes, and hurried off leaving him looking after her, wondering over her erect carriage, the patrician way in which she held her shoulders. Somehow she impressed him even more than the irate customer whom he had to humor because of her millions. Still, if Jane Scarlett broke that buckle she ought to suffer for it.

So Jane went out and bought a five cent package of peanut butter sandwiches, although she loathed them because she had eaten so many of them exclusive of other fare, and took a good draught of ice water afterwards, and determined to eat five cent lunches for a couple of weeks to make up for the price of that crystal clasp.

But there were too many tears in Jane's throat to make a dry lunch like that very palatable just now and Jane, after a bite or two slipped her package in her little cheap handbag and went around on what she called a window-shopping expedition, just to take her mind off the unpleasant things.

She went to the coat section and took another look at the green coat with the brown beaver fur collar that she so hoped to be able to buy before it was gone. She wouldn't get on very fast saving for it at this rate, not with paying for expensive crystal clasps. There! She must forget that. Why in the world couldn't she put it out of her mind entirely and just be comfortable?

It was just then she realized that there was something else on her mind besides that broken clasp. She searched probingly for it and found it was the visit of that young man searching for statistics about the Scarlett family. The more she thought about it the more she became alarmed at the thought that he might be coming after her again. Why hadn't she made it plain that she had told him everything she knew about the family? Oh, what else could he possibly be wanting? Was there something dark and sinister in the history of the family and were they trying to pin it to her branch? Were they possibly trying to pin something upon herself?

Her mind went quickly back over her brief life since her mother died. Was it conceivable that somebody at the school or the boarding house where she had worked had missed something valuable and fixed upon her as the one who had taken it?

But how ridiculous! It was just because of that unpleasant happening about the clasp. She must be all wrought up, to get up ideas like that. And that pleasant young man hadn't suggested any such thing either. What had he said, anyway? Something about collecting statistics about the Scarletts. But a lawyer's firm wouldn't be getting up a family tree, would they? Oh, it was all a mix up. And what could she do about it?

She turned languidly away from the lovely green coat. Why had she thought it so desirable anyway? How hot the cloth looked! And fur around one's neck! Ugh!

She closed her eyes and drew a deep quivering breath. Suddenly she seemed to have reached her limit. Everything had gone against her. If only her mother were living and she could go home and put her head down in her lap and cry it out, and tell her everything!

Well, of course it was idle to think of that! It only meant she would be unnerved for her afternoon's work. Oh, how her head ached and how faint she felt! She must manage to eat another bite or two of those crackers, or drink some more water, or something.

Just then she came face to face with the young head of the stocking department, and his greeting was most effusive.

"Now, look who's here!" he exclaimed. "Could anything be more delightful! I was just looking for a companion to help me while away my noon hour."

"Sorry," said Jane in her most businesslike tone, "I'm just finishing mine. You'll have to look farther."

"But surely I saw you just leaving the button counter not five minutes ago!" protested the young man.

"Are you quite sure you know me from the others?" asked Jane impishly as she turned and slid into an elevator.

As the elevator slipped smoothly down out of sight Jane made a mental resolve to watch herself when homing time came at night, and not be in this young man's way. She didn't want her life further complicated at this stage by this doubtful stranger. She wasn't at all sure she would care to have him around at any time.

So she entrenched herself behind her counter and kept her eyes strictly on her customers of whom there were plenty. She didn't even see young Gaylord when he arrived back at his precinct. She was trying her best to keep so busy that she would not think nor puzzle over her perplexities.

"Oh, are you back already?" welcomed the next girl whose turn it was to take lunch time. "Why, you haven't had your full time."

"I wasn't hungry," said Jane evasively. "Yes madam, we have crystal buttons. What size?"

"Oh, do you really mean it?" questioned the other girl in a whisper. "I was just counting the minutes. A friend of mine has something to tell me and she was afraid her noon hour would be over before mine began. Do you mind if I go now?"

"Go on," said Jane with a satisfaction in her voice that would easily pass for a smile. Jane had forgotten to take the second bite of those neat dry crackers. The faintness that was enveloping her now and then was something primitive, something to be fought and kept under. After all, why should she miss one little meal? She had often gone without several without feeling it much. One got used to going without food. "Yes madam, we have a smaller size of the same button."

The customers were coming in droves, it seemed to her. Why did everybody want buttons on such a hot day? She tried to focus her eyes on a woman who was questioning her, and realized that she was dizzy. What was the matter with her? She wasn't ever dizzy. Was everything getting her? Was she going soft so that she'd be unable to cope with life as it presented itself to her day by day? Of course she hadn't eaten much that morning,— that sickening smell of spoiled codfish over everything! Ugh! She could smell it now! Or was that the lobster she had glimpsed on the chef's long table by the tearoom door a little while ago? If she were up in that tearoom now as a shopper selecting her fare from the menu what would she choose? Not lobster! Not codfish! Not even ice cream! She was beyond all that. Just something hot and thin and heartening. The kind of lunch her mother used to bring her when she was a little girl, and sick. Fragrant toast from homemade bread, buttered and salted and wet with boiling water, and then a steaming cup of tea that smelled like roses. That was what she wanted and nothing else. Could a body be sustained by the thought of the right food when one couldn't actually get it?

She smiled to herself at the queer vagaries of her troubled mind. If her customers could read her thoughts they would think she was crazy. If her floor manager could know what was passing through her mind she would lose her job.

But her mind continued to function steadily on, her fingers worked accustomedly, and the buttons were marshaled into ranks and went out into the world to appear on costumes. But Jane was growing fainter and fainter, and the heat grew more and more unbearable to her till it came to seem as if she could not breathe another breath. Yet she went on, answering the questions lifelessly that were put to her.

It was growing late in the afternoon. She could just see the clock from one end of the counter but somehow suddenly its figures did not mean a thing to her when she looked at them. She put a hand dazedly to her forehead and tried to take a deep breath, but something failed within her, and all at once she crumpled into a little heap on the floor behind the counter.

She had just handed a customer a package, and the woman had turned away. The other two girls were busy one at either end of the counter, and did not notice Jane for a full minute after it happened, and she lay there quite still till one of them coming in haste to look for wooden buttons almost fell over her, and gave a quiet alarm to the floor manager.

The wrapper in her little alcove abandoned her

wrapping and was down on her knees beside Jane with a glass of water she had slipped into her cage, and a bit of a handkerchief, bathing Jane's face, when Mr. Clark came blustering to see what was the matter, his fault-finding frown upon his face as if he would be ready to blame Jane for not foreseeing this possibility and guarding against it.

But when he saw Jane's white impassive face even his Clark-frown disappeared and he blustered at all the others, giving orders right and left. The few customers left stood around staring and saying what awful weather it was, and stretching their necks to see which girl it was who had fainted. One lady produced a bottle of smelling salts. And after a time, which seemed a long time, Jane vaguely opened her eyes and closed them again with a sorrowful little trembling sigh, and all the ladies on that aisle looked and said "Oh!" in various stages of sympathy and interest and curiosity.

A boy presently brought a wheeled chair, as even Mr. Clark could not seem to induce Jane to take an interest in walking, and they wheeled her off to the freight elevator, Nellie Forsythe walking importantly by her side with her hand on the chair, and Mr. Clark circling around it and giving directions, clearing the way with authoritative gestures.

But the passing of Jane took but a brief instant and then the summer crowds closed in and the aisle was as full as usual, only that the ladies who wanted buttons tapped their impatient toes on the floor and wondered why the button counter was manned by a single girl.

Young Gaylord on the stocking side of the main aisle looked tentatively over to the button counter several times late that afternoon, with a view to dating up Jane, wholly because she had seemed so indifferent, but Jane was not in sight. She had meant to slip out through the counter back of the wrapping desk, and so make her way to a street door without his seeing her, but she had no need for diplomacy. It had all been managed nicely for her instead. Jane was lying in a little white soft bed in the hospital of the store on the ninth floor, with a white garbed nurse watching over her, and an electric fan cooling the air about her.

The nurse was feeling her pulse.

"When was your lunch hour?" she asked crisply.

"Eleven-thirty," murmured Jane, wondering why she cared.

"What did you have for lunch?" asked the nurse in a quiet interested voice as if she were saying to a baby: "See the birdie?"

"Why, I didn't have much. It's in my handbag somewhere," said Jane feeling aimlessly around on the bed with one hand. "I didn't eat but a bite. I wasn't hungry." Her voice was very weak.

"I thought so," said the nurse. She vanished into a tiny kitchen from whence came presently an appetizing odor, and then she was back with a cup of delicious chicken broth which she fed to Jane.

"There!" said the nurse when she had finished feeding her the soup. "Now, shut your eyes and take a good sleep. Then they'll send you home in a taxi, and tomorrow morning if it is still hot I'd stay in bed all day. They won't expect you back. I'll tell them you ought to have three days off at least."

"Oh, I couldn't!" said Jane, roused at last. "I couldn't afford to lose time."

"You have a right to three days' sick leave, you know," said the nurse. "I'll tell them you should."

"Oh, I'll be all right with a few minutes' rest," said Jane and drifted off into the most restful sleep she had had for months.

The trumpets were sounding the signal for closing when Jane woke up again, and the nurse fed her more soup and took her home in a taxi.

"I hope you have a cool room," she remarked hopefully as she glanced doubtfully up at the dismal looking boarding house.

"I haven't," said Jane decidedly. "You wouldn't expect it in a house like that in this neighborhood, would you?"

"No, I suppose not," said the nurse regretfully, "but why do your people live here when there are so many nice little suburbs where you could live almost as cheaply, I should think? Do they have to be here? Do they own the house?"

"I haven't any people," said Jane trying to speak resignedly. "This is a boarding house. I suppose somebody owns it, but I don't know why."

"Then why do you stay here?" asked the nurse. "I know a peach of a place. It's eleven miles out and it isn't expensive. It's co-operative."

"There'd be the carfare in," said Jane despondently. "It sounds nice but I guess it's not for me, yet. Not till I get a raise."

"Well, I'm sorry," said the nurse. "If I wasn't going away for the week-end I'd invite you out to stay with me over Sunday. You need a change and a rest or you're due for a breakdown."

"Oh, I think I'll be all right tomorrow," said Jane determindedly. "I've got to be. Tomorrow's pay day, and I've got to pay a dollar and a quarter for a crystal clasp a customer broke herself and then charged me with."

"What a shame!" said the nurse indignantly. "I think if you'd go to Mr. Windle he'd do something about that."

"I'd rather pay a dollar and a quarter than go to Mr. Windle. Good-bye. I thank you for all you've done for me! And for that wonderful soup. It seemed like soup my mother used to make!"

"Well, my advice to you is to go home, wherever home is and stay with your mother."

"Yes?" said Jane somewhat bitterly. "Well, perhaps I will. Who knows? She happens to be in heaven though, and one can't just go to heaven when one feels like it. But meantime I wish I had a lovely cool room with palms and ferns around it and a view of the ocean with cool breezes to invite you up to right now. I'd serve you with delectable cakes and ices and make you understand how grateful I am for what you've done for me."

The nurse smiled and squeezed her hand.

"I'm sorry," she said penitently, "I didn't know, of course. Now don't forget to run up to the hospital room and call on me when you get back to the store. Good night. Be careful what you eat for a day or two, and no more starving, understand, or you'll be worse off than you are now."

Jane smiled and went slowly into the house.

How she dreaded to go up all those stairs. And there was ham for dinner. She knew by the smell. Ham and cabbage again! So she decided to subsist on the memory of the chicken soup and go to sleep at once if the heat would let her.

Up in her room she took off her dress and dropped down weakly upon the bed. Oh, if there were only a way to have a pleasant comfortable room and plain decent food! Well, if she lived through this she would try to manage a change as soon as possible.

Then her thoughts reverted to the morning. The interview with the young lawyer. The man with the kind eyes. He would be somewhere now in a cool place she was sure. He would be about to have a good dinner with pleasant people. He had the atmosphere of such a background. Any girl he knew would be well cared for and wouldn't have to worry. He wasn't the kind of young man who drank and was undependable. How she would enjoy it to have a few friends like that who were decent and friendly and good fun. Well, she mustn't expect anything like that, but if ever she got on at all she would have something to call home. A room in a pleasant house in a wide airy street no matter if it wasn't fashionable. Old fashions were best anyway. Brick perhaps, with high ceilings and vines on the house. Wide windows and pretty curtains. Cool in summer and warm in winter. A little fireplace some-where with the brightness and comfort of firelight! A canary in a pretty gilt cage. But how could she have a canary if she stayed in the store? A canary would have to have someone to care for it.

She would have a pretty rug. Perhaps not an oriental, but one with soft colors. And a bookcase with books she loved. A desk to sit and write letters at, only she knew no one to write to, and a little table to have five o'clock tea on with frosted cakes, when her friends came in! Only she had no friends!

But of course there would be friends if one had a place to invite them to.

There would be deep chairs, too, with soft cushions, and a couch where one could drop down and read and get all the ache out of one's bones. Home! It would be a home! Even if it were but one room it could be home.

Well, if one could make a home out of one room why could she not make a semblance of home here in this third story back?

Here with the smell of cabbage and ancient ham? With the noises of the street, and the thunder of the railroad beyond the back fence? Well, why not? It had four walls. What if they were blackened with smoke, and stained from their years of service? They were clean, for she had washed them down herself when she first moved in. Here with only a box for a wash stand and a tin pitcher and bowl that did not match. There was a calico curtain around it for she had tacked it there herself, and underneath were her other pair of shoes that needed to be half-soled, and her shoe polish and her dust rag. And there was the ugly painted bureau with its paint half gone, and its warped distorted mirror that needed resilvering. It had four drawers where she could keep her simple wardrobe. Some hall bedrooms hadn't even that. And over there in the corner around the nails on which she hung her garments there was another calico curtain. She had bought it and hemmed it and put it up herself. She was thankful for that. It did make her room more like a habitation. Even if it was unbearably hot and smelly in summer and unbearably cold and lonely in winter. It had a touch all her own. But some day she would have a real home that she had made. That is, if she lived long enough to have one. It would take hard work. It would mean that she had to concentrate on a home and nothing else. So far there was no one to make a home for her, and she was sure, sure she would never find a man she was willing to marry who would want to marry her, so why not have a home as a life ambition?

When she dropped down on her hard little bed words came to her mind that she had learned when a child:

"In my Father's house are many mansions. If it were not so I would have told you. I go to prepare a place for you. And if I go and prepare a place for you I will come again and receive you unto myself, that where I am there ye may be also."

And then it came to her that perhaps that was the only home she would ever have. Perhaps the nurse had been right and she was really run down. Perhaps she wasn't going to live very long and was going Home to the many mansions, to where her mother was, to her Father's House!

She closed her eyes and drifted off to sleep, and over and over there rang the words in her ears:

"In my Father's house are many mansions!"

Mansions, not just hall bedrooms!

When she awoke later in the evening she was gasping with the heat, and she stumbled up and dipped a towel in water, hanging it in her window to cool the air a little.

"In my Father's house! My Father's house!"

5

MR. Clark, the floor manager, was worried at the ghastly look in Jane's white face. He carried the memory of her eyes and the look in them with him as he went away from the freight elevator. Was that girl taking it to heart like that about the crystal clasp? Perhaps she didn't break it after all.

He went and hunted up Hilda and made her cry again asking her questions, till he didn't know but he was about to precipitate another collapse in the button department. So in desperation he told her not to worry any more, that Jane had offered to pay for it, but he would fix it so that neither of them would have to do it. It was unprecedented, such generosity from Mr. Clark. Hilda dried her eyes and beamed out a watery smile at him and to his amazement he felt a twinge of something new in his experience. Was it joy? It didn't seem possible. He didn't know joy ever came from acts that were not done for one's self. Perhaps he would try it again sometime if he didn't forget it. Well, anyway he would settle once for all about that clasp. So he took a dollar and a quarter out of his own pocket and went up to the credit department and adjusted the matter so it would never come up again to trouble anybody. Of course Mrs. LeClaire herself should have paid it, but as it was he suddenly felt himself rise far above the millionaire lady in his own esteem. He hadn't suspected himself of having such generous qualities, and he left the store quite pleased with himself. He went home and gave his little three-year-old a whole dime to put in the Sunday School collection and his wife looked at him in amazement and asked him if he really felt well.

That night there were other supper tables besides the Clark one, where Jane's eventful day made a difference. The nurse had been invited to dine with an old school friend in a beautiful house where everything was ordered and cool and delightful. The friend's father and mother were present and the talk was general.

"I had a young patient today who interested me greatly," said the nurse. "She was overcome by the heat and was sent up to me. I found she had had no lunch and I imagine scarcely any breakfast. I fed her soup, and petted her up, and took her home when the store closed. But I found the poor thing lives in the most unspeakable neighborhood. Noisy and dirty and crowded. A boarding house of the worst possible type. How she is going to survive till cool weather I don't see. It's a crime to own a place like that boarding house. It ought to be pulled down, and nice cool livable quarters made for poor folks."

Her friend and her mother expressed sympathy for the poor girl and wished they could do something for her. The head of the house asked a few chary questions, for he had great possessions, mostly in tenement property, and an atrophied conscience got up and stirred with him. He told himself that he didn't know but he

would do something about some of his property sometime.

Kent Havenner came home to the seashore and
grinning announced to his sister:

"Well, I interviewed your glamorous button-vender
today!" He said it in a low tone while the hostile cousin
was telling their mother about her experiences that
afternoon at the Woman's Club.

"Yes?" said Audrey quickly alert. "How did you find
her?"

"Haughty!" said Kent. "She answered my questions
as briefly as possible and walked back to her work."

"Kent, you didn't annoy her in any way?" His sister
studied him searchingly.

"Well, I'm not sure," twinkled Kent. "I think I got
her guessing toward the end."

"Kent, you promised me!"

"Did I? What did I say?"

Then came the cousin:

"What are you two saying? Am I missing something?" she attacked playfully, in a kittenish manner she
had.

"Yes, you are," said Kent with a wicked grin. "You
always miss something when you fail to hear what I
say!" and he sauntered provokingly out of the room.

And the two girls, her fellow workwomen at the
button counter talked her over as they walked part way
home that night.

"Did you know she was called up to the office this
morning?" said Nellie.

"*No!* Was she? Don't you suppose it was about that
silly old crystal clasp?"

"No, it was before that LeClaire woman came in. A
boy from Mr. Windle's office came down to call her. I
heard him. 'Mr. Windle wants to see you in his private

office!' Just like that! And she turned as white as white—! Who is she anyway? Where did she work before she came to our store? She's mighty close-mouthed, I think."

"I don't know. Somewhere up in New England, she said. Maybe Boston. I forget. But if you ask me, *I* think she's a perfectly grand girl."

"Oh, but they never would send for her to Mr. Windle's office unless something was wrong. You can better believe they've found something crooked, or else she's been careless."

"She isn't careless. She's very conscientious."

"Well, say, she didn't faint for nothing this afternoon, did she? There must have been something pretty awful or she wouldn't have passed out that easy."

"Say, look here, it's been pretty awfully hot, and she's been here all summer when you and I were off having a good time at the shore."

"Well, we didn't any of us pass out for the heat, did we? It's my opinion she had some good reason for flopping, if you ask me."

"Maybe she did. I'm sure I don't know. But it's none of our business unless she tells us, and anyhow I like her. She's a good scout. She sold some buttons to a good customer of mine who asked for me, and she charged them up as if *I'd* sold them. I'll say that was pretty decent of her when I was off on vacation."

"Who told you?" said Nellie suspiciously. "Did she tell you herself? Because I'd check up on it if she did. That sounds pretty phony to me."

"No, she didn't tell me. Miss Leech at the desk told me. She said she came and asked her how to give me the credit, because she knew the woman always bought from me. But anyhow I like her, and if I were you I wouldn't be so hard on another girl. You can't tell what kind of a fix you or I might get into, at that."

"I never do anything I'll get caught at!" said the other sullenly.

"Still you might even at that, and then you wouldn't want the rest of us to be hard on you. I think we ought to stick by each other. The work's hard and the pay's small. And anyhow you know Jane Scarlett has always been square."

"Well, yes, she makes it appear that way of course. I'm sure I hope she's all right. But it always makes me jittery to have anything happen like this afternoon. I'd hate to faint. One always looks so washed out and unhealthy. Of course she would anyway without any make-up. I wonder why she doesn't use any?"

"Oh, she hasn't got on to being smart yet, that's all. She'd really be stunning with that dark hair and her big blue eyes if she'd get her hair done now and then. She acts as if she doesn't care how she looks."

The two girls separated at the subway after agreeing that Jane didn't know how to dress, and went on to their separate paths.

But Jane lay in her little hard white bed in her third story back and slept.

And in the night when she stirred and turned over and sighed deeply she kept hearing a voice far away saying:

"In my Father's house are many mansions. I go to prepare a place for you."

6

THE old Scarlett house was high and wide and comfortable. It was built of brick with a hall through the middle. It had wide low stairs with white spindles and a mahogany rail, the kind of staircase that antique lovers rave over. It curled around at the top and made a lovely line of itself, with a nook beneath where a great old mahogany couch with claw legs and rich upholstery nestled. In front of the stairs there was a rare hall table highly polished, where many notable hats had reposed in time past. And over it hung a handsome mirror.

The front door was one of the finest specimens of the old time doors with fanlights above, and a knocker of brass that would have been a valued museum piece.

On either side of the front door there were rooms, one on the left extending the full depth of the house with a full length mirror at front and back between the windows. There was an old-fashioned square piano with a mother-of-pearl floral design above the keyboard, on which the generations of Scarlett children had learned to play, and there were some fine old portraits in oil of distinguished Scarlett men and women. The furniture was beautiful old wood of satin polish, the work of some of the old masters in design. The fabrics which covered the chairs were well-preserved silk brocades of quaint pattern, and there were charming tables and chairs and sofas scattered about.

Across the hall from the front room was a library, furnished with leather chairs and a sofa, a fine old secretary, and rare prints.

The dining room was back of that, with a sideboard that would make treasure-seekers gasp with joy, and a whole dinner set of willow pattern, not a piece missing. The spacious cupboard contained much fine old glass and other interesting pieces, and the kitchen that was housed in a deep gable at the back spoke of years of plenty, in pleasant working quarters.

Upstairs there were five big bedrooms, and two bathrooms that had been added in later years, with an attic overhead that looked like a fairy tale out of the past. Spinning wheels and old chairs, haircloth trunks and chests of drawers. It would be a joy just to rummage in that attic. And in one corner under the eaves, an old table of the kind known as a "stand" on which reposed an ancient Bible with a full record of all the Scarlett births and marriages and deaths. Someone had covered it with a piece of dark muslin to keep off the dust. But that was all. The years had come and gone, and the precious record of a family that had been honored in its time, lay there carelessly unguarded except by a bit of cheap calico that had once been part of a common kitchen apron!

And in that Bible record there was a name set down:

"Jane Scarlett, born to John Ravenal Scarlett, and Miriam Warrener Scarlett April 17th, 19—"

The old house stood in the shadow of great trees, shrouded in thick ivy, its fireplaces empty and dead, its rooms without inhabitant, save for a temeritous mouse or two that ventured in now and then and finding no food hurried away.

And Jane Scarlett, the last of the Scarletts in direct line, lay sleeping desolately in a hard little bed in the third story hall bedroom of the cheapest boarding house she had been able to find.

There was myrtle growing around the edges of the yard, and lilacs overshadowing the wide back porch. The grass was neatly kept and the hedges trimmed by arrangement with the caretakers of the estate, but the garden had run wild, growing weeds and flowers and vegetables at will in one bewildering mass.

Out under a great elm tree an old swing hung, where all the little Scarletts had swung to their heart's content during the years. It needed only a new rope to make it swingable again. And out at one side of the lawn a rustic summer house still stood, repaired occasionally by the caretaker, where the Scarlett girls used to have afternoon tea with their friends. But there was one Scarlett girl who had never been so privileged. Five o'clock teas had never come her way.

There was a gravel driveway from the old barn where once upon a time high-spirited horses were stabled, and victorias and surreys and phaetons rolled proudly down to the stepping stone in front. Then the family got in and drove away. And of later years various cars used by more modern members of the clan took their place. But now the stable was empty and clean. One or two old harnesses and bridles still hung from hooks in the wall. A collection of whips lay on a high dusty shelf, hard pressed by empty oil cans of a later date. And the tool house, just behind the barn, though it still held hoes and shovels and spades galore, was huddled and disorderly, everything pushed back to make way for a couple of modern lawn mowers. It all reminded of nothing better than a well-kept cemetery, giving respect and honor to the past, but meaning nothing whatever to the present but a memorial.

So it had stood for the past seven or eight years while the last owner, Harold Scarlett, had traveled from place to place abroad, at first seeking pleasure, and finally searching for health.

There had been a caretaker all this time who kept the outside of the place immaculate, and whose wife had gone through the gesture of cleaning the inside of the house after a fashion twice every year. But the house had an unloved look, like a dog whose master was dead. It did not seem to belong any more to the cheerful street of pleasant houses on which it was located.

Once, years ago, Jane Scarlett had been taken to that house when she was a very little girl to visit her grandmother who was very old. She retained only a dim memory of a sweet old lady with a crumpled face, kindly eyes, and hands that were startlingly soft and hot and vivid when they touched her.

But she remembered the big old house among the trees as the grandest mansion she had ever seen. At least the grandest she had ever entered. And when she heard of "In my Father's house" she always pictured the many mansions as looking like the ivy-clad brick Scarlett house, and hoped to see more of it in heaven.

The house was located in a place called "Hawthorne," from the many hawthorne trees in the countryside. It was a suburb of a great city, the name of which the child Jane never heard in connection with the house. The old home was always at Hawthorne. But Hawthorne had since became a part of the city itself, and the name Hawthorne was only commonly known through its broad avenue on which the house was located. Perhaps if Jane had known definitely where this dream-mansion was located she might have started out to find it when she drifted on her own and went to find a home and a job. But being only in a vague place called Hawthorne, with the likelihood that it had long ago been sold and thus obliterated from things belonging to herself and her family, it had never occurred to her as possible to go and see it. Moreover her going had depended largely upon chance. She had started out to get away from the country boarding place in whose kitchen she was no longer needed. Heaven had seemed too far away then to hunt for one of the many mansions for her immediate need. So it had never occurred to her that when she found the job at Windle and Harrower's store, she might not be so far away from the starting place of her family. As she lay in her hot room in her narrow bed and tried to be thankful for such blessings as she had, it never occurred to her that the old house where her grandfather, and her great grandfather Scarlett had lived was not many miles away from the place where she was lying.

But even if she had known it, it would not have made any practical difference in her situation.

She was almost dropping off to sleep when she heard footsteps lagging up the stairs. The strangeness of it startled her awake again. The forlorn woman who helped in the kitchen roomed up there, with her slatternly daughter who waited on table. But neither of them would be coming up to bed now. They hadn't finished the dinner dishes.

But the steps came on and paused at her door, and she held her breath and listened. Then there was a hesitating tap. Then again, more insistent.

"Who is it?" Jane managed to ask.

"It's me," the landlady answered belligerently. "I just wanted to find out what's the idea of your staying away from meals this way? Was you expecting to take it off what you'll owe me at the first of the week? You wasn't down to dinner last night nor tonight, and I can't afford to buy good meat and things and then not get paid for them. Besides, if you're coming down you oughtta come on time, and not expect me to keep vittles hot for ya all night. All the other boarders have et and gone. I thought mebbe you'd got asleep and didn't know you was lettin' the meal hour go by."

"Oh, I'm sorry, Mrs. Hawkins," said Jane wearily. "I should have stopped and told you not to save anything for me. I've not felt so well today. The heat kind of got me, and I don't feel like eating anything."

"Well, that's all right, ef you don't want nothin', but it seems ta me you oughtta eat ta keep up yer strength. Don't come round late at night and ast me fer a piece. I ain't gonta be bothered that way. And by the way, I may's well tell ya, I gotta raise the rent of yer room a buck, beginnin' next week. They've raised the rent of the house, and meat's gettin' awful high, an' I can't make ends meet no way ef I don't raise me own rents. I jes' wanted you ta understand."

"Oh, Mrs. Hawkins!" cried Jane in despair, "but I told you when I came I couldn't pay any more, and you said that would be all right."

"Well, I know I did, but I can't do it, I tell ya! Besides I gotta young couple will be gladta come in here an' pay me a buck an' a half more apiece ef I put in a double bed, an' I guess I'll havta do it. I ain't runnin' a boardin' house fer benevolence ya know. I just thought I'd tell ya. You can think it over an' let me know tamorra mornin'. I gotta give them an answer right away."

With the last word the door closed with finality and the slipshod steps went steadily on down the stairs, the workworn hand of the woman feeling her way on the wall as she went.

Jane lay there filled with dismay. What was she going to do? Here she had just been trying to be thankful for this little smelly old room, and now even it was going to be taken away from her!

It came to her presently to wonder about that nice place the nurse had talked to her about. Why hadn't she asked her where it was? But then of course it would have been too expensive. Any place as cheap as this would be awful, just like this. But she'd got to do something. If she paid a dollar more to stay here that would cut out all her margin for sickness, and it looked now as if she might even be sick pretty soon if this weather kept on and she didn't get some kind of a change.

Well, she'd got to do something. Was there any place she could go tonight hunting a room? No, that was out of the question. She wasn't fit to walk and she couldn't afford carfare. She must husband her strength for to-morrow. She *had* to keep going tomorrow. She *must* get that pay envelope.

It was even thinkable that she might be going to lose her job, dropping down in a little heap that way right in the midst of the afternoon work! Maybe they would think they didn't want salespeople like that who could faint on them in the midst of things.

Well, there wasn't any use fretting. She'd better get some sleep. She wasn't hungry. She couldn't eat cold ham and cabbage even if she went downstairs now. She reviewed what the table would probably be like besides the ham and cabbage—and only the worst of that would be left of course. There would be bread, dry pieces that had been left over from another meal, with the mark of a greasy knife on one side. It wouldn't be the first time that one like that had fallen to her lot. She wondered why she ever ate in that place anyway. The food in the cheap restaurants was so much better. Maybe just a room in some decent rooming house would be better, and she could take a bottle of milk and get her own breakfasts, just dry uncooked cereal and an orange. Why hadn't she thought to try that before? It was all an experiment. But as she thought it over she was almost glad that her landlady had raised her rent, for now she had a real excuse to hunt another place.

Well, she would to to sleep now and get all the rest she could, and in the morning she would try and eat whatever breakfast there was, and tell her landlady she was leaving that night. Then she would go down to the store and pay for that crystal clasp, and take what money was left and find some place to live.

Her decision made she fell asleep again, a restless burdened sleep, that broke toward morning, and woke her into a frenzy of despair. Suppose she should give up this room and then not be able to find another at any price she could afford? Maybe she was wrong to give it up. And yet she couldn't pay another dollar a week and go on enduring this hot room and the life here. And it would presently be as cold here as it was hot now. There was no chance of comfort here at all.

So she prodded her jaded muscles to get up and dress, though it was a full hour before her usual time for rising. But then she had a great deal to do before she went to the store. And she must keep moving or her resolve would weaken. She must be determined, to face that woman downstairs.

So she dressed carefully, to give the best impression at the store. They mustn't think she was worn out.

Then she smoothed over the bed, and began to take her things down from the hooks in the improvised closet. There weren't many of them, so they wouldn't be hard to carry. She folded them neatly, three or four plain dresses, and a meager pile of underwear. She was glad she hadn't bought that coat yet. Of course it would have had to be bought on credit anyway, but now she didn't have that to worry about, not till she got another home and was sure of things.

The breakfast bell was ringing when at last she had her garments all folded neatly into her suitcase. Then she pulled down the curtain to her closet and folded it smoothly, with the curtain from her wash stand, and put them in a pasteboard suit box she had brought from the store. She tied the box firmly, and put it and her suitcase by the door. Then she put on her hat, took her handbag and was ready to go. Her rent was up that night, all paid in advance. At least she would not have to pay out anything to move. She would take the suitcase and box with her to the store and put them in her locker. At noon she could slip out and look for a place, or maybe there would be a way to get excused early, if Mr. Clark was in a good humor after that clasp was paid for.

She ate her breakfast quietly enough. She was really hungry, though it was none of it appetizing. She found a little white worm in her shredded wheat biscuit, and the cream was sour. At least it was near-cream. But she reflected that white worms were likely not very unhealthy, especially if you didn't eat them, and that sour cream wouldn't kill her. So she fished out the worm and laid it aside, comforting herself that this was the last breakfast she would ever eat in this house. She might even eat in worse places of course, but this was the last here.

There was toast, burned and cold, and muddy coffee.

She managed a few mouthfuls and then went upstairs to get her things. When she came downstairs Mrs. Hawkins was dickering with a huckster at the door, so she only said as she went down the steps, "Good-bye, Mrs. Hawkins, I'm going!" and then hurried away before Mrs. Hawkins could rally from the shock of being taken at her word.

But the walk to the trolley seemed longer than usual, burdened with the heavy suitcase and box, and the air was sultry with a coming storm. She looked anxiously up at the sky and made for the subway as rapidly as she could. That would land her almost at the store. It would be nothing short of a calamity if she got wet this morning, and no chance to change her garments before she appeared before the floor manager.

But the rain held off until Jane was safely inside the store, and her luggage put away in her locker. Then she appeared as usual in her place behind the button counter. They all looked surprised to see her back again.

"I don't see why you didn't take a day or two off and rest up," said one girl. "Believe me I'd have stayed away and got a good rest."

"Oh, I'm all right this morning," said Jane trying to appear as usual and not realizing how white she was looking. It quite surprised her that so many people were interested to ask after her. It is true that she found a great weakness upon her, but she did not speak of that. It embarrassed her that they should have seen her when she fainted. She was not a fainting girl.

But when Mr. Clark came solicitously up and asked how she felt she certainly was astonished. It hadn't occurred to her that he really counted her a human being like himself.

And then that stocking manager with his permanent wave beautifully set came smiling up.

"Well, little girl, you staged quite a scene last night, didn't you?" he said gaily, as if she were an old friend.

Jane looked up astonished.

"I'm sorry," she said. "It wasn't premeditated. I'm feeling quite fit this morning. Thank you for asking." And then she gave attention to a casual customer who had just lingered to gaze at a new display of buttons.

But young Gaylord was not to be discouraged. He appeared in the midst of the morning's work with a frosty glass of ice water.

"I thought this might help out a little," he said with a cheerful smile, and he handed the glass to her. Jane couldn't exactly refuse. Besides the water looked good.

It was amazing how the other girls flocked around her after that little attention. If that good-looking young man was going to take her up, they wanted to be in her circle.

Jane thought about it as she put her domain in buttonly order and grinned grimly to herself. What would they all say if they knew she was homeless this morning? Well, they shouldn't find it out! But what was she going to do?

At her lunch hour she went out to a good restaurant and ordered a wholesome lunch. Somehow she had to offset that awful breakfast she had eaten that morning. Somehow she had to get a little strength to go on. Fifty cents for her lunch! But it was worth it. Still she couldn't go on paying fifty cents for every meal. Well, when the day was over she *must* find a room, and then she could rest all day Sunday. She wouldn't even wash out a pair of stockings! She would just rest!

She put her head down on her lifted hand and closed her eyes a moment while she waited for her order to be brought.

"Oh, God," she prayed, "when you've so many

mansions, couldn't you help me find a room, just a *little* room, right away?"

Then she lifted her head and looked around her.

Did God really care what became of her? Her mother used to say He did.

And then almost like an answer to that prayer, though she had felt she had no real right to pray for such things for herself, she saw Miss Leech coming toward her smiling.

"Jane," she said hopefully, "are you all tied up for the next two weeks?"

"Tied up?" said Jane, wonderingly.

"Yes, are you somewhere you have to stay and can't get away from, or are you going on a vacation yourself so you couldn't do something for me?"

"Why no," said Jane, "no, I'm not going on a vacation this year. I can't afford it. What can I do for you?"

"Why, you see, I'm taking my vacation beginning tonight, and I've just discovered that the girl I thought I had secured to come and stay in my apartment and look after my canary and my plants and goldfish is going off to Maine herself on a trip, and can't do it. I'm all upset. It isn't everybody I'd be willing to trust with my canary and goldfish. But I thought of you right away when I knew Elinor couldn't stay. Would you be willing to come and live there and look after things? I'd be glad to pay you for it. I feel I could trust you. I've watched how conscientious you are. I would know you wouldn't go off to a dance and let the poor little creatures starve or anything. Can you come?"

"Why, Miss Leech! How wonderful! I'd love to come. But you needn't pay me anything for that. I don't go out to dances and I'd adore having birds and fishes for companions."

"But certainly I'd pay you. I'd feel happier that way. Besides there might be times when you wanted to go back to your own place to stay and it's right you should have something for putting yourself out to stay there."

"But I shouldn't be putting myself out," said Jane. "You see, I'm homeless. I left the room I had this morning. It was unbearable. And I've got to hunt something after the store closes. Your proposition will just give me a chance to look around and try to find something respectable within my means. I'd love to come."

"All right, then, that's settled. You go home with me tonight. We'll have supper together in the restaurant downstairs in my apartment house, and then I can tell you about it. There's a kitchenette and you can get your own breakfasts whenever you feel like it of course."

"It sounds very much like heaven," said Jane with sparkling eyes. "Where do I meet you?"

They arranged the details quickly and Miss Leech went back to her desk, leaving Jane to enjoy her lunch with a lightened heart. Now did ever anyone see a happening like that? And just when she needed it so much. Could it be possible that it had anything to do with her prayer? Well, mother used to believe in prayer that way, but she always said that people who were not abiding in fellowship with Christ had no right to expect such amazing answers to things they asked. She well knew that verse, "If ye abide in me and my words abide in you, ye shall ask what ye will and it shall be done unto you." But she had not been abiding. Neither had His words been abiding in her heart; she hadn't read her Bible for months, and then only a hurried snatch at it. That wasn't abiding. But perhaps the Lord had given her this reply to her request just to call her attention to Himself and let her know He still cared for her. Was that it? She was His. At least she had given herself to Him when she was a child, though since her mother's death she had grown far away from any fellowship. She had almost come to doubt it had ever been anything to her but an idea.

But she couldn't ignore this thing that had happened. God had surely been thinking of her. It was as if a tender hand had touched her, a gentle voice said, "I love you, my child!" Well, she would think about all this when she got somewhere and was rested.

The afternoon went better than the morning. The good food helped, and the relief from worry about the morrow. And when it came time to go up to the office for that pay envelope, and to settle about that clasp, she went with almost a cheerful heart. Even if she did lose that clasp money she would have two whole weeks without having to pay rent, and leisure to look for a room. She didn't need to worry. Of course she wouldn't let Miss Leech pay her for living in a perfectly good room. She hadn't seen the room yet, but any room that was good enough for Miss Leech would be a rest and vacation for her. Especially since she didn't have to pay for it.

The storm had cleared away leaving the atmosphere cooler and Jane felt as if life were more bearable. Though she was glad indeed when the signal came for closing, and she could conscientiously put away the last button, spread the covers over her cases and take her way up to the office.

But Mr. Clark stood at the door of the office and as she entered he motioned to her.

"Miss Scarlett," he said, "don't say anything about that broken clasp. It has been paid for, and you can forget it."

"Oh, Mr. Clark, they didn't make Hilda pay, did they?"

"No indeed! We found it was in no way her fault, and it was also proved that it was not your fault. Don't think anything more about it."

Mr. Clark was embarrassed at his unaccustomed task, for this was actually the first time he had ever assumed a debt of that sort for the sake of anyone who worked under him. It sent the color into his cheeks, and gave him a heady feeling as if God might be pleased with him, though he didn't explain it to himself in those words exactly. But he added hastily, "I'm sure I hope you'll be feeling quite well again by Monday, Miss Scarlett," and then he bowed and turned to speak to another man who came by and Jane went on to the pay-envelope window, and saw Hilda just before her. Hilda with a bright face and no trouble in her eyes.

It was good to look into her pay envelope and find her full amount there. Was this another sign that God was thinking of her, caring for her?

So she went downstairs, got her luggage and met Miss Leech by the door which they had agreed upon and they went on their way to the apartment.

It was just about that time that the postoffice car was delivering a special delivery letter for Jane Scarlett at the old boarding house she had left that morning, and Mrs. Hawkins was explaining in a high key that the girl had left and she hadn't the slightest idea where she had gone, and *wouldn't* be responsible for the letter, though Mrs. Hawkins was careful to take the letter in her hand and study the heading in the left hand upper corner before she handed it back to the delivery man. A firm of lawyers! What would they want of Jane Scarlett? Would it be money? She almost wished she hadn't raised the girl's rent. Well, she was gone and she wouldn't be responsible for holding any letter for her. No, she wouldn't sign for it, either.

So the letter went on its way back to the sender, with "NOT KNOWN AT THAT ADDRESS" written large across its envelope. And Jane had gone into a new world where the message within that envelope could not find her.

7

THEY had a good supper together downstairs in the restaurant and then Miss Leech took Jane up to the apartment. It seemed to her unaccustomed eyes to be palatial. It consisted of a pleasant little living room, a small bedroom, a bathroom, and a tiny kitchenette not much more than a sink and a stove, but still big enough. What luxury! And she was to be here for two whole weeks! It seemed like heaven. She was sure she wouldn't feel the heat here at all, and anyway there was an electric fan.

She was introduced to the goldfish and the canary, and given full directions how to care for them.

Miss Leech left in a taxi a little before midnight and Jane with awe crept into a big soft bed and lay down in wonder. To think she was in such a lovely place and comparative coolness, for two whole weeks! She meant to lie there awhile and think it all over and enjoy it, but she was asleep before she knew it, and exhausted nature kept her asleep until well into the morning.

When she did waken it was to the voice of a little silver-toned clock across from the bed. Nine o'clock!

When had she slept until nine o'clock? But she lay there a few delicious moments longer listening to the new sounds about her. The low rumble of high-powered cars instead of trolleys and freight trains. The deep-throated bell from some steeple not far away, the high fine strains of radio music from an open window. And over it all clear, golden and ecstatic, the sweet flutelike voice of the canary reveling in his morning joy. It was all wonderful, and she found tears burning out from her eyelids. Tears of joy. The pain of having so many things that she had never had before. Would her mother up in heaven know what comfort had suddenly come to her child? Did God plan this for her? She couldn't but feel that He had.

In a little while she got up and reveled in the luxury of a warm bath in a clean tub with all the hot water she wanted to use! Why just that comfort was enough to be thankful for all the rest of her life. How she had hated that tin-lined, roughly painted, light blue bath tub at Mrs. Hawkins', a tub that had to be waited for almost hour after hour on Sunday mornings, and then always had a rim of grease and dirt around its middle.

There were cereals in the minute cupboard which she had been ordered to use up because they would be stale by the time their owner returned. There was a bottle of real cream in the wee refrigerator, and a bottle of milk also. She did not need to make coffee, though she had been instructed in the ways of the percolator. There was bread and butter on hand and some peaches. What a breakfast! And how good everything was!

She fed the canary and the fishes and talked to them as she did it, and the little creatures seemed to be cocking a wise eye at her and recognizing that she was somebody new.

After she had washed her dishes and put things to

rights she turned on the radio and came upon some wondrous music, and a message that reached her tired discouraged soul. A message that Jesus Christ not only was the Saviour of all those who accepted His atonement on the cross for their sins, but that He wanted to be more. He wanted to be the guide and daily companion of each one whom He had saved.

That was a new thought to Jane. She had often wondered if God cared for her, but that He should desire her love and companionship, and long to have the confidence of her soul, had never occurred to her. Was that true? She listened to the message to the end, and during the closing prayer she slipped down beside the big chair where she had been sitting and put her heart in the attitude of prayer. There were no words to her petition, just a longing, just apology in the eyes of her soul, just a wistful yearning for something she did not as yet understand.

By and by she found a pleasant book to read, and in the cool of the afternoon she went out and took a walk in the park that was not far away. Then about five o'clock she began to be hungry and went in to the restaurant and got a good dinner. A chicken dinner. It seemed to her a marvelous day, and when she had finished her dinner she went up and read awhile and then went to bed early. This had been like a real vacation. Why this was the greatest thing that had happened to her since her mother died!

The canary welcomed her with soft conversing cheeps, and she did not feel alone. She was almost happy.

She began to calculate. If she got her own breakfast and a very cheap lunch she might be able to take her dinners down at that restaurant every day. She had got to be well fed or she would collapse in the store again and that wouldn't do. She would lose her job if that kept on happening.

She went to bed and to sleep very early that night. The church bell on the tower not far away rang again, and it seemed to keep time to the words: "In my Father's house. Many mansions in my Father's house."

She was up bright and early next morning, her breakfast got and her work done. The housework was like play, a doll's house. Then she was off to the store.

She tried walking to the store. Miss Leech said she did it every day for the exercise unless it was very stormy. But when she was almost there she began to feel weak in the knees and realized she should not have attempted it yet. She probably had been going beyond her strength for a long time, on insufficient food, as that nurse at the store had suggested. She should give herself another day or two to rest before she tried such long walks. Well, she would take things as easy as possible today, and she would eat a good lunch, no saving of food till she was stronger and quite fit for her work.

She was in her place a little before time, getting her stock settled and greeting the other girls pleasantly, and then, just after the opening bugle, Mr. Clark came hurrying up. His very attitude filled her with alarm, though of course it really didn't matter so much now if she did have to pay for that crystal clasp, now that she was getting a room free for two whole weeks.

"Miss Scarlett," he said, "I've just been up talking with Mr. Windle, and he feels quite strongly that in view of your having had such a bad time day before yesterday you should certainly take your vacation. He says that your record has been so good, and you have been so faithful during the hot months, that he feels we should let you have your vacation *with pay!* He doesn't often do that, you know, but he's making an exception of you because you were sick. So if you will go up to the office right away you will receive your pay check at once and then you will have something to make your vacation a little easier. I think you are looking a little better this morning and I hope by the end of your vacation we shall see a decided difference in you. I hope you have a wonderful time. Good-bye and we'll be looking for you back again."

In a daze Jane took the slip he gave her to take to the cashier and went slowly down the aisle and up the stairs to the office.

She was weak with amazement. She wondered when she reached the office whether she had remembered to thank Mr. Clark for telling her, and whether it would be right to interrupt Mr. Windle to thank him. She decided against that. Two whole weeks with money in hand as if she was working, and a lovely place to stay. Not even a grand hotel at the shore could be as good as that. There were all those lovely books to read, and the radio! Why it was wonderful. God surely had been taking thought for her. She could not doubt it.

And she would have time to look about her in a leisurely way for another room. She wouldn't have to take another terrible place because she simply *had* to have some place in which to stay right away.

Gradually she came out of her daze sufficiently to get excited over her good luck. As she came downstairs she met Mr. Clark and she looked at him with shy eagerness.

"I guess I didn't thank you," she said. "I know you used your influence or this wouldn't have happened to me."

"Oh, that's all right," said Mr. Clark with a wide generous gesture. "Take care of yourself. I hope you have a good time!"

So Jane started out to go back to her new quarters. She wouldn't have to save her strength for work today, so perhaps she could manage to walk back. She could stop and rest in the park on the way. How wonderful to be a lady of leisure!

Two days later the letter that the firm of lawyers had sent to Jane Scarlett at Mrs. Hawkins' boarding house came back to the office with the legend stamped on it that one Jane Scarlett was not at the address given below and her present whereabouts was unknown.

In due time the lawyer who received the mail came with it to Kent Havenner.

"How about this, Kent," he said, "didn't you say this Scarlett girl had given you the address where she was living?"

"I did," said Kent Havenner emphatically, "what's the matter?"

"Not there! Address unknown!" announced the other man. "You sure that's the right address?"

Havenner took the envelope and examined it, comparing it carefully with his notebook.

"Yes, that's correct," he said. "I wonder—?"

"Well, it seems we're up a tree still," said the lawyer. "You thought you had such a good lead, and now our bird has flown. We'll have to begin all over again. Probably she wasn't the right Scarlett after all."

"Well, here, give it to me and I think I can find her. She works in a store."

"All right, hunt her up and be quick about it. I'd like to get that Scarlett matter settled up and off the docket. I'm tired of seeing the documents in the safe every time I go there."

So Kent Havenner went out in the middle of the afternoon and made his way to Windle's store, going confidently to the button counter, expecting to be able to pick out his girl at a glance.

But though he walked up and down the aisle three times and watched every girl that was waiting on customers there, there wasn't a single one who looked like Jane. Could it be possible that his eyes deceived him?

Finally he went up to a girl who was idle for the moment:

"Isn't there a Miss Scarlett at this counter?"

"She's not here today. She's out. She's been sick. I guess that's why," explained a girl who wasn't a regular at the button counter. "There's the head of the department, he might know."

So Havenner interviewed Mr. Clark.

"Oh! She's gone on vacation," explained Clark loftily.

"Well, could you tell me where she has gone?" asked the young lawyer. "It's quite important."

"No! I'm sorry! We don't require our salespeople to sign up for vacation absences. Probably if you would enquire at the office they would know her residence."

Clark eyed the man hostilely. He was dressed too well to be a friend or relative of Jane Scarlett. What could he want of her? Perhaps there were drawbacks in Jane's life even worse than hot weather and ill health. At least he was doing nothing to encourage this young man.

Kent Havenner went on his way. He decided to go to Jane's boarding house. Doubtless the wrong person had got hold of the letter.

So he went to Mrs. Hawkins and she dilated irately on how Jane had left her at a moment's notice just because she asked for a little more money. And no, she didn't know where she went!

"She just walked off with her back up!" said Mrs. Hawkins, and went in and shut her door.

Kent Havenner even went to the trouble of interviewing the office at the store, and found that what Mr. Clark had told him was true. Jane was on vacation and nobody—not *any*body—knew where she was. There was nothing he could do about it, and so he went back to the office to confess himself beaten for the time being. And there was nothing anybody could do but wait till Jane Scarlett came back to the store.

But meantime Jane Scarlett was having the grandest time of her life.

She had portioned out her money so that she could have one good square interesting meal a day, and for the other two fruit and cereal and milk. That would leave her a little more than a week's wages to put by. Then she got a map of the city at a newsstand, and studied the region within walking distance, or cheap riding distance, from the store, and regularly every morning she started out hunting a room.

More and more as she hunted she was filled with distress over the places from which she must choose. Not one had a semblance of homelikeness or comfort. Not at the price she should pay. Yet there must be something better somewhere. Perhaps her ideas were too fine. And of course the place where she was now living made the contrast all the more deadly. Yet she did not ask so much. Cleanliness, a reasonable amount of fresh air, and of heat in winter. The room might be bare and guiltless of paint. The bed might be narrow; if it could only be tolerably smooth, she could stand its being hard. Were just these few necessities so expensive? Surely there must be something bearable somewhere.

But so many hall bedrooms were the same. No heat

in winter, no air in summer. Few and far bathroom privileges.

So one day she went in to the big city station and hunted up the Travelers Aid woman. Yes, she knew of a few rooms where conditions were more tolerable. She wrote a list of them, but warned Jane that they were usually in great demand.

So Jane started out again, and at last found a room that she thought she could stand. It was bare and desolate in the extreme. A bureau, a sagging woven wire cot, a straight chair, and a wash bowl on a shelf in the corner. It was fifty cents more than Mrs. Hawkins' room, but would be vacant about the time she needed it, so she took it tentatively, and hied her back to Miss Leech's apartment to look disconsolately around its comforts and tell the canary sadly how she was going to miss it when her vacation was over. If she didn't have to have a warm coat this winter she could get a better room, but she must have a coat that was really warm.

So she put the thought of a homelike room out of her mind and sat and read Miss Leech's best books, trying to absorb all the pleasure possible so that it would last through the winter that was to come.

Yet while she sat enjoying herself and trying to forget the time that was swiftly coming when she could no longer sit in comfort and read the best books and listen to a good radio, Kent Havenner was worrying himself greatly about her. As he walked the streets or went about outside the city, his eyes were always alert, thinking perhaps he would come on her. That word that she had been ill troubled him. He didn't understand why it was, but he could not get away from the look in her eyes when she had said that all her family were dead. She had seemed so alone, and so quiet and self-contained as if she expected so little out of life and wasn't even getting as much as she had expected.

He tried to put the thought of her out of his mind. There wasn't anything more he could do about her until her vacation was over, but it kept coming to him what if she didn't come back? What if they never found her? Would he have to go on thinking of her and that sort of resigned unhappy look in her eyes?

His sister Audrey had been away in Maine for a few days, but the day she got back he took her for a walk on the beach, eluding the incessant cousin who would have accompanied them, and when they were a good distance away from the house he began:

"Say, Audrey, are you going up to town some day pretty soon?"

"Why, yes," said Audrey, considering. "I was thinking of going tomorrow unless mother has other plans. Why for?"

"Well, I wish you'd do something for me. Go see if you can find your button girl. She's disappeared!"

"Kent, what do you mean?"

"Jane Scarlett! She's disappeared I tell you, and it's important that she be found."

"Disappeared? What do you mean? On purpose? Kent, she hasn't done anything they want her for, has she? I mean I'm sure she hasn't, and if anybody's hounding her for anything and wants me to help, I won't and that's flat."

"Now look here, Audrey, did I say anybody was hounding her? Did I give you any reason to suppose she was wanted by the police? Well, she isn't at all. She's just wanted. That is, there's a letter for her that she ought to have, and it's been the rounds and got back to the office with an inscription that she's unknown."

Audrey looked up startled.

"You don't mean it, Kent."

"S'the truth, kid. And I went myself to the address she gave me and they said she'd left. And then I went to the store and they told me she was on a vacation."

"You mean you've really seen her and talked with her, Kent? I thought perhaps you had just been joking. *Did* you talk with her?"

"Sure thing, sister. Had a very dignified interview."

"Was she frightened?"

"Not in the least. What was there to be frightened about? I went to Windle and he sent for her. I told her I was a friend of Windle's collecting statistics about a family and I wanted to ask her some questions."

"How did she take it?"

"Cool as you please. She looked me through and through and then answered everything I asked her as quietly as you please."

"Well, is there any great hurry about it? Why don't you wait till she gets back from that vacation if it's genuine?"

"That's it, sister. I want you to find out for me if it is really genuine. I want you to go to the button counter and ask for her, and if they still say she's on vacation just get friendly with the other girls and find out when she really is coming back, and where they think she went. You could do what I couldn't, you see."

"Yes, I suppose I could," said Audrey. "But I think you'd have to tell me a little more about the affair before I'd be willing to get into this at all. If I thought they were going to get her into any trouble I wouldn't touch it. I liked that girl."

"No trouble at all, kid. It's just an estate being settled up and they are trying to get information about other members of the family that may be living."

"Did you tell her that?"

"No, I told her only that we were getting statistics. I think she gathered that it was for a book, a family tree or something. I was not supposed to tell the nature of the affair. I was only a factotum, you see."

"You're sure she wasn't frightened?"

"I don't think she was. Not after I began to ask her questions."

"What did you ask her?"

"Her name and where she was born and the names of her father and mother and where they were born and married and died, and the names of her grandfather or any cousins etc. she had."

"Well, that oughtn't to have frightened her," said Audrey thoughtfully. "All right, I'll try and find out where she is. But don't tell cousin Evalina, and don't let's talk about her at the table, because I really mean to invite her down here to stay over the week-end, sometime, and I don't want Evalina barging in and making a fool of you and the girl."

"I should hope not," said Kent fervently. "But say, I don't blame you for being enthusiastic. She's some girl. She has an air as if she was to the manner born and then some. Isn't exactly pretty, either, but might be if she had the money or at least I got that impression."

"Well, I should say you're about as quick at judging character as you think I am. But I'm glad you agree with me. Come on, let's get back to the cottage. If I've got to go to town tomorrow I'd better get busy getting ready."

8

ONE day in the second week of her vacation Jane turned on the radio and heard a woman's voice speaking. It said:

"If you are sad and weary and questioning what life is all about, if you want to find an answer that will satisfy, and help you to go on amid disappointments and hardships and loneliness, come to Mrs. Brooke's Bible hour at seven o'clock every evening in Bryan Hall, for a time of real help and comfort."

Somehow that little invitation seemed spoken just to Jane. It voiced her own longings and promised something that she did not know where else to find. A great desire came to her to go and see what it was, and if it would indeed bring peace to her troubled soul.

She found out that Bryan Hall was only three blocks away from Miss Leech's apartment and she resolved to go that very night and listen. To that end she ate her dinner earlier than usual and was at the place appointed before seven.

As she entered the hall she was handed a little red book which she found to be a copy of the gospel of

John. She turned the pages over interestedly and there was her own fourteenth chapter, "In my Father's house are many mansions—." It made her feel right at home. And then a sweet-faced woman came to the desk and bowed her head in a short tender prayer that made God seem very present.

The leader's voice was brisk and intriguing.

"Please turn to the twentieth chapter of your little red book, and you will find its introduction in the thirtieth and thirty-first verses. Away at the end of the book. Isn't that odd? Let us read:

> 'And many other signs truly did Jesus in the presence of His disciples, which are not written in this book: but these are written that ye might believe that Jesus is the Christ, the Son of God; and that believing ye might have life through His name.'

"You see John is not a biography of Jesus, like the other gospels. It is a book of signs. Signs that Jesus is the Christ, proofs from an eyewitness. And the purpose of writing them is 'that ye might have life.'

"'Oh,' you say, 'I want to see life!' And you may have tried this or that pleasure or pursuit, and actually said 'This is the life!'"

She imitated so well the tone of voice peculiar to that phrase that a boy and girl on the back seat nudged each other and giggled, and even a few older, quietly staid women glanced at each other understandingly.

"But," she went on, "what you may have thought was life may have been a very poor imitation. Turn now to the seventeenth chapter of your little books, the third verse, and read:

"'And this is life eternal, that they might know thee

the only true God, and Jesus Christ, whom thou hast sent.'

"Now, I see some of you looking disappointed. You are saying to yourselves, 'That's not the kind of life I want.' But friends, *there is no other kind* of life, not real life. There is no life apart from Christ. Perhaps the reason you are dissatisfied with life is because you've been seeking it apart from Him and all you have been getting is an imitation. Turn to the first chapter, verse four: 'In Him was life; and the life was the light of men.' Now the third chapter, verse thirty-six: 'He that believeth on the Son hath everlasting life: and he that believeth not the Son shall not see life; but the wrath of God abideth on him.' Now the tenth chapter, verse ten: 'I am come that they might have life, and that they might have it more abundantly.' And chapter fourteen, six: 'I am the way, the truth, and the life.' Of course this isn't animal life Christ is talking about. It is eternal life. It is God's life.

"And there are seven signs in this book which prove that Christ is the only life-giver and that the life He gives is real. The first is Jesus turning the water into wine, just by a look. Wine is the symbol of joy, the ecstatic joy of living. Notice that He told the servants to *fill up* the waterpots. You may guess rightly from that, that the kind of life He gives is *full* of joy.

"You may say, 'I never saw a Christian full of joy.' Well I have, and you'll find that the long-faced people, while they may be full of creeds or theories, are not full of Jesus Christ. Those who are have joy.

"In chapter four you find the second sign. Christ heals the son of a nobleman. Here we find that the life He gives is a spiritually healthy life. There is never any fanaticism or lack of balance in it.

"In the third sign you find Him giving power, in the

fourth, nourishment, in the fifth, peace. *'My* peace I give unto you.' *His* peace is calm even in the midst of betrayal and a cross in the offing. In the sixth sign He gives light. The healing of the blind man, you know. Watch for that when we come to study it, you who feel you are in the dark now. There is no perplexity in your life that His life cannot make plain.

" *'Death,'* you say?

"But the seventh miracle deals with that. That is the crowning sign of all that Jesus is the Christ. He has conquered death itself, and has the authority to say, *'I am* the resurrection and the life.'

"To whom else shall we go to find life? Joy, health, sustenance, power, peace, light, victory over death itself? If we really have Him, His life, there is nothing, *nothing,* that need dismay us. And we receive that life by believing. Let's read our key verse again: 'These are written that ye might believe.' "

When the lesson was over, all too soon for Jane, she carried away with her the little book and the brief notes she had jotted down, and read them over again in her room, resolving not to miss any of these wonderful lessons. Somehow the few minutes' talk had made life seem a wider thing than just her little environment where her thoughts were all centered on herself and her own perplexities. She had had a glimpse into a vast universe, where she was a child of the Father's love, and she longed inexpressibly for that Life that the teacher had talked about. That Life that was joyful, sane, fruit-ful, peaceful and unafraid, guided, secure, eternal!

She took the book of John and sat down to study over the chapters and verses the teacher had used, and let them sink deep into her heart and memory for future use.

For three days Jane enjoyed the evening lessons, and

was beginning to plan how she could attend them after Miss Leech came home and she had to vacate her fine quarters, but just as she was about to enter the hall the fourth evening she heard a voice behind her calling:

"Oh, I say, Beautiful! Where have you been all this time?" Looking around in startled annoyance she saw to her dismay the young man Gaylord from the stocking department. Now, what could he possibly want of her? With all the girls he had at his beck and call, why should he bother her?

Other girls were turning and looking at him and at her; she couldn't just walk in and not return his salute. So she managed a nod, and said: "Oh, good evening!"

She was about to turn and go into the hall, but annoyingly the young man sprang up the two steps between them and came to her side.

"Oh, I say, what became of you? I thought we were going to have a date that next night and then you disappeared."

"Oh, I'm on vacation," she said. "I'll be back all too soon next week."

"Oh, well, how about tonight? I have time on my hands and not a thing to do. A friend I expected to date is sick. Can't you and I see a picture?"

"Oh, thank you," said Jane in a panic, "but I'm going in here. There's something I wouldn't miss for anything."

"Oh, I see!" The young man looked perplexedly up at the building and couldn't quite make out from the various signs at the door just what it might be she was interested in.

"All right," he said gaily. "How about my going along? Perhaps that's the best way to find out what your line is anyway."

"Oh, but I'm afraid you wouldn't like it," said Jane

startled. "It's just a class. I'm sure it's not in your line. Please excuse me. They always begin on time and I wouldn't like to miss a word."

She turned and sped up the remaining steps and into the hall breathlessly. But when she went to a seat she found him beside her, curiously studying the little red book someone had given him as he entered.

He sat down grinning.

"You see you didn't get rid of me so easily," he said, staring around the hall alertly. "What is this anyway? A spiritualistic séance?"

"Ssh!" said Jane shaking her head.

He looked up at the teacher and frowned, and then he looked down at Jane's little red book, and suddenly saw that all the peop e had the same book.

The lesson that night was most interesting to Jane, but somehow it didn't seem to click with the young man. He fumbled the leaves of his book for a minute or two in an attempt to understand what it was about, and then he fidgeted another five minutes. And finally he leaned over and whispered to Jane.

"Say, I'm about fed up on this, aren't you?"

"Ssh!" said Jane shaking her head.

He frowned and tried to listen for another three minutes and then he gave a deep audible sigh.

"Well," he said at last, leaning toward her, his voice by now quite unguarded, and audible to those sitting near, "you win. This is too deep for me. I'm going to the movies. I can't go this any longer. Come on out and find a nice picture!"

Jane was writing down a particularly interesting sentence in her notebook, and looked annoyed.

"Come on, kiddo!"

"No!" she said firmly. "I wouldn't miss this for anything."

"Okay, kiddo. I'm leaving you. See you subse!" and he got up noisily and went out.

Jane was relieved to have him gone. She had been worrying in the back of her mind to know just how she was going to get rid of him after the class was out. She distinctly did not want to go with him to see any moving pictures. She did not want to go with him anywhere. She did not like him. She wondered if that were a wrong attitude. One might suppose she would be grateful for any attention, lonely as she was. Perhaps she was all wrong. But somehow her mother had given her ideals that would not be satisfied by the trifling youth of today. There must be some real people somewhere who looked upon life as more than a good time when work was over. Well, anyway, she didn't have to worry about him any more tonight. And she could get the ending of the lesson without being further distracted.

So she wrote happily on to the end.

She was half fearful as she went out lest she would find him waiting for her outside, insisting upon a picture, and she slid out in the crowd and hurried away, thankful that he was not to be seen.

Those last days of her vacation were very precious. She husbanded each hour. There were certain books in the little bookcase she wanted to be sure and read before she left, and she read three or four hours at a time. Conscientiously she took walks, always choosing the time when she would not be likely to meet anyone from the store. Somehow it seemed more like a vacation than if she came into contact with any of her fellow laborers.

Hungrily she wrote down a list of the books in the little library which she knew she would not have time to read. Sometime perhaps she could find one or another of them in a second-hand store. Or perhaps she could afford a membership in some library. But then when would she have time to read them? Or light and comfort in which to read? She could take a book to a park bench in the early evening and read a few minutes every night, but the daylight would soon be growing shorter, and of course she had her washing to do, and some mending. There wouldn't be much time. Certainly, though, she had a right to a little pleasure. Other people went to the movies, and she could take her amusement by reading, if she only had a good light.

Ah! Here was a thought. It wasn't so many blocks to the big railroad station. Why couldn't she sit in the waiting room for an hour or so now and then and read? Provided she had something to read? Well, she would see when she got settled in her new room.

She wasn't very happy about that room either, but it seemed the best she could find unless she went entirely out of the region near the store, where she could not possibly walk to her work. Perhaps if she got a raise around Christmas she might be able to afford carfare and get a more homelike room. The one she had now was even more bare than Mrs. Hawkins', but it did have a heating pipe running across one end. That might make some difference in the temperature, though she doubted it. However, she couldn't do better just now. And when she got home to the many mansions of course it wouldn't matter what she had gone through down here. *"My* peace I give unto you." His peace would be calm in any kind of environment.

The weather was not so continuously hot now, and when it was intense for a few hours there was always the electric fan to make it tolerable. The respite from the heat had given her a new lease on life, and she had lost the look of strain that had characterized her before she had the collapse in the store. The good food and the rest had given a roundness to her cheeks and a brightness to her eyes, and one morning when she was brushing her hair before the mirror she suddenly stopped and looked at herself.

"Why, I'm not so bad-looking as I used to be," she said to herself. "I guess I was just starved. I'll have to look out for that, even if I don't get a warm coat for winter. I can't afford to look like a ghost or I'll lose my job and then where would I be?"

Carrying out that thought she realized that if she were taken very sick there would be no place for her but a charity hospital, and a charity grave if she died. That was no way for a Scarlett to be, on charity. She must keep well, be self-respecting, and save her money. She had had an honorable father and mother and belonged to a respected family. It was up to her to take care of herself. Or—*was* it? Wasn't it perhaps God's care? If He cared for her that way, the way the book of John seemed to say, then He would provide for her. She must trust and not be afraid. But of course it was up to her not to be careless of her health.

The next day was her last evening in Miss Leech's apartment, and she had tidied it all up. Miss Leech would arrive about ten o'clock that night, and Jane had arranged to go straight to her own new room as soon as she had welcomed her friend home.

The canary's cage was clean, the goldfish had fresh water, the plants were flourishing, and there wasn't a fleck of dust on anything. Jane had her small belongings packed and ready to go. There were still ten pages in a book she wanted to finish, but there would be plenty of time for that after she got back from the Bible class.

She put on her hat and took her little red book and notebook, and went out. The sky was soft with evening. A red glow hovered over the horizon, as much of it as she could see afar at the end of the street, with a vivid bit of coral, golden streaked, dashed across its corner. There was even a little breeze from the direction of the river. A perfect night for the end of her vacation. How wonderful it had been! And she hadn't expected nor intended to have a vacation at all. It just came to her like a blessing out of heaven!

She would not think that this was the end of her pleasant interval. Rather think of it as a beginning, perhaps, of new things. She had found a hope in those Bible classes, and a peace was beginning to grow in her heart as her faith increased.

She walked slowly for there was plenty of time. She wanted to put away in her memory this night, the light in the sky, the cool breeze on her brow. They would be refreshing things to remember if hot hard days came when it scarcely seemed that she could go on. She would go on remembering that in her Father's house were many mansions, and what He chose for her residence here was His ordering, and it was not for her to demur.

There was still plenty of time as she reached the steps up to the building. She mounted slowly. Only a few of the class were as yet going in. She lingered on each step, looking off to the horizon where a flood of gold was pouring into the clearness of the roseate hues. What a lovely picture, even amidst the noise and grime of a city street!

With a last lingering look she turned to go, glad that she was alone, and no one could question her lingering.

It was just then she heard the sound, a voice vaguely familiar, calling her name:

"Miss Scarlett! Wait! Miss Scarlett!"

Without turning she hastened on, startled, dismayed.

Could that be young Gaylord again? She had thought him cured of coming here for her.

But the voice had called her Miss Scarlett, and she doubted if he knew her name. He had always called her "Beautiful!" Who else could it be? Not Mr. Clark. And he was the only one who called her that.

Or was it all imagination? Just some combination of sounds in the street that seemed like her name? She was too sensitive. No one was calling now. She had just imagined it. No, she would not even turn and look back. If it should be Gaylord, somehow having found out her name, she would not let him know she had heard him. She would go in and take her seat. Get a seat by others, where there was no room for him. Then if he had taken a notion to come after her again she would escape his tormenting chatter. She wanted to get all of this lesson. She would surely need it on the morrow.

So she hurried on and drifted into a seat in the third row with others who were filling up the front rows. Surely no one would come up there to search for her! And after she had sat there a few minutes she would get free from the feeling that someone was following her. It was just nerves anyway. She had had a nice vacation and she mustn't allow nerves to dominate her any more.

So she settled down and gave attention to the lesson which began almost immediately, and took her thoughts from everything else.

9

KENT Havenner had stayed in town that evening to see a girl who had sent him word that she would be at her married sister's overnight.

He had been going with her more or less for some months. She was a girl his mother and sister did not like. She used a great deal of make-up, smoked incessantly, drank on occasion, and was moreover divorced. That the reason for the divorce was the fault mainly of her former husband did not make her any more desirable as a companion for Kent in the eyes of his mother, or according to the traditions under which he had been reared.

The girl's name was Evadne Laverock. She was considered very beautiful in a startling way.

There had been some difference of opinion between them for the past four months and Evadne had taken herself abroad for a time. Now she was back and wished to see Kent. And Kent had so far recovered his sense of the fitness of things as not to be quite sure whether he wanted to see Evadne or not. But he remained in town, and telephoned his sister that he had business that would keep him till the late train, or perhaps he would not come home until tomorrow night.

Nevertheless he had not hastened to meet her. He had taken a leisurely dinner at some distance from the house where the married sister was living, and dallied within his own conscience and his common sense awhile before he went out to take a leisurely way to the rendezvous. He did not intend to give in too easily. He would let Evadne make all the concessions.

As he walked along he noticed a number of young people going his way. A score or more of good-looking young girls, at least they were sensible-looking, and most of them had becoming curly hair and bright faces. Some of them were even noticeably pretty, and there was one who had a sweet charm of bearing that seemed to set her apart from the rest. Where had he seen her before? There was something familiar about the way she held her head. There were several young fellows among the girls, some in company with them, and some going by themselves. They were all going to the same place. Up the steps to a building, a hall! Who was that girl with the dark hair? Somewhere he had met her, he was sure. She was distinguished-looking. Evadne wouldn't think so, but she was. He had certainly seen her somewhere, talked with her! Where were they all going? Was this a school?

Then the girl with the dark hair mounted the steps slowly, looking off toward the sunset, and he caught a glimpse of her face. Yes! There she was at last!

It was then he called out! He completely forgot Evadne Laverock, and cried:

"Miss Scarlett! Wait! Miss Scarlett! *Jane!*"

But she went right on up the steps deliberately. Yet she must have heard. If that was her name she would have turned, wouldn't she? He was a fool. Of course it wasn't Jane Scarlett! And yet, if it only was how glad he would be. She was very much wanted at the office, and he certainly would like to be the one to complete the contact and produce her, after the way he seemed to have fumbled the job in the first place.

"Miss Scarlett!"

He was standing at the foot of the steps looking up and other girls turned and looked down at him curiously, but she did not turn. If she had been Jane Scarlett she would surely have heard and turned, wouldn't she?

Of course it was time he went to Evadne Laverock if he was going at all, and yet so strong was his impression as he watched the shoulders and back of this girl disappear into the darkness of the hall above that he seemed compelled to follow her. After all it would take but a minute in a lighted room with a good square look at her to discover his mistake if it was one. So he followed up the steps, and came, after a devious way through a winding hall, to stand in the doorway of the classroom where he saw the lady he was following just sitting down in a seat away at the front. From here he could not be any more definitely sure by the look of her back and shoulders whether she was the girl he sought or not.

So he walked all the way up the middle aisle to the only vacant seat anywhere near her. It was across the aisle one row ahead of hers, in the middle of the row. Here he might hope to get a good view of her face.

And so, after various twistings and turnings, and trying to appear to be watching for somebody coming in the door at the back, he finally got a full view of her and knew it was none other than Jane Scarlett.

But Jane Scarlett was bending over a little red book, finding the place, and then opening a small notebook and getting out a tiny pencil. She was not noticing in the least the people about her. And though he turned his head and looked full at her as long as his natural courtesy would permit him to do, he could not seem to make her look up and recognize him.

At last he settled back in his chair with folded arms and resigned himself to wait till whatever this was was over and he could speak to her. What had he come in on anyway, and how long was it likely to last? Some sort of class? A business course? Was she trying to get ready to do something more lucrative than sell buttons? That was commendable. She seemed a bright girl. The rounded line of her cheek was really lovely.

He glanced at his watch. It was still early. Evadne would not be expecting him yet. And a class of any sort would likely be out in a half or three quarters of an hour.

So Kent Havenner sat still and waited, studying the faces of the quite large group of young men and maidens who were gathered eagerly, with their attention fixed on the woman who was speaking.

Then suddenly his attention was caught by the speaker.

"If you want God in your life you must be willing to comply with the conditions."

Heavens, what was this, some kind of religious quackery?

Then he gave entire attention to the teacher.

"Life is not a mere matter of seventy or eighty years on this earth. Life is eternity-long. Did it ever occur to you how queer it is that we spend about a quarter of the time we count as life in getting ready for it? Going to school to learn how to live? To learn how to earn money and enjoy ourselves? And never give a thought to getting ready for eternity? Some of us try to persuade ourselves that there is no eternity. That when we die we just pass out and are never conscious any more.

"Yet Jesus invites us to a life that never ends. A life that is full of joy with not a disappointment. A life that need make no mistakes under His guidance. And we take no pains to acquaint ourselves with it, nor even try to find out if it be true. This book gives us unmistakable signs of eternity and shows us how to prepare for it."

Kent looked down at the little book in his hand. It was evidently a portion of the Bible. He was more or less familiar with at least the outside of the Bible, but he had never looked upon it as a book that contained any *proofs* of anything. He had always supposed it mere theories.

He listened to the teacher as she briefly went over the résumé of the past weeks' studies, and he followed her in chapter and verse, surprised at the apt quotations.

Now and then he cast a quick glance at Jane and noted her intent interest, the quick kindling of her eye at a new thought. Then all at once he thought of Evadne, and glanced at his watch. She would be wondering why he did not come. He tried to fancy telling her about this place and explaining to her how he happened to be here. He tried to imagine her here with him, and somehow couldn't do it. If she sat over there where Jane sat she would certainly not be gazing up with that eagerness. She would be uneasily looking at her watch, or openly yawning, or definitely getting up and leaving. Evadne was impatient. She would never sit still and listen to words about eternity. Evadne knew the smartest fashions; she knew the price of jewels and other precious things of earth, fine cars, and mansions, and the latest dances, new shades of lipstick—but perhaps she was not figuring on eternity. And if he were to try to tell her about what he had heard tonight while she was awaiting his coming she would but laugh him to scorn.

Was it possibly true as his mother claimed, that Evadne had a vapid mind incapable of serious thought?

And then the old question got the ascendency for the instant, to the exclusion of all that was going on about him. Should he go and see Evadne again at all, or just let the summer's break that had come between them be the end? Did he really want her for the daily companion of his life? Or would he regret it later when he found someone more suited to him?

But the teacher's voice broke upon his consciousness again:

"Did you ever think what it would be in your life to know God intimately and to have Jesus Christ your hourly companion?" she asked. The words fell into his perplexities with almost a shock. It came to him that if that could be true he would have an answer to all his perplexities. He needn't be in danger of making lifelong mistakes. He didn't really want to make mistakes that would affect his whole life, as his family seemed to think he was in danger of doing.

But Evadne was very lovely in her way. He had thought that perhaps his mother was only over-anxious. Also he had hoped that Evadne might change after they were married. But now after the interval of her absence he wondered. Would she? Could she? Did she want to be molded to go his way, or was she determined to go her own?

Looking sharply thus into his inner consciousness he was almost afraid to meet her. He knew her subtleties. She would wind him around her finger again the way she used to do. Just one smile of her red lips, one glance from her topaz eyes and he would be in her toils. Did he want that?

He was practically free from her influence now. They had parted because he had taken a stand against some of her decisions and wishes. He wouldn't go her way in everything.

It had been frightfully hard at first, but he had held out and plunged into his law work, and now he was really interested in it. He wanted to get on and attain great things. And if she came into his life again he knew it would at once mean late hours and gay living, not the steady quiet life to which he had been brought up. She laughed at that. It would mean a constant struggle to hold his own in his work if he were trying to please her. He could not serve two masters.

Well, whatever he was going to do later in the evening, he was working now. He had to contact Jane Scarlett and put her in touch with his law firm. That was his business. And he had been learning these last few months since Evadne went away that business must come first, pleasure afterward. And Evadne had to learn that too if she was going to be around with him. If she did not like it let her go away again. He was getting on well enough without her. Of course he knew that Evadne would not understand why he had to stay in a Bible class and watch one girl, one plain poorly dressed girl who sold buttons in a store, but he was convinced that what he was doing now was his business and it was important. He was quite sure that whatever Evadne was using as an excuse for getting him to come and see her, it could not be important.

How long this session of study would last he couldn't tell, and it was impossible to forecast how long it would take him after this was over, before he was free to go. Better let it rest at that. If he got away from this duty at any reasonable hour he would go to Evadne and have it out with her, find out whether she cared enough for him to go his way or not. If he didn't get away early enough he would just take it that he wasn't meant to contact Evadne tonight, and let it go at that. It was like tossing a penny up, or leaving it to a higher power to choose.

"There is eternal life to be lived here and now. But you will never find it if you try to live for this world also!"

The teacher's words were projected into his thoughts again and seemed almost as if she were answering what he was thinking. "'And this is life eternal,'" went on the sweet strong voice, "'that they might know thee, the only true God, and Jesus Christ whom thou has sent.' Do you want to begin to live this eternal life now, tonight?"

Something stirred in Kent Havenner's heart. Impulsively he wanted to accept that invitation. But how?

And then the class was breaking up. They were stirring all about him, rising to go. How short it had been!

He rose and looked toward Jane Scarlett, and she was looking straight at him, but with unseeing eyes alight with earnest thought. There was no recognition in her glance. She was obviously thinking of what she had been hearing.

He came a little nearer and stood at the end of her aisle as she waited for the girl ahead of her to pass. Then as she came on he spoke in a low friendly courteous voice.

"Miss Scarlett?"

Jane started and looked up. This was not young Gaylord. Neither was it Mr. Clark. Yet she knew the voice. But she had no acquaintances who came to this class. Because of her extreme shyness the few girls who had spoken to her did not know her name. And none of the young men had so much as looked at her nor she at them.

Then recognition dawned.

"Oh, Mr. Havenner! I did not expect to see you here."

"Well, no, it's scarcely one of my haunts,"—he smiled. "I have you to thank for the discovery. But I think I'll come again. It's very unusual, isn't it?"

A blaze of light suddenly shone in her face, making her almost lovely.

"It is wonderful!" she admitted. "But I don't see how I was the means of bringing you here. I only just found it myself a few days ago."

"Well, you see, it happens that you are very much wanted at our office, and I've been keeping an eye out for you for the past two weeks. I even went to your boarding house to search for you, and when I was told that you had left there I tried the store again, but was told you were on vacation. As nobody knew where you had gone there was nothing else to do but wait. But I've been more or less alert for you ever since, for I knew the office was annoyed about my not being able to produce you after having had an interview with you. So when I spied you entering this hall tonight, and failed to be able to attract your attention, I followed you in. I hope you don't mind."

But a sudden troubled look had come into Jane's face.

"Why of course not," she said, "but I don't understand what anybody would want me for. Is something the matter somewhere?"

The young man smiled disarmingly.

"Nothing to be alarmed about," he said. "It was just that the office wrote you a letter, and it came back to them with a stamp that you were unknown at that address. As I was responsible for the address they used, the matter naturally was brought to my notice."

"A letter?" said Jane. "But what would they be writing to me about?"

"Well, I wasn't shown the letter, but I understood it had to do with the settlement of an estate, some papers that had to be signed. Nothing to worry you, I'm sure."

Jane's brows puckered in perplexity.

"Oh, they surely must have got me mixed with someone else. I wouldn't be having anything to do with the settlement of an estate. I couldn't even be a witness, I'm sure. I've never really had much to do with any of the relatives." She gave a little nervous laugh.

"Well, you'll soon have opportunity to know exactly what it is, Miss Scarlett, for I am quite sure the letter will be delivered to you tomorrow morning if you will be good enough to tell me where to deliver it."

"Oh!" she said a bit breathlessly, for she could not yet fathom the why of the letter. "Why, my vacation is over tomorrow morning. I shall be back in the store."

"And back at your same boarding house? I understood the lady to say that you were done with her, or she was done with you."

Jane laughed at the twinkle in his eyes.

"No, I shall not be there. I've found a new room."

"Will it be all right to deliver the letter to you at the store?" he asked respectfully. "I want to make sure it reaches its destination this time."

"Oh, yes, quite all right."

"Then I'll be there. Please don't evade me this time."

They had reached the outside door now, and began walking down the steps, Jane evidently expecting him to leave her. She had that attitude. But Kent did not intend to leave her yet.

"You won't mind if I walk with you a little way, will you?" he asked. "I want to ask you a little about that class tonight. What is it? How did you find out about it? I've never heard of a class like that before, that is, outside of a church. I suppose they have such things in churches, though I don't know much about it from experience. Or perhaps this *is* a church affair. Is it? I was very much interested."

"I don't think so," said Jane, instant interest in her face, and a quick light in her fine eyes that made them lovely once more. "It seems to be just a class. I don't know who sponsors it, or even whether it is sponsored. I just happened to hear it announced on the radio the other night in such a unique way that I determined I would go and see what it was all about, and I liked it so much that I kept coming."

"Well, I liked it too," said Kent with surprising candor. "I wouldn't have expected to like it, but now I'm so interested to see if they can bear out what they said that I'm minded to go again myself. It sort of hit me home right where I live."

"Oh, did you feel that way too? That was the way the announcement made me feel. They said 'If you are sad and weary and questioning what life is all about, if you want to find an answer that will satisfy, and help you go on amid hardships and loneliness, come to Mrs. Brooke's class and get help and comfort.' Well, I went and I'm finding it."

He looked down at her questioningly, searched her earnest young face deeply, and said at last:

"Then perhaps I shall find what I need there too. I'm half a mind to try it."

"Well," said Jane with a timid little smile, "you wouldn't of course have the same trials and disappointments that I have, but I believe, or I'm coming to believe, that there is a remedy in that book for any need one could have."

"I wonder!" said the young man, and walked on by her side thoughtfully.

Presently Jane came to the apartment where she had been staying, and hesitated at the door.

"I have to go in here now," she said shyly. "I'll be expecting that letter in the morning."

Kent cast a glance up at the building. Quite a different affair from the place he had gone to seek her two weeks ago.

"Oh," he said looking at her and the opulent entrance again, "are you living here? I don't blame you for leaving that other place."

"No," said Jane with a sad little twist to her voice, "oh no, nothing so nice as this. I've just been staying here with a canary and some goldfish while their owner was away. I made it my vacation. But it's over tonight. The owner is returning at ten o'clock and I'm leaving for quarters more suited to my pocketbook. I'm sorry of course to go, but it's been a lovely vacation and rested me a lot."

"Oh," said Kent Havenner giving his watch a quick glance, "then you've almost an hour to wait before you move. Have you anything to do in the interval? Because I've been noticing the notebook you are carrying with you and wondering if there isn't some spot where we could sit down for a few minutes and you could tell me about the other lessons in this little red book. I have a great curiosity to know just what the preliminary line of study was. I'm sure I saw you taking notes. Isn't that right? Well, then, would you have time, or are there still some duties awaiting you upstairs?"

Jane hesitated.

"No," she said honestly, "I'm all packed. I've only to go up a minute or two and give an account of my stewardship, and then I'm moving on to my new home.

I'll be glad to give you an idea of what I've gleaned from the meetings so far. Or you could take my notebook with you? Though I'm not sure the notes would be very clear. I had to take them down so briefly."

"Thank you," said Kent with alacrity. "Why couldn't we sit down on that bench I see in there across from the elevators? There seems to be a good light. Would you be able to see your friend from there when she arrives, or is there some better place?"

"No, that's fine," said Jane with relief in her voice. She was afraid he might be going to ask her to go to some hotel or place of amusement, and that she was determined not to do. She might be late and then what would Miss Leech think?

So they entered the lobby and sat down. Jane got out her little notebook and Kent opened his book of John and they were soon deep in study.

Kent Havenner had forgotten all about Evadne for the time being. He was studying an entirely different type of girl, and he had no intention whatever of letting her out of his sight until he knew just where she was located. Not that he doubted her genuineness, but she had been lost out of the scheme of things once, and there was no telling but something might happen again. Besides, he was really interested to know just what type of girl this was who had gotten interest and apparently entertainment out of a Bible class.

Jane opened her notebook at the beginning and made him turn to the different chapters and verses, and then went on. With remarkable clearness, in well chosen words, she spread out the story in John as she had heard it, coloring it all by what it had done for her own soul, and incidentally revealing the sadness and desolation of her own lot. She did not know she was doing this latter.

It would have been the last thing in life she would have willingly done, to have projected herself into his notice.

He watched her face which had suddenly become vivid as she detailed the lessons she had got, and now and then the listener was startled at the applicability of the truths given.

"You couldn't, if you had tried, have told me anything that would so have hit my own case," he suddenly confessed, looking into her sweet eyes with a kind of wonder. His sister had sweetness in her eyes and so had his mother. But most of the girls he knew had sharp, brilliant unsympathetic eyes. He marveled at this girl. This girl who had been living in the very common walks of life.

But his confession brought a sudden consciousness to Jane. Before that she had been talking to him much as if she were talking aloud to herself, going over a lesson that had helped her. Now suddenly he became a stranger, an utter stranger, and she felt herself presumptuous to be talking thus so freely. She was only a button salesgirl. She had no business to be preaching a sermon to this stranger.

The color stole up into her pale cheeks and she dropped her lashes shyly.

"I have talked too much," she said abruptly. "I did not intend to apply this to anyone but myself."

"Perhaps that is the fineness of your ability, that you could use a lesson which has touched your soul to touch mine also. I thank you for it. And is that all?"

"No, there is one more before tonight."

Rapidly she went over the tiny pages, touching upon the main points, and just as she finished she heard a taxi drive up in front of the building and glancing up caught a glimpse of Miss Leech getting out and lingering to pay the driver.

"And that brings us up to tonight," finished Jane hastily, "and there comes my lady. I shall have to go now. Take the notebook if you like and copy it. I can get it again when you bring the letter." She smiled at him and rose with a finality that startled him. There was something about it that seemed so self-possessed, so like a woman of the world who was dismissing him. "Good night!" and she walked gracefully over to the door and possessed herself of the suitcase Miss Leech was capably carrying in.

Kent Havenner sat absolutely still where she had left him, glancing up at the newcomer, but not intruding himself upon the scene. He was pleasantly surprised to notice that the elderly woman who came in, greeting Jane with friendly eyes, was neither a snob, nor a woman of the world in appearance, just a quiet self-possessed business woman.

The elevator came down with a slam just then and clattered its door open, and the two walked into it without looking toward him. He had a feeling that Jane Scarlett would prefer it so.

And so Kent Havenner sat and conned the little notebook till he knew its phrases by heart, caught the turn of words and sentences that spoke of the personality of the writer, the lesson coming through her own heart to his.

It is hard to say just what Evadne Laverock would have thought if she had passed that way and looking in had seen her erstwhile lover who she thought was now under discipline, studying a little book like that and sitting there at his ease as if he had all the night before him, while she waited impatiently for his coming. But there he sat, and several miles away across the city Evadne sat and fumed and waited.

10

MISS Leech was delighted with the look of her apartment, especially with the pot of African violets that Jane had bought at a wayside stand as a little expression of her thanks.

Jane insisted on her going around and looking at everything before she took her departure.

"I hate to have you go," said the older woman looking at Jane approvingly. "It's so late wouldn't you like to stay here and sleep on the couch tonight?"

"Thank you, no. I have a room, and I must go to it and get settled for the morning. I'm so glad you are pleased with everything. I've tried to keep it just as you left it."

"Oh, you have! At least I believe it is cleaner than when I left. I'm afraid you haven't done anything but clean house every day."

"Oh yes, I have!" said Jane eagerly, her eyes lighting up. "I've read two whole rows of books, and I've listened to the radio a lot. I've had a wonderful time, and I've gained five pounds. I'm proud of that. I was really getting too thin."

"Yes, you're looking very well. I'm so glad! I was a little worried about you. I thought perhaps I had been the means of keeping you in the hot city when otherwise you might have gone somewhere in the country."

"Oh, no!" said Jane quickly. "I couldn't. I should have stayed right here and worked hard in the store if you hadn't let me keep your house for you. I had no idea of taking a vacation at all till Mr. Clark came and told me the store was giving me a vacation with pay because I had been sick. I thought that was wonderful of them. But I wouldn't have had any place to go if it hadn't been for you. You see my room was perfectly dreadful. It was breathless and the food was something terrible. Some days I could scarcely eat a bite."

"Oh, my dear! That's too bad. But what are you going to do now?"

"Oh I have another room," said Jane lightly, evading the searching glance of the older woman's eyes. "I hope it is going to be much better."

"Well, I hope so," said Miss Leech. "You must keep in touch with me, and come and visit me for a day or two if you have to hunt for another place."

"Oh, thank you!" said Jane. "You've been just wonderful to me. I won't forget it, ever!"

"Well, I hope we'll always be friends. You don't know what a comfort it has been to me to know I could trust you with my room. It being the only real home I have in the world, of course I prize it."

"Oh, of course. It's a beautiful place. If I ever get rich I shall try to have one just like it, only I'm sure I shall never be as prosperous as all that."

"You can never tell, my dear!" said Miss Leech. "I used to be terribly hard up fifteen years ago when I first got a job, and I tell you I've worked hard for every little thing I own. Except of course a few of the old things, furniture and dishes that came from my home after my mother and father died. So I love it all. And now I shall feel that you have a share of interest in it too, and shall want you to come and see me as often as you can spare the time. Of course I'm getting to be an old woman, and I can't be very good company for a young girl like you, but I shall enjoy you whenever you haven't any better company."

"Oh, I'll love to come," said Jane. "You and I have a lot in common for I've read some of your wonderful books, and so I feel as if I knew the same people you know. And now I must run along and let you get to bed, for I know you are tired after that long journey. Good-bye and don't forget there are some cinnamon buns in the tin box for your breakfast, and fresh eggs in the refrigerator."

Jane picked up her suitcase and the suitbox that held her curtains, and started toward the door, but Miss Leech held out an envelope.

"Here, my dear," she said. "Here is your compensation for looking after my place."

"But indeed, *no!*" said Jane drawing away. "I couldn't think of taking anything for that. I've had a wonderful vacation and couldn't have had it if you hadn't loaned me your room."

"Indeed you will take it, little girl," said Miss Leech determinedly. "I always pay something for having my place looked after, only I never had such efficient service before. And you don't want to spoil my vacation, do you? I should feel like a selfish thing if you refused to take this."

"But you needn't at all. I really don't need it. The store gave me my vacation with pay, so I have enough to get a start."

"That makes no difference," said Miss Leech. "I'm

giving you this little bit because I want to, and you're going to be a good girl and take it. If you don't want to count that you've earned it, then play it is a present I've brought you, and you go and buy something with it to remember me by."

They argued for two or three minutes more, but finally Jane came away with the money. Ten whole dollars! It seemed a fortune to her. Just for staying in a better place than she could possibly have afforded!

Her face was shining with happiness as she got out of the elevator. And there right before her stood Kent Havenner, her little notebook in his hand, and a smile of welcome on his face.

"I've copied it all," he announced pleasantly, "and I thought you wouldn't mind if I stayed till you came down and gave it to you tonight. Here! Let me have that baggage!"

"Oh, thank you, no," said Jane, her face crimsoning with embarrassment to think how shabby her baggage was, and to remember that she had only a very poor rooming house as destination. He mustn't find out where it was. She would be ashamed!

"But yes," he said possessing himself of the box and suitcase. "I'm going to see you to your apartment. I couldn't think of letting you go alone at this time of night."

"Oh, I'm not afraid," said Jane. "I'm used to it, you see. I have to do it often. You mustn't spoil me. I'm a working girl, you know. Please let me have them."

"Oh, no," he said gaily. "You may be a working girl, but you're in my care tonight, and I have a debt to pay you for introducing me to the book of John. I have a hunch I'm going to be pretty crazy over that before I get through."

She walked perforce by his side to the door and tried

to make another stand when she reached the sidewalk, but he only laughed, and gathering the two pieces of luggage under one arm he waved his other hand to a taxi.

The taxi swept up to the curb and he handed the luggage to the driver, as he swung open the door.

"Now," he said as he put her in and got in beside her, "where to? What's the street and number?"

Jane faltered out the address, and added, "But please, I wish you wouldn't feel that you must go out of your way to go with me. I'll be quite all right alone now."

She reflected that after all it wouldn't cost much to pay taxi fare, just this once, and of course it was rather a long way to carry her baggage herself.

But the young man only closed the door of the cab and laughed.

"Sorry my company isn't agreeable to you," he said, "but I've a great desire to see you definitely located for the night so that I shall be reasonably sure to be able to find you in the morning in case you are detained from going to the store. You see I've got to deliver that letter, and I'm taking no chances."

His face was a broad grin, and Jane reflected how pleasant he looked when he grinned, and thought how nice it would be to have a real friend who looked like that and insisted on taking care of her now and then.

"Oh!" she said. And then her face grew troubled as she thought of that letter.

"Is—that letter—so important?" she managed to ask.

"Well, yes, I imagine it's rather important to one member of the Scarlett family, or at least I've been led to suppose that. Anyway it's important that I shall be able to discharge my duty toward the letter, and prove that there *is* a Jane Scarlett, and that I have seen her and talked with her."

"But I can't imagine that I could have anything to do with an important document," mused Jane, the worry stealing into her eyes again. "You see I scarcely know the family at all."

"Well, don't try to imagine, then," said Kent still smiling. "Wait till morning and let the letter settle it. Is this the house?"

He gazed out of the taxi window at the tall bare-looking building before which they had stopped. There was nothing in his facial expression to show what was in his heart about that stark ugly building, nor how unsuited an abode it seemed for that sweet-faced girl, with the delicate features and great serious eyes.

He helped her out and they stood together in the bare uninviting hall while she waited for the landlady or matron or whatever she was to finish talking to a slatternly girl with sly eyes who was trying to get a room for the night without any money to pay for it.

"This is no place for you," said Kent's eyes as he gave a critical glance about and then looked down at Jane's worried eyes. But his lips tried to smile and take it all for granted as if it were an abode of luxury.

"It's—" Jane glanced around her with a disapproving glance, "not so very—grand!" she finished apologetically. "But one can't expect grandeur for a pittance."

"No, I suppose not," said Kent glancing up the straight steep stairway that loomed at the end of the hall, "but it's not very homelike."

"It isn't a home," said Jane with a quick drawn breath of sadness. "One doesn't always have a home. That's why that fourteenth chapter of our little red book of John seems so wonderful to me. 'In my Father's house are many mansions. . . . I go to prepare a place for you.' *They* will be *homes* I'm sure, and there will always be those at the end of the road."

Kent looked down at her in wonder. Such an earnest young face, so sweet and wistful! Audrey had been right. She was unusual. And Audrey had seen that look in her face. She must have. It was a look that once seen was to be remembered.

"I wouldn't know about that," he said seriously. "I've never thought about homes at the end of the road. I'm afraid I've been occupied with thinking of homes along the way, like the teacher said tonight. But perhaps after this I shall think more about it. What chapter was that verse you just quoted about your Father's house?"

"Oh, that's the fourteenth of John. I learned that when I was a little girl. I hadn't thought about it for a long time, until recently, and it came back and—helped me."

She confessed her experience gently with a fleeting smile, as if she scarcely could believe that one like this young man would be interested in such things, or in anything she could say. Yet she was pleased and touched with awe that he really seemed to be.

An unusual conversation to be carried on in, and actually inspired by, that crude rooming house, yet there they stood, he lingering with a strange unexplained reluctance to leave.

Then the matron dismissed the other girl and came forward to Jane. Her eyes narrowed, looking nearsightedly through sparse faded lashes. Suddenly, with a rare smile, Kent lifted his hat, with fine impulse not to embarrass Jane by being a listener to her conversation.

"Well, good night! See you in the morning!" and he was gone.

Jane gave a quick glance out of the door into the warm darkness where he had disappeared, and it suddenly seemed to her that the sun had just been withdrawn from a very bright day.

Afterward when she went up to the fourth floor back room, and discovered its utter desolateness, it did not seem quite so depressing because her mind was on her evening. She discovered that the young man and her talk with him had even superseded and blotted out the coming of her friend Miss Leech. Yes, and the extra money she had not expected to have! Why, there were pleasant things in the world, even though one had no place but this bare room to call home. She had friends, she had more money than she had hoped for, and best of all she had her Heavenly Father's house to look forward to.

But what a pleasant man Mr. Havenner was! How his eyes spoke volumes when he was talking about the class. How he had responded to her own thoughts and feelings. Oh, what would it be to have a real friend like that for her very own!

But of course she mustn't let her mind dwell on him or anything connected with him. He was a great man, that is, he was likely going to be great, a lawyer, and well started on his way toward success from all appearances. And she was only a button salesgirl. She must never forget that. Perhaps sometime in the Father's house above they would meet and talk over their common interest in the book of John, but down here he was separated from her by impassable barriers. For of course he had only been kind and courteous. So she must not dwell on their conversation, nor make anything of it. He was keeping in touch with her just to be sure to get that letter to her in the morning. And that he spoke interestedly of the class and the lesson might only have been an extreme of courtesy. He might not even have meant any of it. Yet she couldn't but think it had been real interest in his eyes, interest for the things of another world.

However, that was not for her to speculate about. She would just be glad that he was interested, or seemed to be, because it made her comfortable and happy to have a bit of fellowship with another one of God's children. Or was he God's child?

But that letter! What was that going to mean to her? Constantly the thought of it recurred to her as something to be dreaded. Of course it might be some mere technicality that had no significance to her personally, though she couldn't imagine a circumstance that would make that possible. But she would be glad when it had come and the dread of it was over. Now, she would do as the young man had advised, just put it out of her mind and forget it until it arrived.

So she turned to the quick settling of her room.

She made her bed swiftly with the skimpy bedclothing the woman downstairs had given her. She got out her little hammer from the ten cent store and tacked up her closet curtain, and then hung her meager garments on the few nails, resolving to purchase a few hooks on her first opportunity and put them up. Then very hurriedly she prepared for bed and was soon discovering what a hard, hard narrow bed she had tonight in place of the lovely soft one in Miss Leech's room. But she was very weary, and it didn't take her long to get to sleep. And it seemed no time at all until her dependable alarm clock was giving her the signal to rise and remember that she was no longer a lady of leisure, but was once more a working girl.

II

WHEN Kent Havenner was out in the narrow street again he walked along briskly, thoughtfully, thinking of the girl he had just left. A most unusual girl!

There were no taxis on this street, and so he must walk until he reached a more frequented district. He was not thinking of where he was going, either, strangely enough. The evening that had begun so definitely as a visit to Evadne, had ended with another girl's wistful face looking at him as she said good night. And he so entirely forgot Evadne that when he reached a street car line that went directly to the railroad station he swung aboard it without thinking. His mind was on the evening's events, trying to think them through to a finish of some sort.

Once he glanced idly at his watch and saw that it was almost time for the last train to the shore, and that if the trolley was not interrupted in any way he ought to be able to make it, but even then he did not remember Evadne.

He made the station just in time to swing himself on the last car of the train, and it was not until he reached into his pocket for his commutation ticket and pulled out inadvertently Evadne's letter that he was reminded of the engagement which he had not kept.

He stared down at the letter in his hand, and finally read it through again. It did not take long. It was just one of her casual scrawls. She never wrote a letter as if she really cared. She always made it appear that it was a privilege to be informed that she was in the vicinity and would deign to receive one.

> Old thing: Am staying over night with Gloria. If you could drop in we could talk.
>
> As ever,
> Vad.

Somehow this reading of the letter gave him a distinct shock. It did not sound in the least like a girl who was sorry for her part of their separation. When he had read it the first time he had only seen in it a concession that she should stoop to inform him she was near and willing to talk. Now a careless insolence was uppermost.

"We could talk." She promised nothing. There was no penitence. And why talk more? They had talked hours upon hours and got nowhere. Why should he expect they would get anywhere tonight? And in the light of the evening he had just spent, her letter seemed most vapid and uninteresting. True it was couched in the accepted parlance of the day, that affected indifference. Was it true that he had ever admired that style of address? Why should reasonable human beings affect a disregard of the decencies and refinements of life? Almost he could see from his mother's point of view.

Well, it was too late to do anything about it now. The train was speeding on its way. Even if he could stop it there would be no way station where he could get transportation back to the city.

And besides, did he care? Had he the least desire to talk with Evadne? If she had anything worth while to tell him she would in time write it to him, or even come and see him. He was satisfied of that. She wasn't in the least backward about carrying out any of her own wishes, and she would find a way. It wouldn't hurt her in the least, even if he wanted eventually to bring her back to his wishes, to see that he was not as keen about her as he used to be. And even if she were now ready, after due coaxing, to promise what he had made a condition of their further acquaintance, he wasn't at all sure that he could trust her promises. Why had he ever thought he could? And what had changed him, without seeing her again? How did he now know so well what she must have been going to say?

Was it possible that it had taken that hour with the little clear-eyed girl from the button counter to show him Evadne's irresponsibility? How was it that a girl like Jane Scarlett in a few brief meetings had opened his eyes to this and more?

Or could it be that that quiet time spent in reading portions of the Bible had somehow toned his spirit to a place where he could discern between real and false?

Well, all this argument with himself was nonsense of course, and why waste the time? Jane Scarlett was only a working girl, with a courageous and a brave outlook, but he mustn't let his thoughts get tangled up with different points of view, and lives. He had enjoyed the evening, of course, and he had to own that he was glad he had got free from the talk with Evadne, but he mustn't get the "Cousin Evalina attitude" as Audrey called it. He probably would seldom see Jane Scarlett again, but he was sure that her genuineness and sweet character had helped him to see the false in Evadne. Maybe it wasn't being half fair to Evadne, but he didn't care. He was going home to bed, and he wasn't sorry. If he had gone to Evadne he would have had to take her to a night club, maybe two or three of them, and how would he have felt tomorrow after that? No, he was glad he had been so absorbed in thinking about what Jane had said that he had forgotten to go in the other direction. Probably tomorrow morning he would have to call Evadne up and explain and apologize, but anyhow he would have a good night's sleep. That was better than going to a hotel bed at five in the morning.

So he settled back and closed his eyes and thought of all he had heard that evening. And without his voluntary bidding Jane Scarlett's face in its wistful eagerness kept coming to his mind.

About the time that Kent Havenner boarded the train to the shore, the telephone in the Havenner cottage by the sea rang insistently, and Audrey answered it.

"Is this Havenner's?" a languid voice asked sharply.

An old familiar fury rose in Audrey's soul at the sound of that voice. Insolent, that was what the voice was, and her heart sank with apprehension.

"Yes?" she said with crisp dignity.

"I want to speak with Kent," the voice drawled, ignoring the one who had answered, though she must have known who it was.

"He is not here at present." More dignity.

"Oh! When will he be in?"

"I'm not sure. He said he might be late."

"Well, tell him to call me up at once when he gets in." The words were a command, as if they were being given to a servant. "This is Vad Laverock speaking," the voice went on. "Tell him to call Maurice 1011-J."

"Very well!" said Audrey without a shade of recognition in her voice, and immediately there was a quick click. Evadne had hung up.

Audrey stood there with her soul boiling within her. Was this what had made Kent stay in town tonight? Had he somehow found out that Evadne was in the vicinity again? Poor fool of a boy!

So that creature was back!

And now would Kent go into a slump again and be worthless as far as business or anything sensible was concerned? Just when he had been doing so well, and was getting interested, really interested in his work! Oh, why did Kent admire her anyway? Painted, artificial, unnatural creature! How terrible it would be if Kent should marry her! Mother and father would feel it so. And as for herself she would be entirely separated from her beloved brother!

Not that Evadne was one who would long endure any yoke like marriage. And that again would bring about another intolerable situation. Divorce was utter disgrace in the eyes of their parents. In fact both Audrey and her brother had been brought up to feel that way about it. Oh, if there was only something she could do to save Kent!

So, instead of going to bed early as she had planned, Audrey took a book and sat up and pretended to read. Though if the truth were known she did very little reading, for she kept continually thrashing over the problem in her mind, hearing again the insolent accents of that hateful voice.

Also she had a situation of her own to ponder. A situation not quite as obnoxious perhaps to the family, but almost as perplexing to herself. Ballard Bainbridge was a scholar of parts. He was so brilliant that some who knew him regarded him almost as highly as he regarded himself. He was handsome withal, and wealthy, a pleas-

ant playmate when he chose to play. But did she want
him in any closer relationship than as a playmate?

The trouble with him was he was a cynic and a
scorner. He had an innate conviction that nobody knew
as much as he did. Not even God, or the president, or
the Bible.

Now Mr. and Mrs. Havenner were not distinguished
church people, nor noted religious workers, but they
went to church at least once a Sunday whenever it was
convenient, and they did not like to hear even a scholar
criticize churches and ministers and religious beliefs. It
did not seem well-bred to them. They liked the man-
ners and customs of an older day, and thought it poor
taste for youth to presume to depart from them. Audrey
well knew that it would be a sore trial to have their
daughter marry a man of that type. And then to have
their son marry an Evadne, linking them up with a
world which they felt had gone mad, and was no longer
safe and sane and conservatively respectable, would be
the final blow. Audrey was dealing with the family
problem for really the first time, and seeing her own
part in it as she had never seen it before.

Now after considering her brother and the terrible
mistake he seemed about to make, she came at last to
face the facts in her own life. What was it she saw in
Ballard Bainbridge anyway? Did she really think she was
in love with him or hadn't the affair progressed that far
yet? Perhaps it was time she looked things in the face
and settled that before things went any further between
them. Could she ever really love Ballard? She admired
him immensely. His brain fairly scintillated with bril-
liancy. His clever sayings were a joy, even if most of
them did end in a sneer at somebody. And sometimes
even a sneer at some pet idea of her own? Could she
possibly fancy herself as going through life continuing

to admire him, and to love him the way father and mother admired and loved one another? Listening to his everlasting cynicism day after day? Fighting the depression that came over her sometimes when he laid low some time-honored custom or faith? Not that she had any very strong religious convictions herself, or wanted to have, but her own nature was sunny and sweet and it depressed her terribly to hear constant criticism and sneers. His nature was wild and turbulent. Everybody wrong but himself, and he set to tell them where they made all their mistakes. Would he ever get over it? Would the time come when he grew a little older and still wiser, that he would realize that he wasn't the only wise one in the whole world? As she looked at the matter honestly, without bias now, she found herself wondering if a woman could really go on loving a man, or even love him enough in the first place to marry him, when she saw his glaring faults as plainly as she did Ballard's. And was it conceivable that if she should ever get up the courage to talk with him about it frankly, that he would consider what she said seriously, and try to look into himself and mend his ways? Would he not rather tell her she was a mere woman, and had no brain or she would know that her criticism of him was all wrong?

Distantly amid her thoughts Audrey heard the late train coming in and suddenly her mind reverted to her brother. Would he be on that train? Or would he stay in town all night as he had suggested he might and go even yet to see Evadne? She knew enough about that girl to realize that the night for her had just begun.

More and more as she considered this her soul rebelled at this possibility for her brother. She couldn't bear to have her precious brother spoil his life. Oh, how did he get in with such a girl anyway? Did he really think he cared for that worthless selfish bit of froth? She had driven him once to take a stand, and then had sulkily gone away to Europe, and apparently not even written to him all this time. Now she was back and was endeavoring to order him around as if he were an old possession of hers. After all this interval would he go back to her? What a sorrowful outlook for the family if he did! Would Kent stand for her high-handedness? He had always been so independent, so decided and self-assured! Would he let this girl wind him around any way she pleased? It didn't seem possible.

Then suddenly she heard Kent's quick step on the path outside. He had *come!*

But her heart went down as suddenly, as she remembered that she must give him Evadne's message. Probably he hadn't known she was in town after all or he would not have come home. Perhaps now he would take mother's car and drive back. There was no telling. She began to wish she had gone to bed and not waited up to tell him.

"Hello!" his voice came cheerfully. "You up yet? What's the idea?"

Then he gave a quick look around.

"Not expecting company at this time of night, are you? Or has that walking encyclopedia of yours just gone? Honestly Audrey, I can't see what you see in that conceited ape of a Bainbridge. I thought you had better sense! If you attach that baboon you and I'll be two people. I can't see him for a brother-in-law, ever. And you won't ever be happy, either, with his exclusive company, for I warn you dad and mother won't be likely to come and see you very often. Maybe you didn't hear him correcting dad the other day, telling him how to run his business on more up-to-date lines. If you had been watching dad and mother then you'd have known about what the atmosphere is going to be if you every marry that bag of wind."

Audrey's face flushed angrily, and then she laughed.

"You're a pretty one to talk. How about the girl you've picked out? What do you think mother will look like if you ever bring that common painted Evadne home as your wife?" She looked at him with flashing eyes, and for an instant his own dropped. Then he looked up again, and laughed half shamedly.

"Now Audrey, that's not a parallel case. I haven't seen Evadne Laverock for six whole months. She's been in Europe. We haven't even written."

"Yes?" said Audrey raising her eyebrows questioningly at her brother, and lifting her chin a bit haughtily.

"Well, she isn't in Europe any more," she said, studying his face as she spoke to see if he had known this, "and she's waiting right now for you to call her up. The number is Maurice 1011-J."

Kent took on an annoyed look immediately.

"What do you mean? Did she call up?"

"She did!" said Audrey, "which is the reason for my staying up, to give you the message, in spite of my good advice. You'd better call her at once. It's getting fairly late."

"Thanks a lot, sister," said Kent in a dignified carelessness, "but morning will be plenty of time. I'm dropping over with sleep, and I'm not keen to call anybody up."

"Well, but really, she was quite insistent."

"I have no doubt of it, but will you kindly let me manage my own affairs?"

"Oh, certainly," said his sister, rising, "with the condition that I may have the same privilege."

"Okay with me!" said the young man yawning. "I wasn't managing. I was just telling you what possibilities were ahead for you if you continued in the way you seem to be going. However, of course, it's your privilege to choose between that know-it-all and your humble family. Good night, kid, I'm turning in. I'm frightfully sleepy!" and he turned and flung up the stairs.

Audrey turned out the lights and went up to her room, but she lay awake for sometime listening. She wanted to make sure that Kent didn't go downstairs afterward and telephone Evadne. It was so inexplainable that he had taken her message so casually. It wasn't like Kent's former way at all.

But though she lay awake for a long time, considering not only the possibilities connected with her brother, but her own as well, Kent did not go downstairs, and presently she heard his regular breathing down the hall, and knew that he was asleep. Well, it was most extraordinary! That he would get a message like that from Evadne and not even bother to call up! Well, if he was really going to be sensible and give up Evadne perhaps she ought to look into her own case and see whether what he had said about Ballard was really true, or just a bit of foolish prejudice. She wouldn't of course want to marry a man who would antagonize her own brother. He might get over it, but then perhaps he was counting on her getting over her feeling about Evadne sometime, and she never would! Never!

At last she went to sleep, her mind more than troubled over her own problem.

She was awakened earlier than usual the next morning by hearing Kent go whistling downstairs. He stopped at the telephone. She sprang up and threw her kimono about her, listening at the door. Was he going to make an appointment for the day with that girl after all?

Then she heard her brother's voice clear and cool.

"Is Miss Laverock there? Oh, sorry! No don't disturb her if she is still asleep. Just give her a message. This is Kent Havenner. Tell Miss Laverock that I couldn't possibly make it last night and I got her message very late, too late to call her. That's all. She'll understand. Thank you. Good-bye!"

Just that. Then Kent went whistling out on the front porch and presently Audrey glanced out the window and saw him walking briskly down the beach in the morning sunshine and gazing off at a white sail on the sea.

Now what did that mean? Was Kent off the girl for life, or just still angry at whatever she had done?

So presently, when Bainbridge called up and wanted Audrey to go sailing that morning she considered seriously before she answered. Should she go and study the young man from her brother's point of view, or should she decline and stay at home?

She finally decided on staying at home. Why should she go when she had no particular desire to do so? Especially as she was not at all sure what her future attitude was to be toward this young man? Why go on any longer until she knew her own mind or heart in the matter! And why force a situation until it came naturally? Didn't the very fact that she was not keen to go with him show that she did not care for him very much? Had she ever thought that she did? There were at least a dozen other young men who came to see her often, whom she would have liked as well. This one had simply come oftener, asked her to go places before anybody else had a chance. Would she really care if she never saw him again? Would she be hurt or sad, except as it might be a matter of pride, if some other girl won him away from her? She had to own honestly that she would not.

So she settled it with her heart that all was well so far. At least she would have a respite for one day and get calm enough to know what she was about. For truly, it did not seem to her that any young man she knew, so far, had stirred her heart to its depths. She could not think of any one whose words of love would set her senses going with delight. Maybe she wasn't the kind of girl who would ever fall in love deeply anyway. Why worry? Why go after love till it came after you? Life was sweet and pleasant enough without it. Why did every woman think that of course she had to get married or her life would spell disaster? There were lots of nice things to do without that.

So she set herself to do some of the things she had put by for a time of leisure, and a happy little peace filled her heart and made her feel that this day was a nice restful interval.

12

JANE awoke the next morning not quite as refreshed from her night's sleep on the new bed as she had been in Miss Leech's lovely apartment, but she got up with interest in the new day. She was going back to work at the button counter and she felt so much better than when she had left for her vacation that she was almost thrilled at the prospect of returning. After all it was so nice that she had a job, and was feeling better and able to get back. It was so nice that she had pleasant things to remember, the books and the canary, and the goldfishes, and the delightful bed, and then most of all that wonderful Bible class.

Memory of Kent Havenner's appearance last night and the pleasant time they had had together talking over the lesson came like a dash of bright color into the picture and made her smile to herself into the scrap of a mirror that hung over her bureau. He had been nice, and he had said he would come again this morning with that letter. However portentous the letter might be, at least it was interesting to have a courteous gentleman bringing it. She would be able to ask his advice or explanation in case the letter was not a pleasant one or involved some sort of action on her part.

So she hurried with her dressing, and went down to the unpretentious cafeteria downstairs, where oatmeal and weak cream featured prominently with orange juice at a premium and not so good at that. She got a simple breakfast. She was rather too excited to eat much. And then she went on her way to the store.

They greeted her quite gaily, those other girls with whom she worked. They told her the latest news of the store.

"And you know that Mr. Gaylord over at the stockings? They say he's married! Can you believe it? And after the way he's been carrying on with all the girls! Why he's made love to half a dozen at least, and Marianne Featherton went around all day today after she heard it, crying her eyes out for him. Isn't she a fool? She says he proposed to her Saturday night! Isn't that the limit? And they say his wife left him six months ago. I don't blame her, do you? Of course Adele Burridge says she doesn't believe a word of it. That she usedta live in the same town where he came from and if he'd ever have been married she'd have heard of it. She's got an aunt living there yet that always writes her all the news, and she says he isn't that kind of a fella at all. But my eye, you don't havta watch him but halfa day ta tell what he is, the way he carries on with all the girls."

"Yes?" said Jane looking at the girl with a quiet calm in her eyes. "Well it's likely he knows the truth himself, and it isn't our business, of course."

"Yeah, course, but I think we should let it be known what kinda fella he is, don't you? How's a right-minded girl ta know? Why, he even came 'n ast me would I go to a dance with him, an' o' course I said yes, a nice lookin' fella like that, an' now here I find he's married, has been all the time. At least they say he is, so what is a girl to do ef she wants ta be half decent?"

"Well," said Jane with an amused smile on her lips, "I should think a girl would have to go a little slow with any stranger and not accept an invitation until she is really well acquainted. A right-minded man wouldn't ask a girl he scarcely knew at all to go out with him, either, until he had a chance to know what kind of girl he was asking. You can't judge either a man or a girl just by appearances, you know, not in these days anyway. Don't you think so?"

The girl shrugged her shoulders.

"Oh, I don't believe men are so particular these days, do you?"

"Well, I wouldn't care for the man who wasn't, would you?"

"Oh, I dunno. It doesn't do to be too particular or you get left outside of everything."

"Not anything worth while."

"Well, I guess you're pretty straight-laced, aren't you? You don't get much fun that way."

"There are plenty of ways to have fun without that," said Jane. "And even if you didn't there's a lot more peace and security."

"Oh rats!" said the other girl. "I should worry about peace and security. You get plenty of that when you're dead!"

"Oh, do you?" said Jane. "I wonder!"

Then a customer came along and she turned away from the conversation, wondering what this girl would say if she were introduced to the Bible classes she had been attending.

It was almost twelve o'clock when Kent Havenner arrived.

He had taken the precaution to cut off a button from

one of his partly worn coats, and he had it ready in his hand along with the letter when he arrived in the store. He lingered long enough to get Jane's attention.

"Can you match this for me?" he asked quietly as she handed a package to a lady.

She looked up a bit startled, but controlled the flash in her eyes and smiled casually enough, her salesgirl smile that she turned on all customers, and then glanced at the button.

"Oh yes, I think so," she said pleasantly and taking the button she turned back to the tiers of button drawers. She soon returned with an open box in her hand.

"Yes, I think these are an exact match," she said and held them out to him.

He scrutinized them amusedly.

"Yes, those are the ones. Charge and send a dozen, please, and here is the address."

He handed out the letter with his card slipped over the address. Not the closest observer could see anything unusual in that transaction. He wasn't embarrassing her among her co-laborers in the least.

She gave a quick look at the letter, took her order book and slipped the letter inside, put a rubber band firmly and deftly about it and wrote the address into her order book from the card.

"It's a pleasant day," Kent remarked pleasantly. "I could be at the door when you go out in case there are any questions about the letter you would like to ask. What time are you usually free?"

She gave him a swift comprehending look that carried gratitude.

"That is kind of you. I'm free at five, or three or four minutes later, unless there is a late customer."

"And what door would be most convenient?"

"The Thirteenth Street door."

"I'll be there at five," he said, and turned swiftly away, as Jane gave her attention to another customer.

There was a faint tinge of pink in her cheeks as she stooped to one of the lower drawers to search for a certain kind of buckle the lady wanted, but no one was noticing her. The whole thing had been so swiftly done that even Mr. Clark, if he had been watching, would scarcely have noticed the transaction. But Jane's heart was beating wildly, and the next half hour before she was due to go to her lunch seemed long indeed. She had time enough to think of all the wild possibilities that letter might contain, and to draw a cloak of dignity about her in preparation for the afternoon closing time when she would have to meet that kind young lawyer, and perhaps ask him troublous questions. But she went steadily on with her work, trying to remember the verses she had been reading that morning: "Peace I leave with you. *My* peace I give unto you. Not as the world giveth, give I unto you. Let not your heart be troubled, neither let it be afraid."

But at last the time of anxiety was over, and she could escape to the cloak room, and read her letter in peace.

It was not long, that important letter with the name of important lawyers in its upper left hand corner. With trembling fingers she opened the envelope and read, the letters dancing menacingly before her eyes as she tried to take in their meaning.

My dear Miss Scarlett:

As a result of the death of Mr. Harold Scarlett, his will must be probated as soon as it can be conveniently done. As there is a possibility that you may be somewhat benefited by this, we are asking you kindly to call at our office at your earliest convenience and bring with you your birth certificate if possible, or any proofs you may happen to have that will prove your identity.

The property has greatly depreciated during the years of depression, and is not the opulent estate that it was in former days. But if you can prove your identity satisfactorily it may be that you are one of those mentioned in the will and will therefore have a voice in whether a modest property belonging to the estate shall be sold, or remain within the Scarlett estate. As there is a possible purchaser in view who is anxious to settle the matter at once, it would be a favor if you could come to the office within a short time.

Very truly,

J. Waltham Sanderson

Jane felt her knees weaken under her and suddenly dropped down on a bench, the letter trembling in her hands. What did it mean anyway? What did she have to do with it all? Did it mean that her name had been mentioned in Uncle Harold's will?

She read the letter over again, trying to fathom the exact meaning of each phrase.

How strange if she were mentioned in the will! Why, she didn't even know that Uncle Harold knew her name! Mother always said that he was very different from her father, he was much younger, he was proud of his wealth and family, haughty and disagreeable. He had made a great fuss when he heard her father was to marry her mother. He had said her mother was not good enough to marry his scholarly brother.

The only time that Jane had been at the old homestead, when she was still a little child, Uncle Harold had been abroad. So he had never meant anything but a name to her, and a very vague one at that, whose life would probably never touch hers. She had understood that he traveled a great deal, and spent his money freely in whims of his own.

So now to have him suddenly speaking to her as from beyond the grave filled her with a strange awe.

She tried to recall all her mother had told her about him. He had married, she knew, and his wife had died a few years ago, just before her own mother died. She could not remember whether there had been children or not. Well, probably if there weren't, or even perhaps if there were, there was some technicality of the law whereby it was necessary for all possible heirs to sign off or something, to make everything legal. Law was a queer thing that she did not understand. It might be of course that there was some clause in the grandfather's will that would take in his other heirs. It must be something like that. It didn't really make sense to her mind, but it was the only explanation she could think of, so she had to let it go at that. At least the letter relieved her anxiety lest someone were trying to involve her in some crooked business, stealing or something like that. She didn't just know what. Anyhow she could do nothing but just wait and trust.

And now she must get a bite of lunch, or she would be collapsing again. She mustn't run the risk of that.

She folded her letter safely into her handbag and hurried to the dairy lunch in the basement where she could get a glass of milk and a sandwich quickly. But all the time her mind was going over this strange new thing that had come to her, trying to figure out what was its portent.

Suppose Uncle Harold had had no children, what would he have done with his property? Suppose there had been fifty or a hundred dollars or perhaps a little more than that left over after his funeral expenses were paid. To whom would he have been likely to leave it? Did his wife have any relatives? She didn't know. Perhaps he would leave it to a hospital that took care of him in his last illness, or a nurse, or some club, or maybe even a church. And perhaps it was necessary in law to have any relatives sign, to make sure that no possible heirs could make trouble afterwards. No, that didn't sound very likely. Law was law, and didn't need possible heirs to agree to what the dead man had willed, surely. Well, it was all right, whatever way it was. She still had her job with a little money ahead, and a Bible class to look forward to one evening a week all winter, for there had been a notice given to that effect just last night at the class. Why should she worry?

Then it suddenly came to her remembrance that the nice young lawyer was going to meet her at the door at closing time, ready to answer any questions she had. She could find out what was closing time in the lawyers' office, whether they kept open Saturday afternoons, or whether there would be a time in the evening when she could go without having to ask off at the store. She really ought not to run any risks at the store of course. Or maybe she could run over at lunch hour, and just eat a cracker on the way in the street instead of lunch.

Then she was back behind the counter and the day swung into a busy afternoon. She tried to forget all about her personal problems and do her work conscientiously, but all the time in the back of her mind was the exciting consciousness that something was going to happen to her, even it if was only a dull visit to a lawyer's office to sign a prosy paper that meant nothing in the world but a formality. Also she was going to meet young Mr. Havenner again after closing time. It would probably be the last time she would ever see him, but he was someone she would enjoy remembering when days were lonely and time seemed long and weary. He was a gentleman. Perhaps a Christian, she wasn't sure. He had really looked as if he meant it when he said he was going to look farther into the book of John and perhaps turn up at the class again.

And yet Jane did not hasten when the bugle blew. She finished putting away her buttons carefully, and took out her purse in a deliberate way. She waited until Hilda and Louise were gone, and took her time getting her hat, and when she finally reached the Thirteenth Street door they were all out of sight. But there stood Kent Havenner leaning against the wall quite casually and not even facing toward the door. He had a folded newspaper in his hand as if he were perusing it. Nobody could suspect, even if there had been anybody watching, that he was waiting for someone to come out of that door. Yet she had a feeling that he saw her instantly when she appeared. He waited until she stepped out to the pavement, and then he fell into step beside her and walked along smiling as if he belonged there, as if she had left him only a few minutes before.

After he had helped her across the street he said casually:

"Well, was your letter all right?"

"Oh!" she said excitedly. "What is it all about? Do you know? And when do I go to the office? They'll be closed after five, won't they? And I *mustn't* risk losing my job!"

He looked at her with an amused wondering glance. Didn't she really understand?

"I suppose that *would* be important," he said.

"Oh, very!" said Jane tensely, and had a secret feeling that he wouldn't in the least understand how important her job was to her very life.

"Well," he said, still amusedly, "you can go to the office right now if you will." There was a twinkle in his eyes as he said it. "Mr. Sanderson is waiting there now for you, on the chance that I might be able to persuade you to come at once."

"Oh!" she gasped amazed, and then her heart suddenly contracted in a panic. Then it must be more important than she had thought! "Yes, I could go now. I don't suppose it will take long to sign a paper, but I'm sorry if I have inconvenienced him to wait longer than usual."

"Oh, that's nothing for him," said Kent. "He often stays late in the evening when he has extra work to do."

Then suddenly he signaled a taxi and put her in, whirling her away to a great high building, and she was soon shooting up to the fifteenth floor in an elevator, her heart beating excitedly. She was glad that the uncertainty at least would soon be over.

"You don't need to be frightened," said Kent gently, looking down at her anxious young face as they got out of the elevator. "You know there is nothing to be afraid of."

She looked up gratefully.

"You are very kind," she said with a faint smile on her pale lips.

And then suddenly they were in the office and a tall elderly man with gray hair and bushy eyebrows stood looking down at her and she felt a great trembling come upon her.

Kent was introducing her now. This was Mr. Sanderson, and he was offering her a chair.

13

JANE dropped down upon the edge of the chair, and her face was very white. Somehow more than ever the business upon which she had come seemed so frightening. If she could only have run out the door and down the stairs and got away she would have done it, and she couldn't just tell why she was so frightened. Somehow the shades of all the things and people that had ever frightened her seemed to cluster around her and focus in that stern-looking Mr. Sanderson.

"You are Miss Jane Scarlett?" he said, and gave her one of his searching glances. "Did you bring a birth certificate?"

"No," said Jane taking a deep breath and trying to speak steadily. "My birth certificate and the few other things I have of that sort I left in a house where I worked for awhile before I came to this city. It would be several days before I could get them. At least I hope it wouldn't be any longer than that."

Mr. Sanderson drew his brows frowning.

"Are you sure you could get them then?"

"Oh, I think so," said Jane. "I couldn't bring a trunk

with me when I came away. I didn't know just where I was going, and the people said I might leave it in their attic."

"Didn't it occur to you that something might happen to that house? A fire or something? Didn't you know that papers like that were very important indeed? Such papers should have been put in a safe-deposit box in a bank for safekeeping."

Jane suddenly smiled. His frowning disapproval, and the utter impossibility of safe-deposit boxes in her life heretofore, made the whole thing seem a farce.

"Why," she laughed, "I didn't have any safe-deposit boxes. I had only the trunk, and no place else to leave it. I couldn't carry it with me, it was too heavy, and I had a long way to walk, at first anyway, and no money to pay for a drayman. But really, I didn't know those papers were worth anything to anyone but myself. And they were only precious to me because they reminded me of my family who were all gone."

The tears all at once welled into her eyes and she winked them away. Just one slipped down and splashed on her white young hand. And there was a mistiness in Mr. Sanderson's eyes, too. An unaccustomed one. Kent flashed a look at him, and then his eyes went back to the girl, the little girl who was facing an unknown dread all alone, and with all his heart he knew he wanted to help her.

"Well," said Mr. Sanderson, clearing his throat, "well, doubtless you did the best you could. And don't worry. Of course there will be some way, either to get the proofs, or to get along without them. Though I understand that there is a relative by marriage who is endeavoring to find out all about this, and try to prove himself an heir. However, we shall find a way, I'm sure. Suppose you tell me exactly what papers you have that show who your father and mother were, and when and where you were born. Can you remember exactly what you have?"

"Oh, yes," said Jane in a clear voice, "there is an old Bible. I think it belonged to grandmother and grandfather Scarlett. It has the dates of all births and marriages and deaths. And there is my mother's marriage certificate, and the certificate when I was baptized, and a little certificate of membership in a Sunday School class when I was very young. And then I have an old photograph album with the pictures of my father and mother and my grandparents on both sides, and a number of the other relatives. Their names are there, written by my father. I think there is a picture of the old home in that album too. A snapshot somebody took."

"Well, that ought to be pretty good proof, if you could produce it," said Mr. Sanderson brightening up a bit.

"Proof of what, Mr. Sanderson?" Jane's voice was very low, but there was a hint of the anxiety in it that she was feeling.

"Why, proof that you are who you claim to be."

"But I haven't claimed anything," said Jane, bewildered. "I just answered the questions that were asked me, and I don't understand yet why I should have been asked. I don't see how I could really prove anything, because you see I have not had anything to do with any of the family at all since I was a very small child, except just after my mother died, when a great aunt seemed to feel a little responsibility for me for awhile, and put me in a school where I could work for my board and tuition. But then she got married again and didn't want to bother about me any more, so she got me a place to work where they kept summer boarders. You see I couldn't really testify anything that would be worth your bothering with me."

"See here, young woman," said Mr. Sanderson getting on his professional roar, "is it possible you don't understand that we are seeking the heir of Mr. Harold Scarlett, and that if you should turn out to be that heir you would benefit by it?"

Jane sat staring at him in wonder.

"Oh!" she said in wonder, "why, I wouldn't be an heir of course, that is, not to any extent, I'm sure. Uncle Harold never saw me in his life, and I doubt if he remembered I was alive. I'm sure he wouldn't leave anything to me. I didn't even know where he was, and he wouldn't know where I was unless great aunt Sybil Anthony told him, and if there was any question of my being an heir she wouldn't have let him know. She would have thought her daughters would come first."

"No!" said Mr. Sanderson sharply, "they would not come first. She was only a half sister of Mr. Scarlett, the daughter of a second wife married late in life. If you were the daughter of Harold Scarlett's older brother, as you state, you would be next in line. You see it is the husband of one of these daughters of this great aunt who is contesting the will, and it is important that your proofs be found as quickly as possible. These more distant relatives will not delay to file their claims, and the man who wants to buy this property must have an answer soon. Would it be at all possible for you to get in touch with this person who cares for your trunk by telephone?"

"Oh! I don't know," said Jane with a startled look. "I have not heard from her for almost a year. I don't even know whether they are living in the same place now."

"Well, if they aren't what will have become of your trunk?"

"Well, I don't know that, either. I never realized it was important to anybody but myself, and I wasn't in a position to do anything about it."

Mr. Sanderson uttered a sound almost like a growl.

"Well, look here, young lady, we've got to get to work on this thing right away. What was the name of this person who has your trunk? And did she have a telephone when you lived with her?"

"Her name was Janet Forbes. Yes, they had a telephone when I was there. But they went to Florida for the winter. I suppose they were coming back if everything went well with them. The trunk was left in their attic. The telephone would be in her husband's name, Aleck Forbes. Blairstown—"

Mr. Sanderson glared over at Kent Havenner.

"See if you can get that phone, long distance, Havenner!" he commanded.

Kent Havenner sat down at a desk and took up the telephone. His quiet business-like voice calmed Jane's frightened heart. She hadn't yet taken in the likelihood of any advantage coming to herself through all this trouble. It all seemed just another bothersome thing she had to do and get through with to satisfy somebody who wasn't anything to her.

But as Kent Havenner talked with the operator, and was at last given someone in Blairstown, Jane's eyes grew wide. This thing they had fantastically called forth out of the air was actually materializing into something genuine.

"Is this Mrs. Janet Forbes?" he asked quietly. "Yes, please, I would like to speak with Mrs. Forbes herself. You say Mrs. Forbes is serving dinner? Well, this is a very important matter. I must speak with Mrs. Forbes for just a moment. I won't keep her long. Yes, please call her to the phone at once."

There was a brief wait and then a sharp voice answered.

"Mrs. Forbes," said Kent, "Miss Jane Scarlett is calling about a trunk that she left with you. Just a moment."

Jane went forward excitedly as he held the phone out to her.

"Yes, Mrs. Forbes. This is Jane. Jane Scarlett. Yes, I'm well, thank you, and I have a good job in a store. No, I haven't written you before because I wanted to get ahead enough to send you the money for the trunk. But now I want it in a hurry, and if I send you money by telegraph would you see that it starts in the morning? Yes, Mrs. Forbes, I want it very much. No, I'm not getting married. I haven't time for such things. But there are some things of my mother's in that trunk that I want to use. Yes, surely, I'll write to you right away, but I'd like the trunk to start in the morning if you can possibly get it off, and by express so it will come quickly. It's really very important."

When Jane finally turned from the telephone she felt as if she had suddenly entered her former life again. How queer things were!

"She is going to send it in the morning!" she announced to the two who had heard all the transaction. And then a radiant expression came into her face. "I am glad!" she said musingly. "There are things in that trunk that I really needed."

Grim Mr. Sanderson grinned wryly at Kent.

"Yes," he said, "if all you say is true I think that you will find that there are things there that you need very much indeed. And now, young woman, when can I see you again? You know we haven't any time to waste. You don't seem to take it in that you are a very important factor in a matter of really important business."

"It doesn't seem at all real to me," said Jane with a wide smile.

"Well, it had better seem so," said the lawyer.

"But," said Jane with a sudden startled look in her eyes, "how much is it going to cost to get this trunk here, and how do I go about it to send that money? Mrs. Forbes said she couldn't afford to send it herself. Her husband has died, and she's had a hard summer. But how much will it cost? I might not have enough."

"Don't worry about that, young lady. We'll attend to that from the office. Havenner, get on the wire and fix that up right away. You got the address and the phone number, didn't you? All right, get that over with, and arrange about the arrival of the trunk, where it's to be sent."

"You want it at your room, where you went last evening?" asked Kent courteously.

Jane nodded, half frightened at the thought of taking her precious belongings out of the past into her forlorn little room. But of course it would have to go there. She had nowhere else to take it.

Kent Havenner went to a telephone in an adjoining room, and while he talked Mr. Sanderson asked Jane more questions about her father and mother, her visit to the old home, and where she had lived since. Incidentally he brought out the fact that since her parents' death she had been for a time in a New England school, the very school where the lawyers had been searching for a trace of her.

Then Kent came back to report.

"It's all fixed," he said. "I wired the money, and then I called up Miss Scarlett's present apartment and arranged with the landlady to have the trunk put at once in her room when it arrives. Is that all right, Miss Scarlett?"

"Oh yes," said Jane looking at him with startled eyes. She hadn't yet got so far as to plan about that trunk in relation to her present lodgings. But this young man seemed to think of everything and know just what to do about it at once. She was deeply grateful.

"Thank you," she said with a shy smile. "And now, is there anything else? When do I come again?"

"Just as soon as you get entrance to that trunk and can bring me your evidence. Have you the key?"

Sanderson's voice was sharp as he asked the question, as if it were a matter that had almost escaped him.

"Oh, yes," said Jane. "I carry it in a little bag around my neck. I was so afraid I might lose it."

Her hand went instinctively to her breast, and then suddenly she exclaimed:

"Oh, I forgot. I have one bit of evidence with me! I just remembered. My mother's wedding ring! It has initials and a date! Would that help any?"

"It certainly would!" said Mr. Sanderson excitedly.

They gathered around her as she drew a fine gold chain from around her neck, and brought out a tiny bag of firm white kid, that might have been cut from a glove.

Jane bent toward the light and unfastened two little snap catches that held its top firmly together, and took out a plain old fashioned gold ring.

There it was, the initials, "J.R.S. to M.W." and the date.

Mr. Sanderson examined the letters carefully under a tiny glass, and at last straightened up.

"Well, I should say you had pretty conclusive evidence there," he said as he handed the ring back to Jane. "So run along, and don't fail to let me know by telephone just as soon as your trunk arrives."

"Oh, I will," said Jane earnestly. And still she was not

quite sure what it was going to mean to herself, even when the papers should arrive. It all seemed too fantastic to be true.

"And now," said Kent Havenner, smiling and looking toward his chief, "I guess that's about all for tonight, isn't it? So, Miss Scarlett, you and I will slip out and get a bite of dinner. Good night, Mr. Sanderson!"

When they were down on the street again Kent hailed another taxi.

"Oh, but you mustn't!" protested Jane. "I can perfectly well find my way back to my—" she hesitated for a word—"home!" she finished with a laugh. "It isn't much of a home, I know, but it's all I have so I have to call it that."

"Yes, well—but we're going to have dinner together first," said the young man, putting her into the taxi, and stepping in after her. "You won't mind going with me for once, will you? I'm tremendously hungry and I know you must be too, and besides isn't the last daily class tonight, and don't we go to it?"

Her heart gave a sudden little leap of pleasure! The class! She had forgotten it entirely in her absorption in this strange new matter that had been thrust upon her. The class! Yes, of course! And he was really going again himself!

"Oh! Yes!" she said. "Of course I'm going to the class. And I'm glad you're going too. But you didn't need to bother about taking me, or getting me dinner. I'm not lost any more, and I'll be sure to let the office know when that trunk comes. I'm all excited about it myself."

"I'm not worrying about that," said Kent, "but don't you realize that I'm sort of your lawyer, and I have a right to take you to dinner once in awhile? I know a nice pleasant place where my sister likes to go. I'll take you there. And it isn't far to the class after that. We'll have a little over an hour to eat. I guess that will do. Here we are!" and the taxi slowed down and stopped before a dignified quiet-looking building, and he helped her out.

"But, this is a grand place," said Jane taking in the inevitable signs of affluence about the building.

"Not so grand as some," said Kent is his easy way.

"But I'm only a working girl, and I'm not dressed up. People don't go into these places wearing their working clothes."

"Oh, yes, they do. I go, and I'm wearing my working clothes. Come on. You'll find it very unobserving."

And so he led her to a table and Jane in a panic of embarrassment entered, looking about, half frightened to death over the quiet unostentatious grandeur.

"This is just a good home place," said Kent as he sat down opposite her and smiled.

"A very magnificent home," murmured Jane in a low voice, and cast shy glances all about her.

"Now," said Kent, "may I order for you? I'm pretty well acquainted with some of the nice dishes they serve here."

"Oh, please," said Jane with relief. "But just get something very simple for me. I'm not used to fancy meals."

And so Jane was launched on a new experience, going out to dinner with a young gentleman, a real gentleman such as her father had been.

14

IT all moved off so very smoothly and pleasantly Jane wasn't embarrassed at all after the first minute or two. Afterward she thought it over and wondered at herself. How at home she had felt there in that new environment! But after all, she reflected, her father had been a gentleman and her mother a lady, even if she herself did sell buttons and live in a little hall bedroom at the top of the house.

Kent quietly took charge of things, talking with the waiter as if he were an old family servant, ordering nice unusual things, thoughtfully giving her a choice between this and that.

And they did not have to wait long. The delicious dinner was set before them in almost no time at all, it seemed, and they were talking.

"You weren't really frightened, were you?" Kent asked when they settled down to eating.

Jane smiled ruefully.

"I'm afraid I was, quite a little," she admitted shamedly. "You see I didn't really know what it was all about, and I'm not sure that I do yet."

"Well, I'm sure I hope you will be quite happy in the outcome, even though it does seem like a fairy tale to you now. It's nice to get real surprises sometimes, and life isn't always all disappointments, you know. Now, tell me about this class. Did I understand aright that it is only to be held once a week after this?"

"Yes, it's only in the summer they hold it every evening. I think they said it is to take a whole hour after this instead of half an hour. But they are going to have a new teacher, you know. Mrs. Brooke is going out west, I think."

"That's too bad!" said Kent. "I had it in mind to attend that class right along, but I don't know that I should care for a new teacher. I thought she was most unusual. Everything she said seemed to have a greater significance than any preacher I ever heard. Who is the new teacher? But then I wouldn't be likely to know one from another. Such teachers are not in my line. I don't remember ever to have had even a Sunday School teacher who interested me."

"I never heard anybody teach as Mrs. Brooke does. But she had told us several times that we will like the new teacher better. She says he is wonderful."

"A man?"

"Yes. I was sorry for that. It didn't seem to me as if a man teacher would understand us quite so well. Mrs. Brooke talked like a mother, right into your heart."

"Yes, she did," agreed Kent, watching the lovely light of interest in the girl's face, and being glad he had brought her to dinner. "Well, if she likes him perhaps he'll pass. We can give him a try anyway. I somehow don't feel like dropping it entirely. So this is Mrs. Brooke's last night! Well, I'm really sorry. Although I haven't heard her but a couple of times, she really opened up new vistas and possibilities in life to me. I almost feel as if I'd like to tell her 'thank you.'"

"Oh, and so would I, if I dared. It does seem strange how I happened on that class from a radio notice. I think really God must have seen my need and sent it."

Kent grinned.

"Perhaps you weren't the only one," he said. "After all, there's the Bible and anybody could have had it and read it without a class of course, only we wouldn't and didn't until she brought it to our notice. But really it was you that brought her to my notice. I'm quite sure I would never have gone into a Bible class of my own accord for anything in the world. So I've you to thank for my interest in this." Then he got out his little red gospel of John and called her attention to a verse that had been given in the last lesson, and asked if she had the reference in connection with it. Then she pulled out her little book, and they conned it all over, like two university students going over their studies together.

Some people came in and took the table a little way from them, looking over and speaking to Kent interestedly. Kent nodded to them but went on turning the pages of John and pointing out something he had read on the train the other night.

After the dessert arrived Kent looked up suddenly and asked:

"Have you thought anything about that property? Are you likely to sell it in case you prove to be the heir?"

"I?" said Jane with a startled look. "Why, no, I don't really believe I'll have anything to say about it. Somebody else will turn up that will take the right, I'm sure, even if it were left to me. I can't think of either my great aunt or her daughters ever giving up any family property to me." She laughed ruefully. "You see they think the earth was especially made for their benefit."

"Well," said Kent, "but if it turned out that it was in your hands to say, would you want to sell it?"

"How could I tell?" said Jane sadly. "I've never seen it. I don't know what it is. If it were really something associated with my people of course it would be wonderful to keep it, but how could a poor salesgirl keep property? It costs money to keep property, even very plain property, doesn't it? There would be taxes and repairs. Oh, no, of course I couldn't keep it, but I'd love to if I could. I've often thought about the beautiful old home where my grandfather lived, and where I was taken as a child, and wished that it might have been kept and I could have lived there. But it takes money to live in dear old homes. I can remember the walls, beautiful wide walls with ivy on them, and there was a swing—"

Kent couldn't help thinking how very sweet her eyes were as she talked about the old days she seemed to love.

"Where was that old home? Do you remember?"

"It was in a place called Hawthorne, not far from a big city. I don't remember the name of the city. That is, it never made any impression on me. Of course it's all written down in my father's diary, and I can look it up when my trunk comes. I'll have to brush up my knowledge of my father's house. Why, it's a good deal like what we're doing in the class, isn't it, brushing up knowledge about our Father's house in Heaven! It's queer how we get interested in this world and drift away from the other life, isn't it? Even when I was very forlorn and unhappy and hadn't a job, and was afraid of what would happen next, I scarcely ever thought to go to God for help. I had no realization that He cared to have me come and talk to Him and ask His help."

"Yes, well, I've done that a lot too, but since I've been reading this Book I've almost come to the conclusion there is another life, and it's worth a lot more than this one down here. I guess I'm glad you led me where I heard about it. Of course dad and mother and my sister go to church, and likely they know all this lingo, only I never hear them talk about it. Maybe they never heard it our way. But I guess it's worth a try. But say, it's time we got going or we'll be late to the class!"

Kent paid the check and they hurried away to the class, Jane suddenly wondering again to find herself escorted as she had seen other girls, and a sudden pang came to her heart. Pretty soon this business about the property would be over and settled one way or the other, and her young lawyer would go his way. He would have no occasion to hover about her and see her here and there and take her to dinner in grand places. When his business no longer linked itself to her, of course he would drift back into his own world. He would probably forget the Bible class too. Or was that quite fair to him to doubt the interest he had acknowledged? Well, she would at least have this pleasant evening to remember, so that when she saw other girls going about with their young men friends she would understand their happy times a little better, and think how she had had at least a little taste of young companionship.

At the class they sat up near the front together, and it was so nice not to be all alone as she had been heretofore.

The lesson that night was beautiful. The two as they listened seemed to be closely bound by their interest, and now and again they would look at each other in mutual recognition of a truth that struck home more deeply than another. If Evadne could have watched her former lover's face that night she certainly would have been filled with scorn and wonder, for never had she seen such a look of awakening on his face, the look of a soul just seeing the light.

At the close of the lesson Mrs. Brooke introduced a young man, their new teacher. They saw to their amazement that he was virile and attractive with a face of radiant happiness. He didn't make a speech, just nodded to them all informally and told them how he loved God's word and that he hoped they were to have many happy hours of study together, beginning next Thursday evening. Then Mrs. Brooke asked him to sing them a song that she might remember as she went away, and sitting down at the piano he sang, a simple rhythmic melody, with the words that wrote themselves in their hearts, and could not easily be forgotten:

> *"Oh Lord, you know,*
> *I have no friend like you,*
> *If Heaven is not my Home*
> *Oh Lord, what shall I do?*
> *The angels beckon me*
> *To heaven's open door,*
> *I can't feel at home*
> *In this world any more."*

He sang it so tenderly, so longingly that it sank deep into the soul life of them all. And then he made them sing it once or twice till they caught it, and went out humming it. It was obvious that the whole group would go home singing that song. The new teacher had won his class. They would all be there next week if at all possible.

Jane and Kent went up and spoke to Mrs. Brooke and said good-bye.

"You've done great things for us both," said Kent, because he was the bolder of the two, and really felt gratitude for what he had received. She introduced them to the new teacher, and they liked his personality at the nearer view. They went out pledged to come again, and perhaps to try and bring others.

"Oh Lord, you know," Jane sang softly, almost inaudibly, as they left the hall and fell into step on the street, "I have no friend like you—" Her voice was very sweet and Kent drew her arm within his own, and looked down at her, and never knew that Evadne had crossed their path on her way to the theater, and was looking back, staring unbelievingly at Kent Havenner walking along with a very simply dressed girl and looking very happy indeed. It really was quite time that she did something about this. She had not counted on such extreme indifference as this.

> *"If Heaven is not my Home*
> *Oh Lord, what shall I do?"*

"You have a really lovely voice!" said the young man. "It is unusual. I like to hear you sing that."

"It is a lovely song," said Jane. "I never heard it before. It seems as if it was made just for me. As if God sent it to show me something. Here I've been mourning all my life that I never had a real home, and perhaps God allowed it just to remind me that Heaven is my home and I mustn't put my hopes on earth. I think that is going to make a great difference in my way of looking at life. I'm not going to fret any more that I've only a hall bedroom to call home. My Father is getting ready my home up there!"

Kent looked down into the loveliness of her exalted face, as if Heaven had opened and given her a quick vision, and a mistiness came over his own eyes. Something contracted in his heart. This was a wonderful girl, and she had hold of something that was worth more than all the nonsense of the smart set with whom he had been trying to enjoy himself for the last two or three years.

Suddenly a vision of Evadne's selfish, hard young face came beside Jane's illuminated one, and he knew all at once that he had been a fool ever to think Evadne was interesting. But he answered Jane thoughtfully enough:

"I guess you're right. But I never thought about these things before. This life has always been enough for me. I've been fairly satisfied with my earthly home, and I never thought of the time that might come when it wouldn't be enough any more. I've got to get busy and grow Heaven-wise, for I don't believe I'm going to feel satisfied down here any more either. That's a great song. I wish you kept a piano in your reception room. I'd suggest that we step in and trying singing it together. I mean to try the tune out the minute I get home tonight."

They were happy eyes that met at the door of the rooming house as they said good-bye.

"I shan't be seeing you till Monday," he said as he paused at her door, his hat lifted. "The firm is sending me out of the city for a couple of days, and I don't suppose I shall be back before late Saturday night. But by Monday that trunk ought to be here, and I'll be stopping around to hear your report. Good night!"

He was gone and Jane was conscious of a sudden blank. But what were his comings or goings to her anyway? She had no right to be disturbed of course. She wouldn't likely have seen him at all even if he hadn't been going out of town. Only going out of town was so definite, and as he was really her only friend, it did make a difference to know that she wouldn't even meet him by chance somewhere.

But she ought not to call him her friend. A friend implied a closer relationship than just a business contact, and that was all there had been between them, or likely ever would be. She must jack herself up in this matter. It was unwise to admire or become interested in anybody who was so utterly out of the range of any possible idea of companionship. He had been nice to her, yes, and she was so lonely and forlorn that she had just enjoyed this contact as much as possible, but she must not let herself be lonely when the contact ceased. That was the way fool girls got their hearts broken, and she certainly did not want to be a fool girl. Her mother had always warned her about counting too much on friendships with men. Even the fact that he was interested in that Bible class did not make any difference. It was wonderful to think he might be a Christian. That would always make a little bond of friendliness. Just to know she knew one of God's children, even if she didn't see him any more was nice. But she must get to work somehow and do something to occupy her mind, and not think about this matter of Uncle Harold's will. Perhaps after hours tomorrow she would go and take a long walk in the park, and bring up at a new place for dinner. That would be a change and give her some other interests.

So she hurried up to her room and got busy putting her things in better order, washing out stockings, and finally writing a letter to the Scotch woman who had been taking care of her trunk. Poor thing, she must be lonely now that her husband was gone! And she was such a kindly soul, and such a wonderful cook. What would she do now, all alone in the world? Would she try to carry on a boarding house alone?

She wrote her kindly letter, tucking in a dollar bill as thanks for the care of her trunk, and saying she liked her job and hoped some day to be making a good salary, although it wasn't very large yet.

Then she hurried to bed and congratulated herself as she lay down that she hadn't thought about that troublesome property nor her young lawyer once since she came upstairs.

15

EVADNE Laverock bided her time for two days, thinking that perhaps her letter had miscarried and would at
length reach Kent Havenner and would bring her lover
in apology to her feet. She loved so much better to put
a man in the wrong, than to seem to be running after
him. But the two days went slowly by and he came not.

The stay in the city at that season of the year was an
utter bore. The house was in a semi-closed state, and
her sister was away at the mountains. Moreover there
were few of her old acquaintances about at this time of
year, and absolutely nothing going on. She must do
something. She could not let Kent drift through her
fingers this way.

She would not call up at his seashore home, because
she simply detested his sister, and she didn't want to
encounter her again even incognito. So she decided on
calling the office.

But all the satisfaction she got from the office was the
information that Mr. Havenner wasn't in at present, and
they did not know how soon he would be in. After an
exasperated attempt to get more information from a

higher source, she arrayed herself for battle and went forth. It was her experience that she could accomplish a great deal more with a man if he could see her. So she put on her most alluring summer street garments, and arrived at the office about eleven o'clock Friday morning.

She asked for Mr. Havenner and was told as before that he was not in at present. Then she asked for Mr. Edsel and was informed that he was engaged with a client, and not to be disturbed. Finally she asked to see Mr. Sanderson. She did not like Mr. Sanderson but she had to get some action quickly, and he was the only one left.

Now it happened that Mr. Sanderson did not like Miss Laverock even as well as she liked him, and he had hoped that she was permanently out of the picture, for he had said to his partner more than once that if ever Kent married that flibberty-jib he personally was going to find some good excuse to get Kent out of the firm, for he would be absolutely worthless if he married that piece of selfishness.

So when Evadne came languidly into his austere private office where he sat frowning at the interruption, and settled her delicate attire in one of his great masculine leather chairs, he almost growled at her as a lion might have done, as if she were too trifling an object to make it worth his while to pause long enough to make even one bite of her.

"Hello, Sandy," she addressed him gaily, "I'm trying to find Kennie and I can't get any service out of your minions. I thought I'd be bold and come to headquarters. What have you done with my Kennie?"

"Your Kennie!" Mr. Sanderson snorted contemptuously. "I wasn't aware you had left any of your property about our offices. To whom were you referring? Could you by any means mean our Mr. Havenner? I have never heard him called Kennie, but possibly his name

might be tortured into that. However, I was not aware that he was your property."

"Now, Sandy!" reproached the girl with a languid giggle, "don't be dense with your Vad! Of course I mean Kent Havenner."

"Kindly omit the 'Sandy,' if you please, and I'm quite sure I never called you Vad, or even thought of you in that way. You are not mine in any sense of the word. If it's Mr. Havenner you're in search of you won't find him here. He's out of town for a few days. He won't be back until late Saturday night if he is then. You'll have to search elsewhere for him."

"Well, but Mister Sanderson, surely you can tell me where to locate him on the telephone? It's very important!"

"No, I can't!" snapped Sanderson. "And I wouldn't if I could. Mr. Havenner went away on business for the firm, with several destinations in view, and he has no time for frills and follies."

He picked up the telephone.

"Miss Worth, is Mr. Hawkins there yet? Well, send him right in. I'm waiting for him."

Then with a stiff bow toward Evadne:

"Good afternoon, Miss Laverock. I haven't any more time to discuss this matter with you. Ah! Mr. Hawkins!" as the door opened to let in a client, "be seated, won't you? Miss Worth, kindly escort Miss Laverock to the elevator." And Evadne found herself summarily dismissed. With head up and angry mien she followed the secretary down the hall without a word, her eyes flashing fire. She went back to her sister's lonely house to plan revenge and meanwhile solace herself with the best a city in summer provides for its worldlings.

Friday was an unusually busy day at the button counter. There were bargains in clasps and buttons and buckles, odd lots and broken numbers, closing out the summer's novelties, and getting ready for fall. There was after-hours work, too, which kept Jane until nearly seven, marking the prices on the bargain sales, getting them ready for morning as advertised.

Feverishly Jane worked to get done as soon as possible. She had a strong hope that her trunk would be at the boarding house when she got back, and she was eager to unpack it and look once more upon the beloved possessions. Strangely enough the articles which might prove her identity in connection with the will of her uncle took second place in her mind now. Her great longing was to touch and see once more the possessions that were connected with her dear mother. It was a great overwhelming longing, and now she began to wonder how she had gotten along so long without them.

But when the work at last was finished and she went to what she now considered "home" there was no trunk awaiting her in the hall as she had hoped, and there was no letter or explanation of any sort. Well, perhaps it would come tomorrow.

She went to bed early so that the morrow would come that much the sooner.

Audrey Havenner had had time on her hands for the last three days. Ballard Bainbridge had been away on a yachting trip with some friends, and while she had not realized how dependent on him she had become for companionship, she found that the days were twice as long when there were no telephone calls suggesting golf, sailing, or swimming. It was not that she was not self-sufficient on occasion, and she had been wanting to do some special reading for a long time, but now that her usual program had failed and she was thrown on her own resources, she discovered that there was altogether too much time for debating with herself whether or not she wanted to let this intimacy with Bainbridge go on to its logical conclusion, or whether she wanted to put a stop to it right here and now, and have her days fully planned by the time Bainbridge came back, *if* he came back, so that there would remain no part for him.

Having looked the facts of the case straight in the face and owned to herself what was the matter, she went and got the books she had been intending to read and settled herself in a breezy hammock on the porch, with a broad stretch of beach and a wider view of the ocean ahead of her. Deliberately she put her mind to the task in hand. She had promised to write a paper for a club meeting in the city which was to be held early in the fall, and this reading was in preparation for that paper. This was a grand time, just made for this preparation. She would work it to the last minute!

But when she got through the first paragraph, some turn of a phrase recalled to her a remark of Bainbridge's, and her mind was off on a tangent at once, arguing the subject from every angle.

In vain she jerked herself back to the duty in hand and tried to go on, but phrase after phrase reminded her of Ballard's line of argument, and now she recalled that he had been the one who had suggested these books for her to read. And his conversation was so like the author that she began to wonder whether he was an original thinker, or was just echoing authors he had read and admired.

She put down the first book, finally, and turned to another, but here again she was reminded of another conversation they had had, and after reading a few minutes she threw the book aside and stared off to sea, her problem all written before her again, the pros and cons, about Ballard Bainbridge. And the more she thought about it the more sick of the whole thing she grew. The facts had grown clearer since his absence, and she began to see how her own natural conclusions and actually her own wishes and tendencies had been deliberately set aside, and his own substituted, until she was getting into the habit of no longer asking herself what she wanted to do, but trying to seek out what Ballard wanted and liked, so that he wouldn't turn that vitriolic scorn of his toward her. She began to wonder if he hadn't just decided to take her over and mold her until she suited his desires, and then take possession of her. Then suddenly her naturally sweet nature, and her love for things beautiful and wholesome rose up in protest and cried out for the happy normal life she had lived before she knew him.

The morning train from the city shrilled along the distant tracks, and all at once a great longing came over her to get away from all these thoughts, and the inevitable decision that was going to be demanded of her by her conscience presently, and just do as she pleased for a while. Just have an old-fashioned good time, doing any pleasant little crazy thing that came into her head.

There was that girl at the button counter whom she had wanted to bring home for the week-end. This was a good time to do it. Kent was away in New England, and not likely to return till early next week. Evalina had gone down the coast to stay with a friend over a few days. She hoped she would not be returning till after Sunday. Why not take the up-train which left for the city in about a half hour, and find that girl and persuade her to come home with her for over Sunday?

She was the more persuaded that this was the thing she wanted to do because when she had spoken of the matter to Ballard a few days ago he had laughed her to scorn. He had called her an emotional philanthropist, and had given her a string of stories about Russia and how the working people were developing there, and how things ought to be that way in this country, and would be presently when the new order of things was thoroughly established. He said that individuals were not responsible for one another. That under a truly modern regime the worth-while people would rise and develop without assistance and those who were not worth while would slough off like scum from a boiling caldron. He told her that she belonged to a higher order of being and should not waste her time and thoughts on girls who were mere button sellers. They wouldn't be that if they were capable of being something better.

Always as he had talked she had felt in her soul that these things he was saying were not true, but it had seemed so much trouble to try to answer him. And really she hadn't given much thought to the subject. Perhaps there was some subtle truth in all he had been saying that made it necessary for her to do some deep thinking and definite studying before she attempted an answer. Well, anyway, she would invite that girl down and get close to her if she could; try to find out just what kind of mind and soul was behind her tensely quiet personality that she had taken such a liking to. And then if Ballard should turn up before the visit was over he would see that she had a mind of her own, and was not trying to follow the almost commands which he had put upon her concerning this desire of hers to know the button girl.

So she sprang up suddenly and sought out her mother who was sitting in the house putting delicate stitches into the hems of some exquisite organdie curtains for the cottage.

"Mother, I'm going to town. Is there anything you want?"

Her mother looked up interested.

"Why, yes," she said. "I was just wishing I had bought more ribbon for those tiebacks. Could you match it? I need five more yards of the pink, and seven of the blue."

"Delighted, mother. Cut off a snip of each and I'll bring it back with me. And mother, may I bring a friend home with me for over Sunday? Do you mind?"

"Of course not. Bring anybody you like. We're having steak for dinner tonight, and chickens tomorrow. Who are you bringing?"

"Well, I'm not sure. Anybody I take a notion. Will that be all right?"

"Quite all right, dear."

So Audrey got herself into a thin smart dark blue frock and caught the up-train to the city.

She matched the ribbon first so she wouldn't forget. Then she walked around the store trying to decide what to do. Finally she marched slowly past the button counter to see if Jane Scarlett was still there, and if she looked as interesting as the first time she had seen her.

Jane was hard at work, flying about, waiting on two people at once, and being very cool and businesslike about it. Audrey stood leaning against the opposite counter and watched her for a few minutes. Then when the two customers departed with their little packages and Jane was for the moment free, she saw her draw a deep tired breath, and mop her face with her handkerchief, as if she were very hot and weary. Her resolve was taken at once.

"You are entirely too impulsive!" Ballard had told

her. "You fly off the tangent on an idea. You should cultivate calmness. You should deliberate before you act."

The counsel came to her now as she started across the aisle straight toward Jane Scarlett, and she smiled at herself. She was not following Ballard Bainbridge's advice now and she was glad she wasn't.

"I want a dozen of those lovely filigree buttons down there in the front of the case," she said in a clear voice.

Jane smiled and gave her a quick look. Where had she heard that voice before? And of whom did it remind her?

But she didn't stop to answer those questions. She reached down and took out the buttons.

"They are pretty, aren't they?" she said pleasantly.

When Jane brought back the package and handed it to her, Audrey looked her straight in the eyes.

"You don't remember me, do you?" she said, laughing up at Jane.

Jane gave her a quick startled look and then a sunny smile lit up her face.

"Oh yes," she said. "You invited me to go home with you to your seaside cottage. You didn't think I'd forget a person like that, did you? I had many a pleasant moment, thinking about that, imagining what it would have been like if I felt I should go. I couldn't forget your face. I thought that was the loveliest impulsive thing anybody ever did."

"Thank you," said Audrey. "I'll treasure that. But now I've come again, and it isn't impulse this time, for I came to town just on purpose. You see I've been thinking about you ever since, and I really want to get to know you. Will you go down to the shore with me this afternoon when the store closes, and stay over Sunday? We can get you off on the early train Monday morning so you will be here in plenty of time for the store opening. And this time my mother is expecting you. I told her I hoped I was bringing someone back with me."

A soft pink color stole up into Jane's white face, and her eyes glowed with appreciation.

"Oh, that would be wonderful!" she said wistfully. "I wonder if I should go! I never heard of anybody doing a beautiful thing like that for an entire stranger."

"Well, we're strangers to you, too," laughed Audrey. "You might not like us at all, in which case you can take the next train back to the city, of course. But maybe you could stand us over Sunday even if you didn't like us, because there is always the sea to look at and a nice breeze to cool you off. Come on, do! I really want you, and I'm sure we can have a nice time together. Do you have to go home first, or could you go right from here? I can lend you a nightie and a hairbrush, or do you have to let someone know you are not coming back till Monday?"

Jane gave a quick thought to the trunk that might arrive.

"I can telephone," she said thoughtfully.

"Well, anyway, I'll be back here and meet you right here at five. Is that all right? Then we can catch the five-thirteen train. However, if you find you can't go at once, why there are two later trains. Now don't you fail me. I'm looking forward to this. Good-bye till five!" and with a bright smile she walked away and was lost in the crowd of shoppers.

Jane, watching her away, was again dimly reminded of someone. Who was it? Just a trick of her walk, the turn of her head. Ah, now she knew. It was Kent Havenner. She was dismayed at the idea. Was she going to be obsessed by the thought of him? How ridiculous.

She must remember that he was only her lawyer. She must not be so conscious of his appearance and attraction. Well, anyway, she had enough else to think about now. Was she really going to the shore for two whole days? Ought she to have allowed that nice girl to persuade her? Or course she could still tell her at five o'clock that she had found she couldn't make it, but she didn't believe that she was going to. She was simply longing for a breath of sea air and a real change, and why not take it? This was a lovely girl. They must be nice people. What would her own mother have said if she were here now?

Customers were coming in now. It was the late morning rush hour. She must forget all this and work, or she would make some foolish blunder and maybe lose her job in her childish excitement. And there was that trunk to think about, too. Perhaps she ought not to go. If the trunk came tonight she ought to be there to attend to it at once. But it would be put in her room and she couldn't do anything about the contents for those lawyers until Monday, anyway. Their office was closed Saturday afternoon.

So an underdrift of thought pursued her as she went on with her work. But there was a light in her eyes, a snap to every movement as the morning progressed, that made people look twice at her and say to themselves, "What an attractive girl that is!"

16

GRADUALLY Jane's thoughts grew steadier. They centered on her clothes. She looked down at herself, glad that she had put on her dark blue linen that morning, because the brown dress she had been wearing all the week had developed a small hole in the elbow and she hadn't had time to mend it. The dark blue was clean, and neat. But she did wish she had something to change into for Sunday. Just a simple cotton dress such as other girls would have had for over a Sunday. She didn't want this new friend of hers to be ashamed of her. Well, it couldn't be helped on such short notice. But at lunch time perhaps she could find some cheap little garments that she could carry in a paper parcel. She needed several new things badly, anyway.

She hurried away to the telephone as soon as she was free for her lunch hour and called up the landlady of her rooming house. She was told that her trunk had not come yet but it would be kept safely for her if it arrived while she was away. That off her mind she took a hasty glass of milk at the soda fountain, and purchased a small package of cracker sandwiches which she slipped in the top of her handbag where she could pinch off a small bit now and then and slide it into her mouth without being noticed. She simply didn't dare attempt going without food for even one meal. She mustn't run risks of fainting.

She hurried to the bargain counters and looked them over with a glance. Yes, there was a sweet little nightie at a very low price, and not so coarse that she would be ashamed to have it seen. Just white muslin with a facing of scalloped pink. It wasn't pretentious at all, either, and she did need one badly. Her only two were so worn that they were constantly needing slits sewed up.

As she turned away from the salesgirl with her package in her hand she saw a counter piled high with light summer dresses. There was such a pretty one of pink dimity with a lovely white collar, and a wisp of black velvet ribbon making a tiny dash of smartness at the throat! But the material was very fine, it couldn't be that the price was that advertised on the card over the table. Or perhaps there was something the matter with it. It looked like a dress from the French department.

She stepped near and began to examine it. No, there did not seem to be any defect in it, except that it was very much mussed. And of course she would have no chance to get it ironed. Or stay! Could she possibly get the woman up in the alteration department to iron it for her in exchange for something she could do for her? The dress was really lovely. Simple and unostentatious. Could she smooth it out a little with dampened hands after she reached the shore?

A glance at the clock showed her time was almost up. Well, she would risk it somehow. There wasn't time to go up to the alteration room and ask, and then come down and go up again. So she bought the dress, and then wondered, while it was being wrapped, whether she had done a silly thing. Just to think of her being so proud that she had to have a new dress! Well, it was bought now, and it was too late to change her mind.

She received her box with a trembling hand, and hurried upstairs.

"Why, sure I'll iron that out for you," said the girl. "Madame isn't ready with the work I have to press, and there isn't a thing for me to do till she is. No, she won't make any trouble for me. How much time you got? Five minutes? Sure, I can make a lotta difference in a cotton dress in that time."

Her skilled fingers were unwrapping the box.

"Say, ain't that a pretty one! And only a dollar ninety-eight! I believe I'll run down to the basement and see if I can't find me one as good. You got a bargain and no mistake."

Jane stood watching the pretty little dress widen out into smoothness, and tried to realize it was her own. Maybe she had been crazy to buy it, just for one day, when she might not have another place to wear it this summer. And yet, it was simple enough to be in style another year. Well, it was hers! And she was glad!

The girl folded the dress carefully and laid it back in the box. Jane put the other package inside and tied the box up. That was a perfectly respectable package to carry, even if she didn't have an overnight bag. She wouldn't look peculiar carrying a suitbox from a store.

She put the suitbox in her locker and hurried back to her button counter, a delicate pink flush on her cheeks. Mr. Clark noticed it as he passed down the aisle.

"You're looking better, Miss Scarlett," he said pleasantly as he signed a return slip for a customer of hers, and it warmed Jane's heart to think of the friendliness in his tone, so different from the severe tone he used to use toward her before she was sick that day.

Then five o'clock came rushing along, and she was so excited she could scarcely get the last things done.

She had managed to slip away long enough to buy a toothbrush and a five cent comb, and now she felt she was thoroughly equipped for her wonderful week-end. Would it be as wonderful as she was hoping?

Just then she caught sight of her hostess standing across the aisle, looking at her with a bright smile, and Jane nodded and smiled toward her.

Briskly she finished with her last customer and came across the aisle.

"I have to go up to the cloak room for my hat," she said. "It won't take me but a minute. There's a chair over there by the glove counter."

She hurried away and was back before Audrey had expected, for she was deeply interested watching the details of closing, and noticing how many salespeople were hindered by customers who came late as she had done not so long ago. They were not all as nice about it, either, as Jane had been.

Jane had found a wooden handle and fitted it to the string around her suitbox, and it looked very neat and trim. They were like two shoppers going on their way to the station. Jane had a sudden overwhelming shyness upon her. It seemed somehow a great presumption to have taken this stranger girl at her word and accepted the invitation. But Audrey was overjoyed.

"It's going to be fun!" she said exultantly. "I was so afraid you were going to get up some excuse and back out of coming, and I had quite set my heart upon it. I want to show you all my pet views, and pleasant spots that I have loved since I was a child. I have a hunch you'll understand why and enjoy them too."

"Of course I shall," said Jane. "I shall just revel in them. Do you know, I haven't been to the seashore since I was three years old and my father took me on his shoulder and walked away out into the water and let the spray dash up around my feet. I loved it. I had a little red bathing suit and I made houses and pies in the sand and built a wall with pebbles and shells. I can't really believe I'm going to see the ocean again."

"Oh, that's just the way I wanted you to feel, and I'm going to enjoy my ocean all over again with you," said Audrey. "We'll go in bathing, too. I think we'll get out in time for a dip before dinner."

"I couldn't," said Jane wistfully. "I haven't any bathing suit."

"Oh, we've loads of bathing suits of all sorts," said Audrey happily. "People are always coming down without any, and mother keeps them on hand, all sizes. It spoils the fun to have somebody left out. Listen! That's our train he's calling. I believe we've caught the earlier train. That means we'll have ten minutes more to go in bathing. Come on, quick! If we run we can get there before it starts!"

Breathless they were seated in the train at last, and there were real roses in Jane's cheeks now.

The two girls sat talking, having a nice time getting acquainted, Audrey pointing out the simple landmarks along the way, and Jane exclaiming over every new sight.

"Such sweet quiet little village streets!" she said wistfully. "I do get so tired of the everlasting pavements in the city, especially on a hot day. I've never really lived in a city before, and sometimes I just long for some green grass, and a cow or two in the distance along a country road."

Audrey looked at her appreciatively.

"I just knew you'd be like that!" she said. "I'm so glad you came."

"Oh, so am I!" said Jane. "But I'm afraid you're going to be ashamed of me in my plain clothes. I didn't have anything grand to bring along, even if I had had time to go to my room and get it. I just have a simple dimity dress I bought at lunch time on the bargain counter."

"We don't wear grand clothes down here," said Audrey. "Nobody minds what we wear. We're down here to get away from that sort of thing. Now, here is our station. Watch and you'll be able to see the ocean in a minute. We pass quite near the beach. There! There it is! Come on, we get out here. It's just three blocks to our cottage on the beach. It will be more fun to walk than wait for the bus. That box isn't heavy to carry, is it?"

"Oh, no. Of course, let's walk!" said Jane, feeling new life in the very air as she trod the platform, and followed Audrey down the sidewalk to the street.

"Oh, isn't it wonderful here! It doesn't seem like the same world we were in a little while ago!"

And then they were facing the sea, and a lovely breeze was blowing into their faces. Jane could think of nothing but "heavenly breezes" to express it.

Mrs. Havenner came to meet them as they ran up on the porch. She was a sweet-faced woman, but, Jane thought suddenly, another woman who had something familiar about her!

"This is my mother, Jane," said Audrey. "Mother, this is my friend, Jane Scarlett. Have we time for a little dip before dinner?"

"Oh yes, plenty, dear," said the mother. "Your father telephoned that he couldn't be out till seven-thirty, so we'll have dinner late. We're very glad to welcome you, Jane, and I hope you'll have a pleasant time with us. Audrey, I mended your bathing suit and it's hanging in the bath house as usual. There's one there for Jane, too, if she hasn't brought hers."

So the girls were soon down on the beach running along like children, and laughing together as if they had known each other always. And strangely enough, Jane didn't even know her hostess' full name yet.

Jane couldn't swim of course. She had never had opportunity to learn, but she stepped into the water like a thoroughbred and thrilled to think she was in the great ocean again after all these years.

At last Audrey announced it was time to go in and dress, and they ran dripping up the beach.

"Goodness! Can you beat it?" exclaimed Audrey. "Mother has a caller on the side porch! Let's go around this side of the house so we won't have to converse. I can't seem to recognize her. A blue dress. It doesn't seem to be any of the natives. I hope she's not staying to supper. I want to have you all to myself tonight. We've a lot of getting acquainted yet to do. We have to find out what we each like, and where we've been, and what we've read, and all that, so if she should be staying, I'll just give you the high-sign after supper and we'll slip away and walk down the beach in the moonlight!"

"Lovely!" said Jane appreciatively.

A moment under the shower, a quick rub, a hasty slipping into attire and then sliding up the back stairs to complete their toilets.

Jane had a cosy room next to Audrey's where she could watch the sea from her window. There were crisp new curtains blowing in the breeze tied with braids of the lovely pink ribbons that Audrey had brought home. Audrey noticed that her mother had taken time to finish these for the stranger guest. Mother never forgot little dainty touches.

Jane looked about on the sweet guest chamber with

awe. It seemed to her that she was in a marvelous dream, and must be going to wake up pretty soon and discover that it was all a dream. But she reflected that if there was a possibility of company perhaps she had better put on her new dress and look her best.

So with a hope that the dress would fit, after all her trouble, she put it on, and was astonished that she looked so well in it. It fitted as if it had been made for her. With a great sigh of relief she got out her little new comb and attacked her hair. It was nearly dry and the dampness had left it softly billowed into loose natural waves. She had always known it was somewhat curly but it had never seemed worth while to take any pains with it. Now, however, she realized how much better it looked in loose waves, rather than brushed sternly back as she had been wearing it.

"How lovely you look!" exclaimed Audrey as she tapped at the door to know if Jane was ready to go downstairs. "I'm sorry you felt you had to buy a new dress to come here, but it certainly is becoming. You look like a young rose about to bloom."

"Oh, if you get poetic about me," said Jane slightly breathless with pleasure, "I'll not be fit for the button counter Monday morning."

"You're too nice anyway for the button counter, you know," said Audrey. "But I'm certainly glad you were there or perhaps I would never have known you."

They went slowly downstairs hand in hand just as a little silver bell was ringing for supper, and Audrey's mother was coming in from the porch with the lady in blue.

It had all happened while the girls were in the water. The next city train had come in and brought the blue lady, and she had arrived at the cottage via the bus from the station, wearing a small blue hat and veil, and carrying a brief coat, and a diminutive overnight bag. The bag and the hat were both still reposing on the porch table outside, so that the lady in blue appeared to be a member of the household as she came in.

Jane heard Audrey utter a soft dismal exclamation as she caught sight of the visitor's face, and she felt that the guest was not as welcome as she might have been. Anyway, she was glad she had worn the pink dimity tonight if there were to be other guests.

Evadne Laverock had stood Kent's silence as long, if not longer, than she ever stood indifference and silence on the part of any of her intimates. She had arisen in her might that morning and determined to do something about it at once. She would find him in one of his haunts and demand immediate attention, and she flattered herself that she knew how to do that effectively. The only trouble was that she knew of but two haunts in which to search for him, his home and his office. He really was most unsophisticated in spite of all she had tried to teach him.

So she arrayed herself in a charming blue costume that her mirror told her was most fetching, and betook herself to the office, very near to noon, which she argued, by all laws of any business she knew, ought to be closing time on Saturday afternoon. She paused an instant at the door before she went in to take in the additional name to the sign on the glass, "Sanderson, Edsel *and Havenner.*" So! They had taken him into the firm! That was what he had been doing while she was away then, getting on in his business! Well, that wasn't so bad! Money was a great necessity, and she could use plenty! So all the more she wished to find Kent.

But when she entered and succeeded in getting belated attention from a very busy secretary long enough to ask for Kent, she was again informed that he was out of the city on business, and would probably not be back to the office until Monday, or later.

Baffled for the present Evadne walked out of the office with a high head, puckering her brows and trying to decide what to do next. She wondered, should she go to his home? She found a telephone downstairs and called up the railroad station, discovering that the train she should have taken had left five minutes before. That was annoying. However, if Kent really was in New England he would scarcely get back before late in the afternoon, and maybe it was just as well. She certainly did not wish to spend the afternoon conversing with his mother, whom she had always felt was a stuffy old woman with terribly Victorian ideas. If she should decide to marry Kent she didn't want to raise any false hopes in the old lady's mind about being a companion of hers. They would never in the world hit it off together. So she decided on the five-thirty train. That was an express, and she could fill in the time shopping. Of course she would need a few things if she were going down to the shore, and she'd been meaning to get one of the new blue leather overnight bags. Her own was getting shabby.

So Evadne filled the intervening hours before her train with agreeable shopping, lunching about two o'clock with a young artist whom she'd dug out by telephone from his natural environment. Their choice was a modern little joint that went under the title of a tavern. After lunch she possessed herself of the overnight bag, with its elaborate fittings of crystal and turquoise enamel, and went searching for a luxurious set of pajamas in pale blue satin with real lace edges. Then she added a few other expensive trifles, including a Japanese hand-embroidered kimono—apple blossoms on black satin with a pale blue satin lining. The price of all these things was simply staggering, but as she had found the charge coin belonging to her sister, it was easy enough to charge them all on her sister's account and trust to the future for settling the bill with her when she should discover it. Evadne was clever about things of this sort. Of course she counted herself honest in the long run, but what was a bill among sisters? Gloria would have done the same by her under like circumstances.

So Evadne had taken the train following the one Audrey and Jane had traveled on, and reached the Havenner cottage just after the two had gone down to swim.

When Kent's mother told her that Kent might be back that evening, though she wasn't sure, Evadne, without waiting for an invitation, exclaimed with an annoyed air:

"Oh, what a bore! And I wanted him to take me somewhere this evening. Well, I suppose I'd better wait. He'll probably come."

Mrs. Havenner with a troubled look in her eyes took the unexpected and utterly unwelcome guest up to Cousin Evalina's room, breathing a relieved sigh that Evalina was away, and not likely to return until the first of the week.

Evadne made herself at home in the room, hung up a gorgeous backless evening dress she had purchased at the last minute, fluffed up her hair, and descended to the porch to watch for Kent, hoping his family would not disturb her.

But Mrs. Havenner, reflecting that this was a Heaven-sent opportunity for finding out whether she had been right in her worried estimate of this girl's character, came out at once and settled down with a bit of sewing in her hand, to talk. So Evadne, realizing that it might be a good stunt to be in loving converse with his mother when Kent arrived, searched her idle brain for topics that might offer possible contact with this antiquated woman, and succeeded in bringing forth some in which they had not a thought in common.

They were laboring through a forced conversation when the dinner bell summoned them, and they arrived in the wide cool sitting room from which the stairs ascended, just as Audrey and Jane came down.

17

EVADNE eyed Jane. Who now was this little unsophisticated child with a face like a seraph, and a bearing like one to the manner born? Hadn't she seen her before somewhere? Or had she? Was she a sister, or a cousin? No, she was sure Kent had no other sister than Audrey. It must be a cousin. Or perhaps just a neighbor.

But though Evadne thought she had never seen Jane before, Jane knew suddenly that she had seen Evadne. She had seen her across the aisle in the store, charging the saleswoman of the trimmings-counter with having picked up her purse and secreted it. The saleswoman was weeping and protesting her innocence, and Mr. Clark was doing his best to alternately soothe her, and calm the customer's fears, promising that a thorough search would be made, and sending for Mr. Windle himself—who happened to be out of town at the time. But Evadne had raved on, denouncing the whole store for her loss. Until suddenly the salesgirl from costume jewelry came rushing over excitedly with Evadne's purse in her hand, asking: "Is this yours, madam? You laid it down under a box of clips and I just found it."

Jane could not forget that selfish empty little face as it had been wreathed in anger. Perhaps this very memory served to give that haughty little lift to her chin, and that steady unsmiling look to her eyes as she acknowledged the introduction that the other girl didn't even take the trouble to acknowledge. Evadne was trusting to her intuition that this girl wasn't of any account whatever.

Mr. Havenner came in as they were sitting down and was duly introduced to the two girls as "my father," by Audrey. And so far Jane had not yet heard the family name.

Mr. Havenner gave Jane a swift appraising look and then his glance rested on Evadne with a scrutiny that few guests at his table received. And it was noticeable that his face did not light up as he studied the indifference of the girl. His wife could see that his former opinion of her remained, and she gave a little sad suppressed breath of a sigh as if it coincided with her own opinion.

Jane felt all this, almost as if another language were flashing these things around the table, though it was invisible to the guest herself. She wondered not a little who she was. It was evident that Audrey did not know her very well, and that she was an almost stranger to them all. Yet it was also evident that the girl herself did not care in the least what they thought of her. She was only killing time, waiting for—what?—to happen.

The answer came very soon. There were sounds of footsteps at the front door, and the new girl sprang into action.

"Oh, would that be Kent?" she said. "Let me go to the door and surprise him. He'll be so delighted to find me here!" and she jumped up from her chair and dashed into the living room without waiting for permission.

Kent!

But there must be other Kents in the world beside the one she knew, Jane reflected. She recalled the startled look that she had shot at Evadne without knowing she had done so. She sent a swift furtive glance about the table. The family were sitting perfectly still, not even looking at one another, each one engrossed in his plate. There was disapproval in their very attitude, but it was evident they were trying to be very discreet and not show their annoyance. There was an utter silence in the room, and the chirpy murmurs of the guest and the rumble of the man at the front door could be distinctly heard.

Suddenly the mother roused to consciousness of the other guest.

"I think it's getting a little cooler, don't you?" she asked of Jane, with a charming smile, that somehow made Jane feel as if she were not classed with that other forward guest in the living room.

"Well, it certainly is cooler than where I've been all day," said Jane with a lovely smile in answer to the mother's smile.

And then they could hear Evadne coming slowly back.

"It's a man for you, Audrey," she said, dropping lazily into her chair again. "And he seems to be terribly possessive. He wants you at once!"

"Oh?" said Audrey indifferently. "Did he happen to say what his name was?"

Evadne looked a little surprised.

"Oh, yes, something that began with a B. I forget what it was. It doesn't matter. I was convinced that he knows you well, and wants to see you at once."

Audrey laughed lightly.

"How amusing!"

And then without the slightest sign that she was answering the man's demand she looked toward the waitress.

"Molly, please find out who is at the door, and give him a chair. Say I am engaged at present, but will be out in a little while."

Evadne watched her in amazement.

"I don't think he'll stand for that treatment," she remarked amusedly. "He seemed to me to be the touch-and-go kind."

"Yes," said Audrey, still amusedly. "Well, it's a matter of indifference to me whether he touches or goes. I've sent him a chair however."

Mr. Havenner barely suppressed a chuckle, and Jane kept her eyes upon her plate, struggling with her sense of humor.

"You're foolish," advised Evadne. "He's stunningly handsome."

"Really?" said Audrey. "Oh, but you know I see so many like that!"

Then Molly appeared in the doorway.

"It's Mr. Bainbridge, Miss Audrey. He says he hasn't a minute to spare and he wants to see you right away. He says it's very important."

Audrey fixed a level gaze on the worried maid.

"Tell Mr. Bainbridge I have a guest at dinner and I cannot come at present. Tell him not to wait if he is in a hurry."

"You must be pretty sure of him," remarked Evadne.

Audrey smiled sweetly.

"Is that the way you treat the ones you're pretty sure of?" she asked with a pleasant lifting of her lashes. And then she turned to Jane.

"Are you going up to New England next week to the regatta?" she asked innocently.

Jane stared at her an instant and then her face broke into a wreath of impish smiles and she answered:

"Well, I haven't quite decided. Perhaps if you would be willing to go with me I might go. We could have fun, couldn't we?"

"We certainly could. I know some of the men who own those yachts, and no end of people who are going."

"Let me see, what date is that?" asked Jane demurely.

"The eighteenth," said Mr. Havenner unexpectedly. There was a sedate twinkle in his eyes that his daughter knew was a sign that he was extremely pleased at something.

"Oh," said Jane, "that might be all right. But I can't say definitely until I get home to my calendar."

"Well I certainly do hope you can go. I think it would be swell, and if you decide you can, I'll switch all my dates and go along."

"Well, I'll do my best," said Jane with a bright little air as if she had been used to making dates like this all her life.

Audrey looked at her in wonder. What a clever girl she was to be able to put over a thing like this without even a hint. She felt a thrill of pleasure to think that the girl she had picked at sight was turning out to be even more than she had hoped.

"All right," she said, fairly sparkling with eagerness. "That settles it. If there's the least possibility of this being pulled off I shall go down the first thing Monday morning and buy that perfectly darling dress I saw in the store today. It was in the French room and I know it must had been a scandalous price, but I'm determined to have it. Mother, it was one of those perfectly tailored smart things that look so simple it seems as if a three-year-old child could make them. But it is made of the most gorgeous material you just know it must cost all kinds of prices."

The mother gave a little gasp as she looked up, and then swallowed her surprise and managed a smile.

"That sounds wonderful, Audrey. I'd get a couple of them if I were you, dear. You don't come on a thing like that often, you know."

Suddenly the father looked up with a very wicked twinkle in his eye.

"Hop to it, Audrey girl!" he said pompously. "My entire bank account is at your disposal."

Jane almost lost her composure then. The look on Evadne's face was so full of so many things. Astonishment, incredulity, wonder. For the first time that evening she seemed to be really interested in them all. "They are just taking her for a ride," giggled Jane to herself, "and she doesn't seem to know it. Well, they probably have some reason, and it certainly is wonderful to see a girl like that getting razzed."

But these dear people, the father and mother, and Audrey, were kindly, and not naturally sharp-minded. What reason could there be for their animosity? Was it their son? Were they afraid for him? For surely this girl would not be good for any young man, a girl with a cruel twist to her character!

"Thanks, dad," said Audrey. "Come on, Jane, if you have finished your lemon pie. Let's take a run on the beach and work off some of our extra spirits. May we be excused, please? We have a date with the moonlight!"

Audrey arose as her mother nodded assent, and catching Jane's willing hand led her out of the room by a side door, out of the house, and down onto the broad stretch of smooth white beach, with the shimmering opal-tinted expanse of sea stretching as far as eye could reach.

"Weren't you great!" said Audrey. "You certainly played up to my lead in fine shape. I nearly ruined it all by laughing, you did it so well."

"Well, I wasn't quite sure I *should*," said Jane. "It didn't seem quite true. Of course I couldn't go to a regatta, and I never expect to see one, but I couldn't resist the temptation to answer like that. I don't suppose I'll ever see her again, but it was fun."

"Yes. Wasn't it? Isn't she the worst ever? I can't stand her. She's waiting on the chance of seeing my brother tonight, and he may not come home till next week. He's off on a business trip. I wanted you to meet him. He's a dear! But some other time perhaps! Now, we came out to run, let's run!"

So they dropped hands and flew down the beach till they were entirely out of breath. At last they slowed down and walked more quietly together.

"I'm afraid you will think we are terribly rude, the whole family, I mean. We don't usually ride our guests that way. But it happens that this particular one has been most obnoxious to us all in more ways than one, and I think dad especially was trying her out on one or two points and studying her."

"Yes," said Jane, "I thought it must be something like that. Has she any right,—that is,—is she—engaged to your brother, or anything?"

Jane could not shake off a certain sense of embarrassment as she spoke of the brother. How silly, just because his name was Kent! It couldn't be her Kent, it just couldn't! Things didn't happen that way. Even if it were, he wasn't hers. Why should she care? But she must remember to ask Audrey her last name at the next lull in conversation. It was absurd to be visiting here and not know it.

"Engaged? Goodness, I hope not!" said Audrey vehemently. "Still, you never can tell. A girl like that has ways of getting around a man that are inexplicable. Oh, it would break our hearts if my brother should marry her, or even be engaged to her."

"There are a lot of couples who must have been deceived in each other," said Jane. "I don't see what some of them see in each other. Of course we see a good deal of that in the store, and it makes me disgusted. There are some really good-looking young men there that act the fool with every girl they meet. A girl can scarcely know whom she can trust. So many men are all for themselves!"

"Oh gracious!" said Audrey. "That makes me think of the man who came to the door while we were at dinner. And we slipped out the side door and ran away! Now I suppose he is sitting there yet, waiting for me, or else he is very angry and has gone away forever! Well, I really don't care. He was getting to be a nuisance. But I don't want to be rude. Would you mind running back with me part way? I don't like to leave you away off here alone, but if you don't want to come in right away you could linger down by the lifeboat where we were this afternoon till I can get rid of him and come to you."

"All right," said Jane. "I'd love sitting in that boat and just looking out to sea. I wish you wouldn't hurry. Stay as long as you want to. I'll be quite all right. Don't come back unless you want to use me for an excuse to get away from something."

"Ah! It's rare to have a friend who understands!" said Audrey, catching Jane's hand and squeezing it. "Now, let's go!" and they were off again down the beach.

Jane climbed into the stranded lifeboat and settled herself, gazing off into the silver sea, across the molten stretch of sand. She spread her rosy dress about her and could scarcely believe it was herself sitting there by the sea. So much sea, so much moon, so much silver and gold, and not a rift of a cloud in the sky!

Presently her thoughts went back to the dinner, and the strange girl, and the young man named Kent who was supposed to have come to the door and didn't. Oh, could it be her Kent, her lawyer? Of course not. That would be too fantastic.

But if it should be, and he came home while she was here, what would he think of her? Wouldn't she appear to be just in a class with that Laverock woman at dinner? How dreadful!

It seemed awful to think of him as interested in such a girl—if it should really be the same man. She couldn't believe it. She just wouldn't. And she wouldn't think about it nor him any more. She would just enjoy this wonderful silver vision. Why, this was as near as an earthly mind could ever vision the Heavenly shore! Would it look like that when she died and was nearing the shore of Heaven? She could almost see the towers of a Heavenly mansion, off there in the silver-blue sea.

"Oh God! Keep me from getting mixed up with this earth so that I shall forget that this world is not my home!"

Then as her thoughts sped back into the past week she began to hum softly and then to sing louder:

> *"Oh Lord, you know*
> *I have no friend like you,*
> *If Heaven is not my Home*
> *Oh Lord, what shall I do?"*

Her voice rolled out sweetly in the wide silver night. She felt as if she were talking to God. She had a strong consciousness that she was all alone with God, that no one else could hear her. It had been literally years since she had been as much alone as this. She always felt that she would be overheard if she sang. She had never dared even in church or the Bible class to let her voice out to its fullest. But now she felt that the soft murmur of the sea would drown any sound she made, so that it could not possibly reach up to the house, and there was not a creature in sight either way.

She leaned back against the tiller of the boat and sang on. When she had finished the simple song she sang others, some which she had heard recently at the Bible class, and more from the store in her memory, until the past came trooping about her and peopled the lovely silver world with those she had loved and lost. There were tears in her eyes now, and her voice broke occasionally, but she sang on with that full-throated beauty that she scarcely had known she possessed. She was just singing to the Lord. At last she paused and it was as if all the sacred truth she had been taught by her parents, all the wonderful new Bible truths that she had been learning the past few days, blended together and thrilled her young soul till it wanted to speak aloud to God. Instinctively she went back to the new song which had been ringing in her heart more or less ever since she had first heard it. She sang it as if she were singing to God from the depths of her being; slowly, soulfully, beautifully, through to the end:

"Oh Lord, you know,
I have no friend like you—!"

and coming out of the silver night it sped up the beach and down the beach like the cry of a saved soul suddenly learning its isolation from all around it. The wistful longing of her desolate young heart rang out hopefully with the final lines:

> *"I can't feel at home*
> *In this world any more!"*

And suddenly, as she ended, the melody rang on from the beginning again, with other voices like an echo taking up the strain:

> *"Oh Lord, you know,"*

Startled, yet still feeling herself alone, and as if angels, or some trick of her own imagination, had supplied the harmony, her voice took up the air again and she sang as if inspired.

It was only an instant before she realized that they were real voices, those voices, and not a figment of her imagination, not angels, like those that came to the shepherds of old, not supernatural as for a minute it had seemed, but human. They were live real voices singing with her. Tenor, bass, and now Audrey was humming an alto with them also!

She sprang up and looked around, but kept right on singing. She dared not stop. There they were, standing just a little back of her boat on the sand. She couldn't see their faces enough to distinguish who they were, till they drew nearer, singing as they came.

It was then that she saw Kent, and a great gladness filled her heart. She didn't stop to realize how astonishing the situation was, nor what he might think of her to find her here. She was just glad, and a flood of light filled her face and lit her eyes as she looked toward him with instant welcome, answering the radiance of welcome already in his own face for her. It was only a moment that they turned the glory light upon each other. Then Jane came to herself and began to take account of other factors in the situation. Who was this man with Kent? Could it be the man who had come to the door while they were at dinner? No, for she had seen this man before. Who was he? Ah! She knew now. It was the new teacher of the Bible class, Mr. Whitney! And no wonder he could sing like that, his own song that he had sung for them!

Oh, and they had all heard her sing alone, and maybe she had made mistakes! But how grand it was for them all to be there singing it together! And no wonder Audrey and her parents seemed familiar to her! She could see now, even in the moonlight, how very much the brother and sister resembled each other. Strange that she had not recognized that at once! She certainly would not have come here if she had! What should she do? Disappear?

"Sing it again," exclaimed Audrey, as the last notes died away on the brilliant night. "I'm just getting on to that alto. It's lovely. What tender beautiful words!"

So they sang it again, and it seemed even more exquisite yet.

Jane was standing down on the sand now with Audrey's arm around her lovingly, looking off to the edges of the silver sea where little golden lapping wavelets caressed the silver sand. And suddenly she was aware that two other figures were coming slowly toward them down the beach, a woman and a man.

18

THE woman was dressed in blue, with golden hair that gleamed in the moonlight, and all at once something clutched at Jane's throat with cold frightening fingers, and drove the gladness away from her heart. What impossible situation was this anyway?

Here she had been rejoicing that Kent Havenner had come, when she had no possible right to rejoice. He belonged definitely to this other girl in blue! This insolent girl. No wonder Audrey didn't like her. But it didn't make any difference that she was a disagreeable girl. She evidently had a right to him. She had made it plain that she came down here to see him, had planned to surprise him at the door as if they had an understanding between them. And of course she, Jane, had no claim whatever upon Mr. Havenner, except in a business way, and possibly as a member of the Bible class. She never had had any claim, social or even religious, which should give her a right to such a tumult of joy as had come to her when she recognized him behind her singing. The blood burned hotly in her cheeks and she was glad that moonlight would somewhat camouflage her face and hide her confusion. For she was ashamed. Almost as if her joy had been written flamingly across her face, she was ashamed! A nice girl did not admire a man so much as that at first. A man who was really nothing to her, a man she did not know except as an honorable respectable business man. It was all wrong that it set her heart to singing. She had no right. Even if he did not definitely belong to any other girl yet, she had no right to be so happy about his approach. It was probably because she had had so little really enjoyable companionship, that she had idealized him. And she must snap out of it! Right here and now she must get wise to herself, and take this all in a matter-of-fact way. He was nice of course. But she would miss even the nice time she might have for a couple of hours tonight if she got silly about this thing.

She would just act to him exactly as she had always acted since she knew him,—after all the acquaintance was so very brief—and then when she got by herself she would read herself such a lecture as she never had before, and try to get some sense into her head. Meanwhile this was a nice time that God had sent her, and she must not spoil it. This teacher and Mr. Havenner, and Audrey! How nice that she was his sister! Still, of course she mustn't count on coming down here again. But while she was here she would enjoy everything, and not make them ashamed of her before these strangers, whoever they were.

The last notes of the quartette died away and there were the other two, standing a few yards away from the boat!

It was Evadne's voice that broke the sweet silence, trilling out an empty little laugh.

"My word!" she said lightly, "what a lugubrious

song! It sounds as if you all were about to pass out! Why can't you sing something cheerful?"

"I should say!" echoed Ballard Bainbridge. "Where did you rake up a deadly song like that? It sounds as if you were on a sit-down strike in a mine or something. You should sing something cheerful on a gorgeous night like this. How about this?" and he struck into the most modern air he knew, with a pompous voice so filled with pride of itself that it sounded as if it were stuffed with Indian meal, or dry mashed potatoes.

There was utter silence while he sang, and Evadne stood beside him posed in the moonlight, wishing that it were the fashion to take pictures by moonlight and that someone had a candid camera. She knew she must be rather stunning with that light on her gold hair, and that handsome man beside her. So Audrey thought he was hers, did she? She'd better look out or she would lose him. Evadne had ways with her that could ensnare any number of men at once, no matter how impervious they thought they were to charms. She was glad that Kent was there where he could watch her. She had had no words with him as yet, for he had come in by the back door with his friend, and gone out again with Audrey by that same door. Evadne was not sure whether he had known she was there, for she had been sitting on the end porch, facing the other view of the beach, when he came in. But he knew she was here now, and she exulted in the thought that he would see her for the first time under such favorable circumstances. It had been a good hunch that had led her down here to his home. She was triumphant also that she had a good-looking man by her side. That was always an asset. Of course she did not know how he despised that particular young man.

But Kent did not seem to be attending to the solo that

was being rendered so affectedly. He was stepping quietly over to that Scarlett girl's side, and taking her hand, smiling down into her face. Evadne darted a lightning glance at him. Was this only a gesture to show her that he had friends also? He was talking earnestly to Jane, as if he knew her well, smiling at her, and she at him. They were not disturbing the singer. They did not make a noise. But they were carrying on a silent little aside and enjoying it. She set her stubborn lips hatefully, and flashed her jealous eyes, boding no good for any who displeased her.

Then the song was ended, and the singer beamed about waiting to be commended, but Evadne was busy and no one else cared to commend him.

"Let me introduce my friend Mr. Whitney," spoke up Kent eagerly. "This is Miss Scarlett, Pat. And over here, Miss Laverock and Mr. Bainbridge. My sister Audrey you have met."

The stranger acknowledged the introductions courteously, and then Kent, still at Jane's side, said:

"Now, how about a walk on the beach while the tide's out?" and possessing himself of Jane's arm he whirled her about and started briskly up the beach, she falling quickly into step beside him.

"Shall we follow?" asked young Whitney of Audrey, and they started on a few paces behind the others.

There was nothing left for the other two guests but to follow. Ballard Bainbridge strolled lazily along, mortified that his song had made so little impression. He considered himself a fine singer.

"I'm afraid our efforts were scarcely appreciated," he said loftily. "That is the trouble when one tries to uplift depression of any kind, it is so seldom understood."

"Well, I thought your singing was swanky!" declared Evadne, lapsing into her lingo. "I never come out here but I'm depressed. It is a great pity that these young people have been brought up by such antiquated parents. I thought Kent had gone out into the world enough to get over his early training, but he seems to have lapsed badly since I went abroad."

"Yes, I suppose that is what's the matter with them," agreed Ballard, drawing Evadne's arm into his and settling it comfortably close, their shoulders touching. "They are so bound by laws and customs and rules! It will be great when a new order of things is finally established in our country. Children will be no longer parent-ridden, they will be brought up by the state, and able to express themselves as their wills prompt!"

"Do you really think we are coming to that, Ballard?" asked Evadne, leaning a little closer to him and looking up into his face. "Oh, you do encourage me so! When I look about upon the people who are so tied down by the wishes of others, by old customs, by what is so mistakenly called courtesy, it is so pitiful, and seems so hopeless."

"Yes, it is pitiful," said Ballard Bainbridge, looking down into Evadne's vapidly pretty face, and laying a possessive hand over her small one that lay relaxed upon his arm, "certainly pitiful, but not hopeless, my dear Miss Laverock."

"Oh, call me Vad, won't you?" said Evadne in a wheedling tone. "I shall think you don't love me if you call me Miss Laverock so formally."

"Oh, but I do love you," said Ballard with a fulsome smile. "I find you are the answer to my heart's desire. Even in the little time I had with you up on the porch I found myself wondering how I have lived so long without you," and he slid his arm about her and drew her closer, stooping and laying his hot lips upon hers. This was what Audrey never would let him do.

Slower and slower their footsteps lagged as they exchanged vague views about the world today and what was coming in the future, a future wherein one's passions and desires should be the only criterion, and there should be no more thou-shalt-nots.

Now and again Evadne, clinging to this new-found man, a lover after her own heart, glanced up occasionally to see if Kent were observing her, for she had acquired so cunning a skill in dealing with men, that one never fully absorbed her whole consciousness. But Kent was far out of sight, and the other two were just vanishing around the curve of what was called "the Point."

Jane's heart was fluttering happily. She told herself she was having a nice time, just like other girls. A young man who was a real gentleman was walking on the beach with her, just as he might walk with any girl. He knew she was only a button girl, and yet he was treating her like a lady, just as if she were any nice girl out for the evening. There wasn't a tinge of condescension in his manner. He was acting as if she was his equal in every way. And that was the height of courtesy, to forget social separations and just be friendly.

He was holding her arm and guiding her to the firm smooth places on the beach, walking briskly and calling her attention to the lovely lights on the ocean, to the pathway of moonlight that trailed out across the waves, telling her about a little ship that went curtseying over the billow, explaining what it was, whence it came and whither bound.

"It certainly looks like the way to the Heavenly city out there, doesn't it?" he said suddenly, stopping for a moment and gazing across the water over the bright path.

"Oh, it does!" said Jane wistfully. "My, if it really was, I would certainly start walking!"

He was looking down at her, watching the expression on her face there in the moonlight.

"Yes?" he said sympathetically, but suddenly drawing her arm a little closer within his own. "Not just yet, please!" he added. "We—don't want to spare you so soon. We're just getting to know you."

She looked up startled, almost thrilled at the friendliness in his tone.

"Oh! that's nice!" she said with a faint little smile on her lips. "I—was afraid—perhaps you wouldn't like it that you found me here, just a client from your business life. You know I hadn't an idea this was your home I was coming to, or I never would have come. Your sister just picked me up out of the blue and brought me. I never even knew her name till we got here, and even then only her first name. But if I had found out before you came I should have tried to make some excuse to get right up and run away. Especially when I knew there was company."

"But why, pray? Do you dislike me so?" asked Kent, smiling down into her eyes.

"Oh, no!" disclaimed Jane fervently. "It was just that I thought it might mortify you to find a button girl in your home. It was all very well to be kind to a stranger, a working girl, when it was a part of your business, but you can surely understand why I would not have wanted to force myself upon you socially if I had known. I would have felt it was a discourtesy to you."

There was something lovely in Kent's eyes as he met her earnest upturned ones.

"Yes, I understand," he said gravely, and then slipping the hand that held her arm down to her own hand he gave it a quick warm pressure like a clasp. "Yes, I understand you, but—I do not feel that way in the least. I look up to you almost reverently, because you were the one who led me to the way of Truth. And I think maybe you will be glad to know that today I've made an important decision. You see I came down from Boston on the train with our new teacher, Pat Whitney, and we talked a lot on the way. He made me see what it is I've needed all my life, and gave me a vision of my own heart that was full of sin. I never called it sin before. I thought it was only youth, and good spirits, and a desire to do as others did. But now I think I understand it better. I see all these wild impulses to have my own way, and work out my life for my own glory, and my own pleasure, were really a turning away from God, and what He had planned for my life. And I realize now that that is not the way of happiness. For a long time I've been unhappy, and dissatisfied, and I didn't know what was the matter. When I would get what I went after for a time, it didn't satisfy, and I was restless and full of longing. But tonight I saw what the great trouble was. I needed my Saviour. I've taken it in at last that it was my sins that made Him have to suffer on the cross." Kent spoke slowly in a low tone, and as if he had almost forgotten Jane was there, as if for the moment he were in a world apart. Then he drew a deep satisfied breath. "But now I've accepted Him, and a great burden of uneasiness has rolled away from me. My whole outlook on life seems changed. I want Him to have His way with me from now on. Do you know Him this way? Have you ever taken Him as your Saviour?"

"Oh, yes," said Jane softly. "Once a long time ago when I was a little girl my Sunday School teacher talked with me, and I accepted Christ. But that was long ago, and during the years I drifted very far away from Him. My mother was a Christian, but after she died I felt bitter toward God for having taken her away from me. I stopped praying, stopped reading my Bible, until I heard that announcement over the radio and went to see what it was about. But—now—I've come back. I told Him so a few nights ago. I think He accepted me and forgave me. I don't know a whole lot about it all yet. But I want to learn."

"Then that's a tie between us that is greater than any social differences," said Kent gently. "Besides, there aren't any of those differences either. Your Scarlett family is just as good as any socialite living. But when one is related to the Lord Jesus Christ, in a tie of blood, it counts far more than mere human rating."

"Oh! I'm so glad about you! I wanted you to know Him!" said Jane ecstatically.

"Did you—dear!" The last word was breathed so softly it was scarcely audible. Afterwards Jane was sure she had only thought it, or perhaps only wished it, and she chided herself for the thought, yet it had seemed so reverent, like a blessing, that she could not feel about it as she would if it had been upon another's lips.

Kent reached out and caught both her hands and pressed them warmly and close, and then drawing her arm within his own again they walked on together in silence for a few seconds, a brief sweet silence.

It was the sound of other voices that broke the holy quiet between them.

"Did you know that Pat Whitney is preaching near here tomorrow? About two miles above our cottage at a little shore church. Would you like to go and hear him in the morning?"

"Could I?" she asked eagerly. "Oh, I would love to. Will your sister think it is all right for me to go?"

"I'm sure she will," said Kent. "I'll see that she

does,—if she doesn't," he added grinning. And then his face grew sober again.

"Do you know who the others are?" he asked with a nod backwards and a little anxious pucker to his brow.

"I know their names."

"Yes, well, their names are enough. They won't be in sympathy. Not either of them."

"I—thought so—! That is, I don't know the man at all. I hadn't even met him till you introduced him. The lady was at dinner. She didn't sound as if she would be."

"No!" he said thoughtfully.

And then they could hear the others coming nearer, and they swung around to take the homeward way. Arm in arm, talking earnestly, they passed Pat and Audrey, and then a little later Evadne and Ballard.

Evadne waved a hand of greeting and called out to Kent:

"How about changing partners, Kennie?"

But Kent merely waved a casual hand in acknowledgment and passed on with Jane, scarcely looking up.

Evadne walked on greatly dismayed and deeply angry. She had not counted on a rebuff like that! She would certainly pay Kent well for his action. Kent belonged to her, body and soul, or so she had for a long time supposed. This had started out as a much-needed discipline for him; she had had no idea he would turn her sword upon herself. Yet with Evadne, a man looked never so interesting as when he was hard to get.

However, the man with whom she was walking now was not to be sneered at. He was far more congenial than Kent ever had been.

And because Ballard saw that his new companion was ready to go to Kent whom he despised, he roused himself to challenge her interest. And Ballard was attractive. He reflected that this girl was far more to his liking in her ways than Audrey. At least he would enjoy her for the evening, and probably give a salutary lesson to Audrey, who was getting too much out of hand.

So he walked Evadne far down the coast, put her on a local ferry, and carried her to another resort where a noted hotel offered a ballroom and plenty to eat and drink. Evadne danced far into the night, dined and wined to her heart's content, and was brought back in the wee small hours of the morning, deposited at the door of the cottage, and met by Audrey's mother, though she had hoped to have been met by a repentant Kent. She had planned to shock Kent by her own condition of intoxication, though to tell the truth it took a great deal to put her beyond her own control. But to meet Kent's mother at that hour, with a thickened speech and the breath of liquor heavy upon her lips was another matter. Mrs. Havenner escorted her to Cousin Evalina's room, thankful that she had not as yet returned, and then herself lay down, but slept no more that night. Was this the girl who intended to marry her son?

19

MEANTIME Audrey had been walking in a new world, listening to an evangel.

Pat Whitney was fresh from extensive study in a seminary where the gospel of the Bible was taught in its purity, by lips of holy men as noted for their scholarship as for their spirituality. He had been for four years in close companionship with a body of young men who lived in the consciousness of the constant presence of Jesus Christ, and to whom the Holy Spirit was a real Person of the Godhead. The study of God's word had been a delight, and he had no joy greater than to talk about it and impart its meaning to others who did not know all its wonders. Yet he spoke so simply, so humbly withal, that he gave no sense of being dictatorial.

Audrey had been attracted by him the minute she saw him, and wondered if his attraction was all in his looks, or if in reality here was another Ballard who thought he knew it all and wanted to make everybody bow to his knowledge.

But before they had talked many minutes she was sure he was not conceited, and she had also decided that he had a fine sense of humor, a quality in which young Bainbridge was greatly lacking. When she reached that point she forgot to try to card-index him. She only knew that he was delightful and not the least bit of a pedant.

But they had not gone far before they were talking on the subject that was ever uppermost in his mind, the great wonder and glory of salvation for a lost world. And it was Audrey herself who introduced it, all unaware.

"And you," she said, "what *are* you? A business man? No. I'm sure not! A lawyer? Somehow you don't look it. A professor? An astronomer? An archaeologist? Not a minister! *I* have it, a writer! Is that right?"

He smiled.

"You're wrong," he said. "I'm not a writer, though there may come a day when I shall want to set down some of the wonderful things I have learned, after I have had more time to put them into practice. No, I'm not any of those great things you have mentioned. I'm just a plain servant."

She turned an astonished gaze at him, trying to fathom what he could possibly mean.

"A servant of the Lord Jesus Christ," he said with a ring of pride in his voice, "Whose I am and Whom I serve!" he added reverently. "He loved me and gave Himself for me, and now I live to give the good news of Him to others."

She looked still more puzzled.

"You mean you're some kind of missionary?" she asked. "Surely not! You don't look like any missionary I ever saw."

He laughed.

"Perhaps you've been unfortunate in your missionaries. But no, listen! I'm just a plain teacher of the Bible.

You may call me by whatever title you choose. It doesn't matter. I like to tell people that there is a Saviour who will save from sin, and give life and joy and peace and brightness in this dark world."

"That sounds wonderful!" said Audrey. "Tell me right away how to get that."

And there, walking by the summer sea in the moonlight, he told her how he had found the Lord, and what He had been to him, and before their walk was ended he had made Audrey long inexpressibly for the peace which he himself had.

It was a bright talk, interspersed by laughter now and then. Audrey soon recognized that here was a strong man going a hard way, and *liking* it. Happy he was in an eternal joy, and with the constant consciousness of his Lord walking with him! It was the most amazing thing that Audrey had ever heard, and she kept him talking about it by asking many questions, unwilling to pass to other topics.

They came back at last to the wide inviting porch and found Kent and Jane talking and looking off to sea. They grouped themselves on the steps and lingered, waiting for the other two who had been in their party at the start. Mrs. Havenner brought out lemonade and tiny frosted cakes. They had a little party, and kept wondering why the others did not return.

The mother had lingered watching her own two, and studying the two strangers, approvingly. She thought of the two who were out and away somewhere, with relief that they were not here.

At last Kent said:

"Well, Pat, if you're going to preach tomorrow it seems to me you ought to have a little sleep. How about it if we turn in now?"

"Preach?" said Audrey opening her eyes wide. "You didn't tell me that about yourself!" she accused.

"But did I have to tell everything, lady?" he grinned. "I only tried to answer what you asked. It didn't really matter, did it?"

"He's preaching over at Silver Beach Chapel," explained Kent, "and you won't get much information about himself out of that baby, sister. He's got too many other important things to tell."

"Yes, I found that out," said Audrey. "But I'm going, of course. What time?"

"Well, Jane and I are walking by way of the beach," said Kent. "We thought we would start about ten-often in the morning and take our time. I imagine Pat won't mind our tagging along. If he does, the beach is wide."

"Delighted to have the company of *all* of you," said Pat happily, his tone including them all, but his eyes smiling down into Audrey's.

Perhaps if Mrs. Havenner had happened to be out there just then and heard what they said, it might have saved her lying awake and worrying about her son, after she had escorted the disheveled Evadne to her room.

But in the morning at breakfast she found out what was going on, and watched the four start out for their walk with relief in her eyes. Later she told her husband and they drove over also to hear the young man preach. But they had not been gone long before things began to happen at home.

Evadne had of course not come down to breakfast, and nothing had been heard from her before the family left for church. Mrs. Havenner instructed her maid to give the lady a cup of good strong coffee if she should appear before they reached home, and she went off thankful that none of the family knew what time this unwelcome guest had come in.

But they had scarcely been gone from the cottage half an hour before a car drew up at the door and deposited Cousin Evalina there, and then drove off again.

Evalina gathered up her bags and essayed to go up to her room, but when she entered she was amazed to see a handsome dress of sheer blue stuff lying in a heap on the floor, and a number of other articles of apparel scattered about.

Indignantly she turned toward the bed and there lay the golden-haired Evadne in a drunken sleep. Evalina had had little experience with drunkenness, but she did know enough to recognize the heavy stupor that enveloped the sleeper, and the strong odor of liquor on her breath. She was indignant beyond words that her room, *her* room, had been commandeered for such a purpose as this. For any purpose in her absence! Evalina considered that as long as a few of her garments were left behind her, the room was occupied by herself, and belonged to her, and never considered that she was not even an invited guest, but had come unannounced and taken possession.

But when Evalina drew nearer to the bed, and studied the face of the interloper, she recognized who this girl was. This was Evadne, Kent's girl, who had run away to Europe and left him.

She had always thought it was somehow Kent's fault that he had allowed a girl as sophisticated and beautiful as this one to get away from him, after he was practically engaged to her, and everybody was expecting an announcement. So her first reaction when she recognized Evadne was triumph, pleasure. So, the girl had come back!

Did Kent know it? Where was Kent? Had he taken

her to a dance or a night club or something last night and got in late? She cast her eyes about and took in every evidence that could possibly tell her anything. Then she laid aside her own wraps, put her suitcases in the closet out of sight, and tiptoed softly out of the room. She must find the family and get an idea of how the land lay. Perhaps they were wanting her to take the other guest room and let this guest have the one where she lay asleep.

But Mrs. Havenner was not in her room. Audrey was not in her room. Nobody seemed to be anywhere. Further investigation showed evidence of a second guest in the other guest room. Her anger rose. What did they think they were going to do with her? Of course they hadn't expected her back until tomorrow or next day, but it seemed a strange performance. She hadn't said definitely she was going to stay all the week!

She went downstairs but none of the family were there. She looked up and down the beach, and even traveled out to the bath houses, but there was no sign of anybody, and only dry bathing suits greeted her eye as she swung back the doors of the bath houses.

Well, of all things! What had the family gone and done? Leaving Evadne alone asleep! And perhaps Kent was upstairs in his room asleep also. She would go and find out!

So she climbed the stairs again and swung Kent's door open. No, no one was there. Well, this was extraordinary. She decided reluctantly to interview the maids. She hesitated to do this because neither of them had what she considered a proper respect for her. They resented her suggestions, and served her most reluctantly. But this was a case where it was most necessary to find out the exact situation. So she raided the kitchen.

"Molly, where are the family?" she demanded of that worthy as she came into the dining room to set the table.

"Oh, they've all gone to church!" said Molly with a toss of her head and a kind of triumph in her voice, as if going to church were a regular habit of the Havenners.

"To church?" asked Evalina with a lifting of the eyebrows. "What do you mean, to church?"

"Why, they've gone to church to hear the young preacher," she related with evident relish, drawing out her tale to its utmost possibility.

"The young preacher! What young preacher?"

"Why the young preacher Mr. Kent brought back with him from Boston or somewhere. His name is Whitney!"

"But I never heard of him!" said Evalina indignantly. "Where is he preaching?"

"I heard them say he was preaching down to Silver Beach Chapel!"

"Silver Beach Chapel! That little dinky place! Why, nobody that was worth anything would preach there. You must have heard wrong, Molly. They couldn't have gone there!"

"Yes, ma'am, that's what they said. The young folks walked down the beach, but Mr. and Mrs. Havenner went in the car later."

"Young folks! What young folks?"

"Why, Miss Audrey and the young preacher, and Mr. Kent and that other girl that's staying here, Miss Scarlett. Miss Jane Scarlett, that's her name!"

"Jane Scarlett! You don't mean *that* girl is here, Molly?"

"That's what they call her, Miss Evalina."

"Mercy!" said Evalina, She turned as if to leave the room and then she remembered and turned back.

"But Molly, what about this young woman who is in my room? How did she get there? Who put her there?"

"I donno, Miss Evalina. She was at dinner last night, and then she didn't come down to breakfast with the rest. Mis' Havenner said I was to give her strong coffee when she comes down."

"But why was she put in my room?"

"I donno, Miss Evalina, deed I don't! She come along before dinner, and Mis' Havenner took her up there to take off her hat, and then after dinner they all went out somewheres. Mr. Bainbridge was over too, an' the young folks all went out on the beach, but I went out when I got my dishes done, and I don't know nothing more."

Evalina looked thoughtful an instant and then she said, as if in explanation to herself:

"So Mr. Bainbridge was here, was he? To dinner?"

"Oh, no'm! He come askin' after Miss Audrey, and she sent word for him to wait, but she didn't go out for a long while and then she just walks down to the beach with Miss Scarlett."

"Where were the young men? Where was Kent?"

"Oh, he and the preacher-man hadn't come yet. They come afterwhile. I heard them singin' hymns down on the beach. The preacher has an awful pretty voice."

"Singing *hymns?*"

"Yes, singin' hymns. Some awful pretty ones!"

"Well, but what became of Mr. Bainbridge?"

"Oh, he was out on the front porch talkin' to the lady with yella hair that's upstairs asleep. You gonta be here ta dinner, Miss Evalina? Shall I put on a place for you?"

"Certainly!" said Evalina, and swept upstairs severely.

Evalina went into her bedroom with a very firm expression on her face. She glanced at the clock, and saw that it could not be long before the church-goers arrived at home.

She closed her door with decision and stood gazing for a minute at the sleeper who seemed not to have stirred since she left her. Then she walked firmly and heavily over to her washstand, and taking a large clean washcloth from the drawer, wet it thoroughly in the coldest water she could get from the faucet, and going determinedly over to the bed she sloshed that wet cloth swiftly over the face of Evadne until she gasped, and let out a scream.

"There! That's all right!" said Evalina. "Nobody's going to kill you. I'm only doing this for your own good. It's high time you were awake and dressed. I know you'll be glad I did it pretty soon."

Thus she instructed the invincible Evadne until amid much groaning and struggling and protest she had her thoroughly awake. Evadne's first rational act was to fling the wet cloth which had just been freshly soused at the faucet, straight into Evalina's face, and thus, caught by her own weapon, hoisted with her own petard as it were, Evalina was forced for the moment to retire from action and rescue her best dress from water stains. But she did it with set lips, uttering no sound.

Evadne sat up and blinked at her, using language that was not in the usual Havenner vocabulary. But Evalina merely gave her a withering glance and went on rubbing the front of her skirt dry. At last Evadne reached the end of her repertoire and stared at Evalina.

"Who in heck are you anyway?" she stormed.

"I'm part of the family," said Evalina complacently, "and you happen to be occupying my bed."

"Oh!" said Evadne contemptuously, stared back at it, and laughed. "So what?"

"Nothing, only it's almost time the family came home from church, and I thought it was time you got into some clothes and were ready to meet them. Dinner will be served in about three-quarters of an hour."

"What in heck do I care?" said Evadne insolently. "Who do you mean will be back from church? Where are all the folks anyway?"

"Why, Kent, and Audrey and the preacher and that Scarlett girl they tell me was here all night."

"Oh!" said Evadne, startled really awake now. "Say, who *is* that Scarlett girl? Where have I seen her before? She just simply walked off with Kent all the evening and I never did see him at all."

"She's nothing in the world but a button salesperson from Windle's store. What did you let her walk off with Kent for? She's nothing but a *working* girl."

"A *working girl?*" Evadne's eyes were wide with anger. "Do you mean to tell me that Kent Havenner would go off with a working girl when *I* was here?"

"Well, I expect Kent has been pretty angry at what you did. You can't expect to have him smile right off the bat when you come back after a silent six months in Europe."

Evadne stared at her.

"Do you mean to tell me that Kent Havenner has no better sense than to use a little baby-faced working girl dressed in pink dimity to make me jealous? *Me?* Well, if that's all it won't take long to bring him back to his senses!"

Evadne flung herself out of bed and began to dress swiftly. But she went on asking questions.

"What's Audrey trying to do to his royal highness, Prince Bainbridge?"

"She? Oh, I'm sure I don't know. They've been pretty thick all summer. He brings her quantities of books to read, and they quarrel a lot, but I think she's about engaged to him now."

"Well, you'd better think again," said Evadne. "I'm thinking of taking him over myself if I need an understudy for Kent. He's a looker and presentable. He dances well, too, which is what Kent never did."

"You were out dancing last night!" charged Evalina.

"What's that to you?"

"I had to wash your face to get you awake," remarked Evalina significantly. "I wouldn't advise you to play that act of getting half-stewed around here very often. Kent's father and mother are very old-fashioned."

"Don't I know that? I can get along without your advice, thank you. But say, can't you take your glad rags out of here, and let me have this room to myself? For I'm thinking of staying here several days. This is going to be some campaign!"

"I'll say it is," said Evalina, "and you'd better keep in with me if you want to win, for there isn't anybody else you can depend upon, I'm afraid. They're all a narrow lot here!"

"You're telling me!" said Evadne.

"There! They're coming now!" said Evalina. "See! They're *walking* back! I thought they'd come in the car, but I think I heard that come in some time ago. See! There they are up by the pavilion."

Evadne went to the window and looked up the beach.

"Yes," she said sourly, "and that Scarlett girl is walking with Kent again! The insolent thing! I know her by that pink dress! Little bold thing!"

Evadne turned and went on rapidly with her dressing. Not that she had so much to put on for her garments were few and scanty, but there was her make-up to repair, without its usual nightly anointing.

Nevertheless Evalina was surprised that she was ready so soon, calm and cool and haughty, a beauty crowned with golden curls walking lazily down the stairs.

"Good morning, folks," she called noisily as the church-goers came in. "Been out boating or swimming already?"

Nobody answered her. They were talking to one another.

Then Evadne marched straight up to Jane and addressed her.

"What are you doing here, anyway?" she asked, as a prince might have addressed a cur. "I wonder, do they know who you are? How did you steal in here unaware?"

Jane turned a bewildered look at the woman of the world.

"Evadne!" said Kent in a shocked voice. But she paid no heed to him. She only raised her voice a little higher so that even the servants in the dining room could hear.

"Haven't I seen you selling goods in Windle's store? Answer me! Don't you sell buttons at Windle's?"

And then Jane's careful training by her mother stood her in good stead.

"Why, yes," she said with a nonchalant smile. "Certainly. Ask Audrey, she has bought buttons of me. Why? Did you want me to use my influence to get you a job?" She gave a little twinkling look at the astonished Evadne.

From the back door that led to the garage Mr. Havenner had entered unseen a moment or two before this conversation began, and now there came a chuckle, appreciative and hearty. Mr. Havenner had a great sense of humor, and Mrs. Havenner, her face full of worry, slid over by his side. It always relieved the tension when her husband laughed.

Pat Whitney, too, had a twinkle in his eyes, and let them dance at the angry lights in Audrey's eyes, as if to say, "Why worry? It isn't worth all that, is it?"

Kent, furious, opened his mouth as if to speak, and just then the dinner bell rang, and instead he closed it and turned to Jane.

"Well, I guess that means we won't read that article till after dinner, doesn't it, Jane?" he said, and taking her arm led her out to the table.

Jane was tremendously embarrassed, now that she had met her crisis and said her little say. She was afraid perhaps she had overdone it, and was too rude. Yet what else could she have done? Burst into tears and left the room? Taken the next train home? Wouldn't that have embarrassed her hostess more than this?

So quietly she walked out to the table, thankful for the courtesy which was placed at her disposal, as if the whole family were doing their utmost to offset the insult that had been offered her.

Evalina had been on her way downstairs just as Evadne began her attack, and Evalina had stepped back to await developments. What a brave girl to go to the root of the matter right at the start! Surely they would all see now what the world thought of people who took up with poor working girls! This was going to be rare!

But a moment later when Jane gave her gay little answer Evalina drew back farther into the upper hall. How did the girl dare to speak that way? It showed what a bold thing she was.

Her cousin's chuckle from the doorway did not fail to reach her ears, and an angry look crossed her face. Then with set lips she went down the stairs in a stately way, and marched over to Evadne effusively. That poor girl should see that she was not alone.

"My dear!" she purred as she came on, "was that the dinner bell I heard? How welcome. I'm simply starved! Aren't you? I don't believe a soul offered you even so much as a cup of coffee this morning."

Together they sailed out into the dining room and took the seats Mrs. Havenner indicated, each inwardly indignant that the little button girl was given the place of honor at Mr. Havenner's right hand. They sat and stared at the circle of bowed heads while Pat asked a blessing on the food.

The dinner was a very quiet one. Evadne scarcely opened her lips: She had the air of one who had been outrageously insulted.

The talk was mostly of the service that morning, grave, sweet talk in which neither Evadne nor Evalina had any part. They simply stared at each one who spoke in inexpressible astonishment. Now and then Evalina broke out with some bubbling remark irrelevantly, concerning something nobody cared anything about. Frequently Kent would recall some interesting phrase or sentence from one of their Bible classes and ask Jane if she remembered what Mrs. Brooke had said about that, and Jane, doing her best to overcome her shyness, answered well, so that the young minister asked her several questions.

"You know I'm to have that class now," he explained to Mr. Havenner, "and I really feel very reluctant to follow such a wonderful teacher as Mrs. Brooke. It seems too bad they have to lose her."

Somehow they got through that dinner, got out of the dining room, and then Kent and Jane took themselves out of the way, with Audrey and Pat following not far behind, and no one said a word to Evadne about going along. No one paid any attention to Evadne, except Evalina. She felt the poor child was being treated abominably. She went upstairs, rooted out a pack of cards from her trunk and brought them down to the porch, setting up a card table in a conspicuous place where everybody who went by on the beach could see them. There they sat and played cards all the afternoon, though she well knew it would annoy her cousins beyond expression. They were not very spiritually inclined it is true, and did not hesitate to play cards on occasion themselves, but they did not think it looked well to have it going on in their house *on Sunday*. They were quite good religionists.

Evadne played with sullen eyes looking off down the beach watching for the wanderers to return. What she would have said, how she would have looked, it is hard to say, could she have seen the four, ensconced in a comfortable group around an old wreck of a dory, Pat with his Bible out, Audrey looking over his shoulder, and Kent and Jane each with a little red book, while Pat unfolded the meaning of the wonderful words.

"Well, I never knew the Bible was a wonder-book like that!" said Audrey as she arose at last and shook off the sand to start for home. It was almost time for the young people's meeting when they reached the house. They rushed in and took a bite from the buffet lunch that was set forth, cold chicken, biscuits and jelly, cake, and little raspberry tarts, fruit and milk and iced tea.

Evadne had counted on the evening and the moonlight to make up for a lost day. She had counted on a chance to lure Kent out onto the beach and feed him a large piece of humble pie. Make him eat it and like it, and apologize!

But lo and behold the whole crowd of them were going to church again! Even the father and mother!

"We don't hear a preacher like that very often," father Havenner said. "Better hear him when we get the chance."

So Evalina and Evadne were left disconsolate. Had it not been that Ballard Bainbridge arrived a few minutes after the departure of the church-goers, Evadne would have been desolate indeed.

Of course Ballard did ask for Audrey first, but he seemed content to substitute Evadne, and they sauntered away together into the moonlight. There were places, it appeared, where they could get plenty to eat and drink, especially drink, even on Sunday.

And so Evalina was left alone, with no apologies whatever.

What she did was to sit on the porch and turn things over in her mind until she came to the conclusion that this cottage by the sea was no longer going to be a pleasant refuge for her, not for the present anyway. The Havenners had let her see by their manner ever since dinner that she had done an unspeakable thing by taking up for Evadne, and she felt that life was not going to be pleasant there the rest of the summer. So, as the dusk drew on and the sea grew silver and beautiful, she withdrew to her room, and proceeded to repack her things. She had decided to leave early in the morning. There was an old aunt who spent her summers in the mountains who might be persuaded to welcome her for a time, now that many of the summer people were leaving, and the bridge players were not so numerous. At any rate she was going. She had outstayed her welcome here. It was better to go before they asked her to. So she folded her things and laid them neatly in suitcases, and was safely and soundly in bed and asleep when the family got home from church and sat in peace on the porch to talk for a little while. But she was not so sound that she did not hear much that was said by the young people. One thing she heard definitely enough, and that was Kent's plan to take Jane in on the first early train that she might be in plenty of time to get to the store. She resolved when she heard that, that she would not to go sleep until Evadne came back, and that she would tell her at once. Perhaps Evadne would go on that same train with them, and spoil their plans. It was terrible for Kent to get so interested in this working girl!

But Evalina was very weary. The excitement of the day, added to her early trip, had utterly worn her out, and she fell asleep and never knew when Evadne came in, never heard her creep into bed, and didn't even waken very early in the morning.

When she did wake up and looked at her clock she saw it was too late. Kent and Jane would be gone. Her plans were all awry.

When the two finally did get up and go downstairs to a very late breakfast, they found themselves the sole inhabitants of the cottage except for the servants. The Havenners had gone up the coast in their car to visit some friends, and all the young people had gone to town! Kent, Molly said, would not return for several days perhaps. Evalina and Evadne were left in state to enjoy themselves.

Evadne had promised already to go sailing with Ballard Bainbridge at eleven o'clock, and as she had no relish for staying at the Havenner cottage, she packed her effects and took them with her, knowing she could get Ballard to drop her at some livelier resort. Not that she was going to abandon her fight for Kent. No indeed! Not for a little working girl, even if she was smart and saucy! But there were other ways of working that Evadne knew and she would go to more promising fields for the present, eventually getting Kent by himself where she knew she could use her keenest charms upon him.

After Evadne was gone Evalina lost no time in taking the next train, and she could almost hear the maids in the kitchen as her taxi drew away from the house exclaiming:

"Well, thank goodness, she's gone! And good riddance to her! May she never come back!"

BACK in the store again selling buttons, Jane felt as if she had been in a glorious dream and was suddenly let down to earth again. She was almost dazed with the shock of it.

There had been no time for her to go to her rooming house. She had called up before Kent left her, to know whether the trunk had arrived yet, but could get no satisfaction from the girl who answered the phone. The girl didn't know, and the landlady had gone out to market. So they had to wait.

"It wouldn't likely have come on Sunday, anyway," said Kent. "Never mind. But you'll call me up just as soon as you hear, won't you?"

Jane promised with a wistful smile. Too well she realized that the little chance of a telephone call would probably be the last she would see of Kent. Pretty soon this business about the Scarlett will would be settled one way or the other, and that would be the end.

All day she worked fiercely to keep the ache of loneliness out of her heart, trying to make herself see how foolish she had been to let herself get interested in

Kent. Of course there was excuse. She was lonely, and had no friends who were congenial. She ought to have been willing to take up with anybody who offered a passing friendliness, like that young Gaylord. But how could she? If what the girls said about him was true it was just what she had surmised. Her feeling about him wasn't merely her prejudice. And she would rather go alone all the days of her life than take trivial favors from a trifler.

Well, she had had one good time anyway, and she must not let this ghastly feeling that it was all over and she was back in loneliness overcome her. It must not. What was her new found faith worth if it could not sustain her even through loneliness? Perhaps she would go and see Miss Leech a little while after hours. But no, she couldn't do that, for the trunk was her first concern. If it didn't come tonight she would have to do something about it. Perhaps she ought to call up Mrs. Forbes again and see if it had started yet.

So the day wore on to its close and Jane went back to her desolate little bare room. But there was no trunk there.

After a poor Monday-dinner she went out to a telephone pay station and called up the railroad express office, but they said they had received no such trunk. Then alarmed she called Mrs. Forbes again, but Mrs. Forbes was sick in bed. A strange voice answered. She couldn't come to the phone. Jane sent a message to her. Had the trunk gone yet? But after a long wait the girl came back and said no, she didn't think it had. She said Mrs. Forbes had fallen downstairs and struck her head, and she wasn't quite "all there." They had asked her about the trunk but she didn't seem to know. Sometimes she said it had gone, and sometimes she said it hadn't, and finally when they pressed her to think hard and tell what had happened, she had roused to say pitifully: "Tell her she'd better come and get it herself. The man won't know which one it is."

It was all very bewildering, and Jane's heart sank. What should she do? She couldn't get away from the store. And Kent would be expecting those papers to come soon. Mr. Sanderson had had his secretary telephone the store just before four o'clock to tell her to bring them up tonight if they arrived after she got back to her boarding place. He would be very much annoyed if they hadn't come yet. Should she telephone Kent? She shrank exceedingly from doing so. Now that she was away the shame of her having appeared at his home in his absence had come over her with renewed power. He must not, *must not* think that she was running after him. At the same time if this matter was really as important to somebody as they seemed to think, had she any right to wait longer?

Of course it might be true that the trunk had started before Mrs. Forbes was hurt, and it might arrive all right tomorrow. But if it did not, and the lawyers questioned her, she would have to tell about her telephone conversation. So, it was better to let Kent know at once.

But what would the Havenners think of her? Oh, she *couldn't!*

So she debated the matter over and over, and finally with fear and trembling called the Havenner cottage. At least if her courage failed her she could say she called up to thank them for the nice time they had given her, although of course she had done that most thoroughly before she left that morning. And suppose Mr. Havenner, or Mrs. Havenner should answer the call. Would she have the nerve to ask for Kent, or should she just leave a message? It would have been so much easier if she could have called him at the office. Then no explanations would have been needed.

Then suddenly Kent's voice answered her:

"Yes?"

"Oh, Kent!" she began. "I thought I ought to let you know—"

"Oh, Jane! I was wondering if you had any news. Has the trunk come yet?"

"No, it hasn't," she answered in a worried tone. "And I was so troubled about it I telephoned again, and I find that Mrs. Forbes fell downstairs and had a concussion of the brain. They don't know whether she had sent the trunk or not, and they can't seem to find out from her. She is still in a state of delirium, or daze. When they asked her about it again she answered that I'd better come and get it myself, that nobody else would know where it was. Now, what do you think I ought to do? I could go, of course, but I might lose my job, and I really can't afford to do that. I thought perhaps you might be able to find out from the express company whether the trunk ever started or not. Could you?"

"Why, of course. I'll phone right away, and I'll call you back. Where are you? At a pay station? Can you stay there half an hour if it takes me that long? All right, I'll call you back. But say, in case you should have to go—yes, I really do think it is important enough to you to risk asking for a day or two off. But—I'll call you back in a few minutes."

Jane sat down, her heart in a tumult, her mind in a turmoil. If she was going to tremble and get all stirred up every time she heard his voice over the telephone it was just too bad. She never supposed she would be like that, and she had got to snap out of it mighty quick. "Oh God my Father, Oh Jesus Christ my Saviour, deliver me from this foolishness, and make me a right-minded person!" she prayed quietly in her heart.

Then she turned her mind to the possibility of that journey. If she had to go, had she money enough? How much would it cost? More than ten dollars? She couldn't afford it of course, but it seemed as if she must anyway. Why, here she was planning to use the little pittance she had put away with a hope toward that lovely winter coat! When would she ever get any more?

Well, she would get the cheapest ticket possible. Maybe she could travel at night and save one day away from the store. She wouldn't need to take a Pullman. She could sleep curled up in a day coach.

Then she thought of her clothes. If she only hadn't bought that sweet little pink dimity and that new nightie she would have had almost enough to cover the ticket! But she was glad she had bought them. Somehow the memory of that blessed time beside the sea, those heavenly talks, those Sunday services, those moonlit walks, had cheered her soul and made her stronger for whatever hard things there were ahead of her now. But what should she wear on the train? This blue linen would be the right thing, but it was mussed now, and perhaps they would expect her to go at once. There would be no chance to get anything new, even if she had the money. And of course the pink dimity wouldn't do. Perhaps she would have to wear the brown dress. It was clean, but she would have to mend the rip in her sleeve that had kept her from wearing it last week. She could wash out a collar and iron it dry. No, it would take less time to press the dress she had on. Well, it wasn't as if she were going to a grand place. These people back at Mrs. Forbes' house would remember her, if they remembered her at all, as merely a girl who helped with the dining room and kitchen work a year ago. If she was clean and neat it wouldn't matter.

So she let her mind settle everything, while her heart waited for marching orders.

Then suddenly into her thoughts shrilled the telephone bell. She went to it at once.

"Jane? You there? No, they haven't sent that trunk yet. They say that they went to the house but the woman who knew about the trunk had met with an accident, and they were told they would have to wait till she was better. No one else could identify the trunk. Now, you poor child! I'm afraid you'll have to go. I've telephoned Mr. Sanderson, and he thinks it's quite important that you have those papers tomorrow. He says to make your claim legal you should have your proof in at once. There are only two more days before the time will be up, and the property can go to other claimants. That would make a great deal of trouble getting it back."

"Well, why not let it go, then?" said Jane wearily. "Why should I bother? It won't be very much anyway, will it?"

"More than you think, little girl. And anyway, it isn't right not to get this thing done as it should be done. There is no point in letting other people get things that were legally left to you."

"But you know I haven't asked permission to leave the store. I might have trouble about that. You know I've just had a vacation."

"Oh, yes. I thought of that, and I took the liberty of telephoning Mr. Windle, and he said that it was quite all right for you to go, and he would personally explain your absence in the morning to the head of your department. I hope you didn't mind my doing that. I thought it might save you a little anxiety, and I know you won't have much time, if you leave tonight as I think you should. Could you leave tonight?"

"Oh, I guess I could," said Jane, half frightened. "But I certainly thank you for asking Mr. Windle. That is wonderful. I did dread asking to be let off."

"Well, that's all right. I'm glad you're not sore at me. Now, I've looked up your train and it leaves the main station just five blocks from where you live, at eleven-forty-five. Can you be ready by that time? That's good. Well, then, meet me down at the front door of your rooming house. I have to go back to town on an errand and I'll be glad to put you on your train. Now, take it easy and I'll see you at eleven-fifteen at your own door. It's lucky you phoned just when you did or I might have been gone. Good-bye. I have to run for my train."

She hung up the receiver and caught her breath in amazement. What a wonderful man he was! How he had taken her little affairs and put them through in the face of all odds! Ought she to let him do this? But how could she help it? He had taken it all right out of her hands as if it was his right.

Well, perhaps as her lawyer it was, who knew? She hadn't of course chosen him for her lawyer, but so all the more she must do as he said. But why was all this so important? Was it really true that she would get some money? Was this property they talked about that somebody wanted to buy, worth enough to pay her railroad fare to get the trunk? Well, perhaps she was just silly and ignorant, but why was it so vital that these people be kept from getting something they wanted? She had no faith whatever that there would be much. But of course, if there was a hundred dollars or more, it would be wonderfully nice to have it.

So she hurried to her rooming house, thrilling as she

entered to think that Kent would be there pretty soon waiting for her.

She went up to her room and got together a respectable costume for her journey. And then money occurred to her again. Would she have enough for that ticket? She counted it out. How lucky she had not yet put it in the bank. She couldn't have cashed a check tonight! There would have been nobody who knew her well enough to do that. She took out the little cotton bag she had made to pin her valuables into her dress, and counted out the cash. Two ten dollar bills, two fives and three ones! She handled it wistfully. It had made her feel so safe and happy to have all that to fall back upon if she should be sick. And now this would likely take every cent and she would have to begin to save all over again. That would be the end of the lovely green coat with the dear brown fur. Well, never mind. What was it Mrs. Brooke had said? "Nothing can come to you, that is not permitted by your Father." Therefore this must be all for the best, somehow.

Well, it was good to have something like that to trust in when you couldn't understand.

So Jane hunted through her small store of garments till she found those she needed, rejoicing that there was a clean collar after all that she had forgotten. And at last she was ready as she could be. Then she turned and knelt down by her hard little bed and asked God to go with her, and guide her, and help her to find her trunk, and get safely back again. And then while she still knelt it came to her, what if something had happened to that trunk? What if it was lost or stolen or strayed? Nobody would steal it intentionally of course for there wasn't anything in it that would be valuable to anyone but herself. Oh, if those false heirs knew about it, and knew what was in it, they might have connived to get hold of it and destroy her evidence. But they didn't. At least she didn't see how they possibly could. But she added to her prayer: "Dear Father, please take care of that trunk. I wouldn't like to lose mother's pictures and things! It's all I have left of home!"

Then she rose and glanced at her cheap little watch. In ten minutes she would go downstairs and Kent would be there, and she would enter upon a new experience in her life. It had been a long long time since she had taken a journey on a train. And oh, if she didn't have money enough what should she do? Would she have to be subjected to the humiliation of having to borrow from Kent?

She lay down for five minutes and closed her eyes, trying to quiet her excited nerves.

And then at last it was time to go downstairs. At least, it was almost time, and she would rather be early than late.

But when she reached the lower floor there was Kent sitting on the hard little bench that served for visitors, smiling and watching her with relief in his eyes.

"You're all ready?" he asked. "I'm glad. I came over a little early, thinking there might be something I could do for you."

"Oh, thank you. You're so kind!" she faltered. "I think there's nothing left to be done but to get my ticket. Do you have any idea how much that would be likely to be? I wonder if I have enough."

He smiled and held out an envelope.

"Here are your tickets, lady. All paid for. The firm looks out for this. It's part of the expense of probating the will. Keep your money for a better purpose. Now, shall we go? I think there might be more restful places for you to pass these few minutes than sitting on this hard bench, though I suppose we should be thankful for even this."

He grinned and picked up the brief case he had with him, and then possessed himself of the package from Jane's hand.

"Come, let's go! Do you have to tell your landlady you are leaving for a few hours, or not?"

"No," said Jane, "I told her I was spending the night away, but if the trunk should arrive during my absence would she please look out for it. She doesn't care whether I go or stay. It's odd to feel that no one cares. You know I think that must be pretty bad for some young girls that haven't had any bringing up."

"I should say!" said Kent. "But you're not that. Plenty of people care for you!"

"For me?" said Jane with unbelieving eyes lifted, "I'm afraid you're mistaken."

"No, I'm not," said Kent assuredly. "Mr. Windle told me not two hours ago that he valued you very highly, and he was glad to give you as many days as you needed. That he felt you were a very lovely girl."

"Oh," laughed Jane, "Mr. Windle wouldn't know me from a fly on the wall if he should meet me in the store. But just the same I value his appreciation."

"And my mother thinks you are a wonderful little girl!" went on Kent. "She thinks you are charming, and very pretty, and smart as a whip. She especially appreciated some of the bright things you said, and the way you met trying situations."

"Oh, I really do love to know that," said Jane. "She is dear! I fell in love with her the first minute I saw her."

"That's nice," said Kent with satisfaction. "And my sister thinks you are the nicest girl she ever knew, and a lot more expletives I haven't time to repeat. Here's our taxi."

"Oh, but we could walk," said Jane. "You are being much too nice to me. You will spoil me, you know, and then all these nice things won't be true."

"Oh, but that's not all of them," he said as he got in beside her and closed the door. "Molly and the cook think you're the grandest thing that ever walked the earth, and dad said he was glad to see I'd been able to look at the right kind of girl at last! And that's not all either. Pat thinks you're a marvelous singer, and a real Christian, and he's so glad we're both going to be in his class this winter. There! If that isn't enough I could tell you what *I* think, but I'm afraid that might take too long, and we don't want to miss your train."

He helped her out and they walked through the big bright station.

"How about a spot of ice cream?" he said as they came to the station restaurant. "I think we've plenty of time, and I'm hungry, aren't you? I didn't half eat my supper tonight I was in such a hurry."

"That would be lovely," said Jane, "but I'm afraid it was my fault you didn't have time for your supper."

"No, it wasn't. That was before I had heard from you. I missed my usual train out and took a bite in town before the next train left."

Such a pleasant little time they had together, talking of the sea and the moonlight, and what a wonderful preacher Pat was.

"Audrey thinks he's swell," mused Kent, "and I'm glad she does. I can't abide that egg of a Bainbridge she's been affecting. I was afraid she would lose all ability to judge character if she kept on companioning with him. I certainly was pleased she liked Pat, and so was dad. You know, that's another thing we have to thank you for! If you hadn't gone to Mrs. Brooke's class I never would have heard Pat, and known him in Boston, and brought him home with me. Oh, all things are working together for us with a vengeance these last few days. I'm going to have all kinds of a good time with Pat. He was just what I needed."

Soon they went down the long steps to the train, and Kent led her to her car and introduced her to her seat.

"I got you a whole section," he said. "Then you don't have to worry about anybody getting up above you. I'll tell the porter not to make up the upper berth, so that you can have all the air there is."

"Oh," said Jane, "you shouldn't have got me a berth at all. I could just as well have sat up. I can sleep anywhere."

"Oh, yes?" he said grinning. "And look like a little washed-out lamb in the morning, too, I'll bet. Well, you've got a berth. And now, I guess I'd better be going. Good night, and I wish you success. I'll be praying!" That last was in a soft voice just for her ear. Then he gave her hand a quick warm clasp and was gone, down a little narrow alley at the end of the car. Jane felt suddenly all alone and very small and inefficient. What a difference it made to have someone look after you!

Well, there she was again, harping on Kent Havenner. After all it was God, not Kent Havenner. If Kent had been just a nice pleasant man, without some consciousness of God, he probably wouldn't have looked at her, even for the sake of his business. He probably would have been going after girls like Evadne Laverock.

But Jane had little time for meditation. The porter asked her if she would like her berth made up at once, and told her she could sit on the other side of the aisle while he did it. So it was not long before she was getting ready for her night's rest behind heavy green curtains.

But it wasn't hot there. There seemed to be clean breezes in every corner. Probably it was all air-conditioned. Well, she would be thankful for every bit of rest and comfort that came her way. The memory of it would help her sometimes when the days were hot and unbearable in the store, or when she lay on her hard little bed in that hall bedroom and wished for morning because she could not bear the heat of her room.

So she folded her cotton kimono about her and snapping off her light lay down on the incredibly soft bed, resting her head on pillows such as she had never owned.

She fully intended to stay awake awhile and enjoy this luxury, not waste her time in sleep, but before she knew it she had drifted away into unconsciousness, her last thought the words of Kent as he said: "I might tell you what I think of you myself, but it would take too long—" She wished she might have heard what he thought. But no, that remark was probably just a polite nothing. He knew so well how to say such things gracefully. It was an art to say pleasant things as if you really meant them. Perhaps he did mean them in a way, only she must be very, very careful never to think of them as if they were anything special for herself. He would have said the same to anybody.

And then oblivion came down with a vision of Kent's kindly smile lighting her path through the unknown way of tomorrow.

21

MEANTIME Audrey was having troubles of her own. Ballard Bainbridge was on the warpath.

Audrey had just settled herself with a new Bible she had gone in town that day especially to buy, and with a list of notes Pat had given her propped up on the table beside her, and a brand new pencil with a lovely green handle, she was about to begin a new and fascinating bit of education which she had come to feel in the last twenty-four hours that she sadly needed. Then Molly came up to her room to say that there was a caller downstairs.

Audrey arose with a sigh when she heard the name Bainbridge. Now it had come, what she dreaded. She would hear plenty of comment upon the new people, she would be lectured severely for her behavior Saturday and Sunday, and urged to amend her ways. She would hear that detestable Evadne held up as a model. Audrey could see in her suitor's eye Saturday night the retribution that would be coming to her.

Almost she was tempted to send down word she had retired and couldn't see him tonight, and then it occurred to her that that would only be putting off the evil day. She would have this to meet eventually, why not get it over with once and for all and be done with him? She needed no further time to think. She knew now she would never marry him, nor even care to hold him for a playtime friend.

So she slipped on a plain little dress and went downstairs as quickly as she could, anxious to get it over with and get back to her study. There were certain verses she had promised Pat she would look up and memorize before the class Thursday night. She had no more time to waste.

She appeared suddenly before the prancing impatient young man, and his expression grew blank as he looked at her.

"Oh," he said, "I hoped you'd be dressed. There isn't overmuch time. I'm taking you across the point to the hotel where Vad and I found a marvelous dance floor Saturday night. Champ is taking us in his car and he'll be here inside of ten minutes. Hustle up and change as quick as you can. Put on the gaudiest thing you have. They certainly are swell dressers over there."

Audrey held her head high. It happened that she had heard from her mother the condition of Evadne when she came back Saturday night.

"Thank you, Ballard," she said firmly, "I can't go anywhere tonight, and I certainly wouldn't care to go over there, of all places."

He frowned.

"Don't waste time!" he said. "Go and get ready and talk on the way!"

But Audrey did not stir.

"I'm not going out tonight, Ballard. That's final. I am exceedingly busy. And I'm saying again, I do not wish to go over to that hotel. Its reputation is anything but savory. And I wouldn't care to have anyone know I went there. I *wouldn't* go. I guess perhaps you don't know in what condition you brought home Miss Laverock Saturday night."

"Oh, what utter nonsense!" raved the young autocrat. "It's time you got over such archaic notions. Certainly I know. Vad wouldn't have got into that condition if she hadn't wanted to, would she? She had a reason all righty."

"Yes?" said Audrey. "Well, I have a reason for not wishing to go out with you tonight, or any other night. I am done! Please consider that final!"

"Aw now, Audrey, I didn't think you'd be jealous! You've always seemed bigger than that. Just because I went out a night or two with Vad, do you have to act like a child? In fact it was you started the whole thing if you'll remember. I called for you to take you out for a plane ride, and you refused to come to the door to speak to me. In fact you simply ran off with another man and left me. Could I be blamed for taking the lady you handed over to me?"

"I'm not blaming you, Ballard. I simply say I do not wish to go anywhere with you tonight, and especially not to the place you have selected. In fact I may as well tell you that I have been discovering lately that you and I haven't even two ideas in common. I know you expected to change me, to mold me to suit your own ideas, but I have just come to realize that I don't wish to be molded. Not by you anyway. I don't agree with your ideas about modern life and the new order of things that you are always talking about. And I don't wish to discuss them any more. I'm done! I'm sorry if I seem to be unpleasant, but I felt it was best to be frank."

"Now, Audrey, don't be a simp! Go and get your best togs on and we'll talk on the way."

"No," said Audrey. "Positively *no!* You'll have to excuse me from now on. I'm really sorry that I've let you waste so much of your valuable time on me. But you see I never quite understood until a few days ago just how I felt about the matter. I kept putting off thinking about it, hoping, perhaps, that you might change. I don't know just what it was I thought. I guess I was too lazy to think. But now I know what I think, and I'm telling you."

"But Audrey, I'm really very fond of you."

"Is that so?" said Audrey wearily. "That's a nice way to part, I'm sure. But I guess it was because I found out that I wasn't really very fond of you, that made me come to this decision. You know two people who are not of one mind about things in general couldn't possibly go on together very long without a clash, and I had reached a clash, Ballard. I really had. I couldn't go on and hear you denounce the things my father and mother count precious, even if I didn't always myself. I couldn't go on and hear you talk about morals and laws being all nonsense, and the Bible untrue, and God a fake. It was getting on my nerves. So, Ballard, go and find Evadne Laverock and take her with you to the places you both like. Or find somebody else like-minded—"

"But see here, Audrey, that's it. I told Vad I was coming to get you to go with us, and she's got a man for you she's sure you will enjoy. He's a man who has never gone in for sophistication before, and he wants to step out. We thought you would be just the one to induct him into a delightful evening. Now, Audrey, be a good pal and help us out. I can't go back to Vad and tell her I failed. I never fail, you know."

"Don't you?" smiled Audrey. "Well, this time you

have! But I suspect you needed that to teach you that you aren't as wise as you think you are."

"What do you mean by that?"

"I mean that I've found something vaster and more exciting than all your theories and all the books you loaned me. I've found the Book of books and it's fascinating. I wouldn't give it up for all the pleasures of the world. I've found a friend and a Saviour, and I'm happier than I ever was in my life before."

"You talk like a fanatic! Don't tell me you've got religion, Audrey, after all the trouble I've spent upon you!"

"Well, I don't know whether I've got religion or not yet, but if I haven't I soon will have, for I'm going after it with all my heart. Only I don't call it religion, I call it Christianity. I understand there are a great many fallacies masquerading under the name of religion, and I want something real. If you'll excuse me now I'm going back to what I was doing. I really haven't any more time to waste in talking about nothings. I'm only sorry I ever wasted any that way. And now I bid you good night!" And Audrey swept up the stairs and left her erstwhile lover alone, staring after her. Did she really have that much spirit? What a pity it wasn't active in something worth while instead of chasing after out-worn dogmas! Well, let her go awhile! Doubtless she would tire of religion and return to her natural world. Young people didn't live like ascetics the way they used to do in bygone ages!

But what was he going to do now? This was going to be awkward. He had wagered a goodly sum on the expectation of bringing Audrey to prove his power over her. And incidentally to get rid of the young man whom Evadne had attached for the evening.

Slowly he walked out of the house and down the

steps, greatly to Audrey's relief as she listened. She even hurried downstairs to lock the doors so that he could not return and call her back to conflict. She was most eager this time to dip into her new Bible. Would she really be able to find all those wonderful things that Pat had showed her yesterday? Or were they all in his own fertile brain?

So Audrey settled down again to her study, and her mother coming anxiously in an hour later found her hard at work.

"Oh, I'm so glad you're here, and alone!" she said with a relieved sigh. "I thought I heard Ballard Bainbridge come in, and yet it was so still here I couldn't think what had happened."

"He did come in, mother. He wanted me to go to a dance over at that awful Red Lion Hotel with Evadne and some strange man who needed lessons in sophistication. Imagine it! I think I told him pretty clearly where to get off, and I hope you won't be troubled with him around here any more. I'm about fed up on him."

"Oh, my dear!" said her mother, dropping down in a chair and bowing her head in her hands, the tears running down freely. "I'm so relieved! I was so afraid you were getting fond of him, and I didn't know what to do, with both of my dear children running right into danger that way. Oh, I'm so glad you're done with Ballard."

"So am I!" said Audrey impetuously. "I was getting more and more involved and didn't know how to get out. It took a fool girl like Evadne, and a little button salesgirl, and a real man who teaches the Bible to show me the false from the true, but now I guess I'm wise to my follies. Mums, why didn't you ever make us learn the Bible and know what it means when we were kids? It's simply great! It would have done more to keep us straight than anything else you could have done. Why didn't you?"

"Oh, my dear, I don't know," wailed her mother. "I guess I never knew much about it myself, but I've always respected it. My own father used to read it for hours, and seemed to love it. Is that a Bible you have?"

"Yes, I bought it in town today, and I'm going to study it regularly. Pat Whitney is helping me. I'm going to his class Thursday evenings. I think it's great. Why don't you and dad take it up? I believe you'd like it better than bridge. I really do. Neither of you ever cared much for cards. And this would be something unique. Not just like what everybody else is doing."

"Why, I wonder if your father would like it. I'll talk to him about it. I always thought it was hard to understand, and maybe it was better to let ministers interpret it for us."

"Oh, but it's not hard the way Pat teaches it!" exclaimed Audrey. "If I'd known it was like that I'd have studied it long ago. He makes it very interesting."

Her mother sat watching her wistfully.

"You like Mr. Whitney pretty well, don't you?"

"I think he's simply swell, mother. Only I feel so awfully ignorant when I'm with him, more ignorant than I did even with Ballard. You know he always took it for granted you were ignorant anyway, even when you knew a thing pretty well. But Pat is so humble he never assumes that he is dead right. He just tells what the Bible says and I think he must know it all by heart. Whereas Ballard didn't believe the Bible was anything but a bunch of lies. Now go to bed, mother. You're all shivery and shaky and you need a good night's sleep. You don't need to worry any more about me. I'm cured. No more Bainbridge for me. And as for Kent, I shouldn't wonder if he had had almost enough of

Evadne too. He seems to like Jane a lot, doesn't he? You liked Jane too, didn't you? I thought you would. I think she's sweet. So lay down your burdens and get a good night's rest, and let's do something nice, make plans and things in the morning."

Mrs. Havenner kissed her daughter and went away with a smile on her face, and Audrey plunged into her study again. She didn't want to stop until she had looked up all the references that Pat had given her, and proved that everything he had told her was true.

22

WHEN Jane awoke the next morning she did not know where she was for a moment, and then the motion of the train and the softness of the bed on which she lay recalled her to the present, and she realized that she was on her way to get her trunk. What a lot of changes had come into her life lately! A vacation and a week-end at the shore, and now this wonderful trip in a Pullman train!

Then she realized that it must be near morning and she pulled up her shade and looked at her watch. Yes, it was late. The train would be at her destination in half an hour! She must get dressed at once!

She hadn't really undressed fully, so it did not take her long to be in neat array and ready to get out. Then she went to the washroom and washed and made her hair tidy. Everything she had to do, even the washing of her face, seemed a part of a play in this complete little dressing room, and she longed to linger and enjoy it. But she knew she must have her hat on and everything ready to get out at once when the train reached her station. It did not stop long at small stations. She mustn't run the risk of being carried on to Boston!

So in a very short time she was ready, hat on, little box packed and watching each station. As she drew nearer to the well-remembered locality, things began to seem familiar to her. She watched the farms she knew slip by. The Gilmans had painted their house by the lake. The Fosters had built a garage. How interesting it was to see changes in the places she knew so well.

And then they reached her stopping place and she got out and walked slowly down the long platform to the station, noticing the line of new busses that were drawn up on the side next the street. The whole place looked pleasant to her just because it was familiar.

"Good morning! Did you have a comfortable sleep?" said Kent suddenly, getting up from behind a pile of baggage and coming forward to greet her.

"Oh!" she said blinking at him, half frightened lest she was losing her mind. How could he be here?

"You didn't expect to see me here, did you? I'm real, indeed I am. I traveled on the second car ahead of yours and that's how I happened to be out ahead of you. You see, I wanted to surprise you. I thought it would be fun to greet you and see how surprised you would be." He ended with one of his pleasant grins.

"But how, why—?" she began, and looked almost as if she were going to cry. "Did you have to travel all this way and lose all this time from your work? Couldn't you trust me to come back?"

"Oh, Jane! Of course! Yes! But you see I had some business up the road a little farther which I can transact while you are repacking your trunk and saying hello to your friends. I thought it would be nice for me to be here and make arrangements for that trunk to be sent. Mr. Sanderson thought so too. He said there was no telling what contingencies might arise about that trunk, and I ought to be here to help you out with it. You see it is quite important that we get those proofs on file. There is only one day left now, and we don't want to run any risks. Incidentally, too, I'm to wipe out another errand that has been troubling the office for a week. It's only thirty miles above here, and ought not to take long, a mere formality, but had to be attended to by one of the firm, so they wished it on me, besides the job of personally conducting you on this treasure hunt. Now, young lady, the next act is to get some breakfast. Do you suppose this restaurant is any good, or should we go to a hotel?"

"I'm afraid this is rather expensive," said Jane shyly. "It used to have that name."

"Then let's go in. It ought to be good. I'm hungry as a bear, aren't you?"

"Why, I wasn't going to bother to get any breakfast," Jane grinned back. "I was too excited about being off traveling alone."

"But you aren't off traveling alone any more, lady, so what? Do I get any breakfast or not?"

He seated her at the table and started in with orange juice, oatmeal and cream, beefsteak and flannel cakes and coffee.

"Don't forget the maple syrup," he said as he handed the order to the waiter.

"Now, Jane, what is the order of the day?" he said, leaning back and looking at her with satisfaction. "Do we take a taxi to the residence of Mrs. Forbes at once, or are there preliminaries?"

"Why, I was going to walk," said Jane thoughtfully. "I don't know that they would know me if I came in a taxi."

"It could be done I suppose, if time is not too much of a factor. How far is it?"

"About two miles."

"Oh! In that case I think we'd better take the taxi. It seems a good thing that I came after all in spite of the rather cool welcome you gave me, if you were going to economize at that rate. We've got to get back to the city tonight, lady, if possible!"

"Oh! Of course! I didn't realize!" said Jane. "But listen. I didn't give you a cool welcome. I was just surprised. I just didn't understand it."

"You weren't very glad to see me, were you? Honest?"

Jane's cheeks suddenly got very red.

"Yes, I was," she owned, with her eyes down half shamedly. "I was a great deal gladder than I wanted you to see!"

"But why?"

"Well, I thought this was a matter of business, and I had no right to just friendly gladness. Besides I was a little scared."

She lifted her eyes with a swift glance and downed them again, quickly.

"Why you everlasting little fraud, you!" laughed Kent. "You weren't willing I should get any satisfaction out of coming. I see. Well, I'll take pains to rub that in on you some day and make you bitterly repent. Now, tell me the rest of your plan. Should we arrange with a truck to follow us at a reasonable distance to get the trunk, or arrange with him to come at telephone call?"

"Maybe that," said Jane. "I was beginning to be afraid there might be something queer about their not being able to find that trunk. It might take time to find it, you know. Oh, I'm so glad you came along!"

"Thanks! So am I. Now, shall we go, or will you have another batch of griddle cakes?"

"Oh no, thank you. Let's go!"

So they went.

While Jane went up to see Mrs. Forbes, Kent sat on the porch of the Forbes residence and visioned Jane going about there as a little serving maid, a little lonely girl with only an old Scotch woman for a friend, and a lot of hard work to do.

The old Scotch woman lifted a frail hand in greeting, and smiled a faint smile.

"I'm sorry—" she faltered, "couldn't get it—off."

The sullen maid who had let her in explained to Jane that Mrs. Forbes' accident had happened the same evening she had telephoned for the trunk. She had been coming downstairs with some blankets that she had brought from a room she had been cleaning for a new boarder. The blankets needed mending and she was going to do it that evening. She caught her foot in a torn blanket, and fell the full flight, rolling down to the foot and striking her head on the railing several times.

"No ma'am. She hadn't been up to the attic yet to look for the trunk. She was awful busy and she thought it would be time enough to do that when the man came for it in the morning. But when he came she didn't know nothing at all, and couldn't answer a question, so we couldn't give him no trunk, and she didn't never get so she could show us, so the man stopped comin'. Yes ma'am, you could go up an' find it if you know where you left it."

Jane was greatly relieved that Mrs. Forbes had not fallen going after her trunk, and she tried to talk cheerily to the sick woman.

"Never mind, Mrs. Forbes," she said gently, "I'll find

the trunk, I'm sure. Is it just where I put it before I went away?"

The sick woman looked dazed.

"I think it is. Though mebbe my husband—he mighta moved things around—a bit—afore we went south."

She closed her eyes as if it had been an effort to say so much, and Jane arose.

"Don't you worry," she said, "I'll go up. I'm sure I can find it. I have a friend downstairs who will help me. He's strong and can help me bring it down."

"All right! You go find it!" said Mrs. Forbes, and shut her eyes again.

Jane called Kent and together they went upstairs to the attic.

At first, when they got up to the attic, Jane's heart sank as she looked toward the corner where she knew she had left her trunk, for there wasn't any trunk there. Only a pile of old broken chairs and an old-fashioned bedstead and bureau. The whole arrangement of the attic seemed to be changed, and it was crowded full of things, furniture piled up to the ceiling. Cards tacked on the backs of several boxes with a name and address showed that the Forbeses must have allowed somebody to store all their furniture there.

In despair Jane walked around, poking into corners. Kent followed her, suddenly realizing that this expedition might not turn out to be as successful as he had hoped after all.

"If it wasn't so dark here!" said Jane desperately. "I'll run down and see if I can't borrow a flashlight."

Presently she came back with a candle, and holding it aloft Kent finally discovered several trunks back under the eaves behind a lot more furniture. He flung off his coat and got to work, and presently cleared a path to the trunks.

"There it is!" cried Jane in a relieved tone. "Oh, I'm so glad!"

Kent hauled it out and brushed the dust off his hands.

"I certainly am glad I came along," he remarked, "even if you're not!"

"Oh, but I am!" said Jane. "I never said I wasn't! What would I have done without you?"

"That's the talk. Now, lady, here's a bit of advice. Don't you think it would be wise in you to open this trunk right here and now and make sure that nobody else has done so in the interval and removed any of the contents? We don't want to have to return again tomorrow if we can help it."

"Oh, I never thought of that!" said Jane aghast.

"Have you the key?" asked Kent anxiously.

"Oh, yes." Jane produced it promptly.

There followed another anxious moment while Kent wrestled with the lock, and then the ancient hinges groaned as he flung back to the top.

"Full to the brim!" said Kent as he arose and brushed the dust from his knees. "But are they yours? Make sure of that. Are the special things there that we need?"

He took the candle from Jane and held it high while she knelt before the trunk and laid out pile after pile of folded garments, touching them tenderly because they reminded her of her beloved mother.

"There's mother's wedding dress!" she said softly as she laid out a long white box.

"That's nice!" said Kent in a voice that was soft with sympathy.

"Yes. And here is the Bible!" said Jane, feeling deep into the trunk. "And the photograph album!"

"That's good!" Kent's voice rang with satisfaction.

"And here's the box with the papers, birth and wedding certificates. I don't believe a thing has been touched!" cried Jane in excitement.

"That's grand!" said Kent. "Now, the next thing is to get back home as fast as we can. Had you planned to take this trunk to the office or to your rooming house? Because if you want to take it straight to the rooming house we'd better take out these things that are important and carry them by hand, hadn't we? We could get a box or a suitcase in this town somewhere, I suppose. But why don't you just take the trunk along to the office and unpack it there. You know it might turn out that there was something else in it we needed."

"Oh! Could I? Wouldn't it be dreadfully in the way?"

"No indeed. We have an extra room, and nobody would need to see it. We could pack it right up again after Sanderson has all he needs out of it, and take it in the taxi with us back to your rooming house tonight. Let's see. It is nine-thirty now. If I remember aright there is a return train leaving here about eleven. If we can get that we'd be home around seven. I'll telephone Sanderson and get him to wait. We'll keep track of the trunk and have it right with us. It isn't large and I can have it checked on our train. How's that?"

"Wonderful!" said Jane. "Oh, I'm glad you are here. I wouldn't have known what to do next."

"All right! Let's get to work."

"But you have to do something else for the office," reminded Jane.

"Yes, well, that's secondary. I'll talk to Sanderson first."

"I suppose I could take the trunk to the office myself if you would tell me how to manage, and then you could stay and do your work," suggested Jane dubiously.

"Yes, you could," said Kent, "but I'm not going to let you. You see there are so many things that men can do in the way of dealing with railroad men and taxi drivers that women wouldn't be able to work, at least not quiet inexperienced girls like yourself, and I'm not taking any chances."

Jane's heart sang a little song of joy, though she tried to still it, making out to herself that she was only frightened lest she would somehow bungle this and disappoint the office. But the song sang steadily on, and its reflection shone in the look on Jane's face.

Kent put the things back in the trunk and locked it. Then he turned around to Jane.

"Now, you are a little glad I came along, for some other reason than just to help you do this work, aren't you? I see it in your face. I hear it in your voice. And how about letting me kiss you? Just once, anyway. You know I love, Jane. And this looks to me like the quietest place we'll have for several hours for me to show you how I love you. May I?"

Jane's face flamed a joyous rosy tint. She looked up and her eyes were alight with beauty.

"Oh!" she said. "Oh!"

But she did not draw away. She did not say no.

And then he folded her in his arms and laid his lips tenderly on hers, holding her close for a long moment.

"But—I'm only—a poor—working—girl!" gasped Jane with glory in her face. "And you are—"

"Go on," he said, looking adoringly down at her and holding her closer, "what am I? I've been wanting to know what you thought I was and I couldn't find out."

"You are—" Jane started again shyly, "a gentleman!"

"Oh, is that all?" said Kent looking disappointed.

"Well, that is—a great deal," went on Jane, "but—

beside that—you are—" She paused and looked up into his eyes adoringly, "you are *dear!*" she added softly.

Then he grasped her closer and laid his face down to hers.

"You are *precious!*" he breathed. "You are the dearest thing that ever came into my life!"

A little after, when she could get her breath to speak again she said:

"And yet, I am a working girl and you are a gentleman! Why, I worked in the kitchen in this very house. I used sometimes to scrub this attic floor when we were housecleaning."

"Yes," said Kent, smiling down into her face just below his own, "that is the reason why I wanted to kiss you here, right here where you did humble work. It is beautiful to me. It reminds me of the lowly way your Lord and mine came to earth for us. It helped to make you what you are, a fine, strong, all-around womanly girl. Not a little fool like most of the girls I know. I've tried to think I loved some of them and I couldn't. Beloved, I love you!"

And then he kissed her again.

Suddenly he drew back.

"But I haven't time now to tell you all the reasons why I love you. We've got to get to work and catch that train. Do you suppose they will let us telephone here? I'll get an expressman right away. If you've anything more to say to your old lady, go say it and we'll get off as soon as our truck goes. I'll phone Sanderson from the station."

It was astonishing how quickly things got moving, once they were downstairs. The expressman arrived hot haste. Jane said good-bye to Mrs. Forbes and left a crisp five dollar bill in her hand in sympathy for her in her illness, received a shower of blessings from the poor paralyzed tongue, and they were away to the station.

Kent talked with his chief, agreed to telephone to the nearby town instead of going there, and was able to arrange the business satisfactorily.

Then suddenly the train came, and Kent saw the trunk on to the baggage car, came back and got Jane just in time to swing on to the Pullman with her, and they were embarked on a blissful journey, which seemed all too short to them both when it was over.

Later that evening they arrived at the office with the trunk on the taxi with them, and a porter whom Sanderson had bribed to stay late helped Kent take the trunk in.

It was almost like a sacred rite as the two men stood by watching the girl unpack her treasures. Sanderson found a mist in his eyes more than once, as one and another trifle full of memories was brought to light. For Jane had forgotten their presence, at least the presence of Sanderson, and was talking now and then to herself, evidently recalling dearest memories.

"And there is my first little dress, and my baby bonnet!" she would say, almost in a whisper. "And mother's wedding gown!"

She lifted the cover of the box for a brief second and disclosed a satin dress of other days, its modest train and high puffed sleeves carefully folded back with tissue paper, its wreath of orange blossoms lying on the top. And where the satin had slipped back a little, soft folds of malines, the wedding veil, were disclosed, bordered with a dainty edge of real lace.

Sanderson stood with his hands clasped behind him, and blinked away the tears, thinking of another bride who had been his, and of the dreary years that had come between that vision and now, ever since another scene with a casket had taken her away from him forever.

At last he received the big Bible and handled it almost as if it had been a sacred vessel of some sort. And when Jane brought forth the pictures and the important papers they all sat down at a long polished table and laid them forth. Sanderson was very much impressed. The pictures brought out a good many facts.

There was Harold Scarlett when he was only a baby, and Harold Scarlett when he was a boy in school, and again when he was in college, and then as best man at his brother's wedding. The wedding picture, too, was a proof in itself. For there stood Jane's sweet mother in her bridal array, looking almost like Jane today, and there was Harold Scarlett standing in the group, smiling a gay irresponsible smile at the world.

There were later pictures. A couple he had sent from Europe, one taken at Monte Carlo, another at some famous resort in the south of France. And then a few clippings and a newspaper picture carefully pasted in and labeled by the hand of Jane's mother. It was all most convincing. And then there was a photograph of the old Scarlett home.

Jane looked at it lovingly.

"I was there once," she said ruminatively.

"Why!" said Sanderson looking at it sharply, and then turning to Kent Havenner he said in an undertone, "Identical! That settles it!"

But Jane was too busy with the dear old pictures and did not notice.

"Well, now, young lady, I'll see that your claim goes through quickly," Sanderson said in a kindly tone. "You can leave these things here with me for a few days, and when all is settled up I'll return them to you. No, I don't need the wedding dress. But yes, the marriage certificate, and the other papers. Now, Kent, help Miss Scarlett pack up, and you can take the trunk with you. I've all that we shall need. You've done good work and done it expeditiously. Good night! I'll let you know, Miss Scarlett, as soon as all is completed."

So Jane packed her trunk again and Kent took her home.

"I'm not going to let you stay long in this dump!" said Kent as they neared the rooming house.

"Oh, it's all right," laughed Jane. "I've so much other joy I'm sure I shan't mind any more."

"Darling!" he murmured and held her hand close. And then the taxi stopped and he had his hands full getting someone to take that trunk up to Jane's room.

"Remember, it won't be for long," he murmured in her ear as he said a staid good night.

23

IT was the very next afternoon that Evadne put herself in her grandest battle array and started out to get her revenge. She began by trying to call up Kent for she had intended to ring him in on it too, but Kent was not in his office. He was out on business for the afternoon they said. That was the same answer they had given her for the last two days, and she felt there was intention in it, which made her all the more wrathful.

She arrived at the button counter while Jane was waiting on two very nice ladies who were buying buttons and clasps for their fall outfits, and she stormed up to the counter and interrupted.

"I want to speak to you, Miss Scarlett!" she demanded.

Jane glanced up at the sound of the voice and gave her a startled glance.

"Just a moment," she answered.

Evadne waited impatiently for as much as a full minute, then she repeated her request.

"I'm busy just now," Jane said quietly.

"Well, that doesn't make any difference," said

Evadne, raising her voice still higher, "I'm not going to wait on you all day. I've important things to do. I've something to say to you that won't wait, and if you can't stop what you're doing and listen to me, I'll say it now where everybody can hear. I've just come to tell you you can lay off my fiancé, that's all. He belongs to me, and you've no right to try to take him over."

The button customers looked at her curiously, and gave a startled glance at Jane whose cheeks were rosy red, but whose demeanor was still quiet and controlled. Save for the color in her cheeks she paid no heed whatever to the tirade that was going on, but other people were giving plenty of attention and Evadne had known they would.

"Some people might not pay any attention to such actions on the part of a mere working girl, but I don't feel that way. Such carryings on as there were last Saturday night and Sunday are not to be endured. I intend to see that there isn't any more of it. I just thought it was fair to warn you that if you have anything whatever to do with him any more, I shall go the limit in having you punished. You're a menace to the public and it is a benevolence to others to put you where you can't do any more of it. A life sentence wouldn't be too long for such as you!"

By this time Mr. Clark had heard the loud voice from afar and had arrived on the scene. Ladies were rushing from this aisle and that to peer above one another's heads and see what was happening now. Evadne was looking straight at Jane, for all the other salesgirls at that counter had hastily gone as far away as the limits of the counter would allow. Everybody else, too, was looking straight at Jane, whose face was calm and restrained, but turning very white now. Mr. Clark's eyes upon her, his lifted eyebrows almost demanded some explanation from Jane.

But Jane only finished writing her slip for the buttons she had sold to the two ladies who had charged their purchases and gone. Then she looked up straight at Evadne.

"I don't understand you," she said coldly.

"Oh, yes, you do!" taunted the angry girl, well knowing that she had the upper hand. "You understand me well enough. You know who it was you went walking off up the beach with Saturday night, and took to church all day Sunday. You knew perfectly well he was my fiancé and you just exulted in taking him away from me and making me a laughing stock. And I'll have my revenge, I swear I will!"

Suddenly Mr. Clark stepped up to Evadne.

"Excuse me, madam," he said, "but wouldn't it be better to wait until closing time and talk quietly with this girl, if you have to talk? You'll be making *yourself* a laughing stock, doing it so publicly. And we really can't allow this to go on in the store, you know."

"Very well, then, make this girl answer me. I told her I wished to speak with her privately and she was insolent. She said she was busy."

"That was her privilege of course when she was working."

"Oh, indeed! Well, if you are going to be insolent too I shall have to demand to see the owners of this store. For I intend to have an answer from this girl before I leave."

"Have you anything to say, Miss Scarlett?" asked Mr. Clark, with an almost pleading expression in his eyes.

Jane swept him a grateful glance.

"Yes," said Jane, still quietly, and not looking in the least frightened. "I would just like to say this. If the gentleman to whom you refer as your fiancé is really so, surely you could trust a man such as he is! If you know him as well as you seem to think you do, you would know that he would never do anything unbecoming to the man who was your fiancé. That's all, Mr. Clark. Would you like me to go off the floor?"

"No, Miss Scarlett, stay where you are and go on with your work. Madam, I shall be glad to take you up to Mr. Windle if he is not too busy at present to see customers of the house."

Mr. Clark led the angry Evadne away, into another aisle, and the customers closed in around the button counter, stretching their necks to see who this girl was, but Jane had disappeared into the tiny wrapping cubby-hole behind Hilda, with her hands on her hot cheeks, taking deep breaths and praying in her heart for help.

She got it too, and presently came out calmly and went to work again.

"My, but you were swell!" whispered Louise, fluttering up to her between sales. "I wish I could be cool like that and carry off a situation. I would have gone all to pieces and got furious. I would have slapped her old painted face for her. That's what she oughtta have got. Say, did you really snitch her man from her?"

Jane laughed.

"Of course not," she said. "What an idea! Forget it, Louise. I'm sorry I had to be the cause of a disturbance in the store, that's all. Say, are there any more of those blue enamel buttons with the rhinestones in them?" and Louise was turned aside and went hunting blue enamel buttons. But Jane had come to the place where she had begun to tremble and wanted to sit down and cry. However, she remembered that she had a stronghold that would not fail her and went on to the end of the day.

That night when Jane came out of the store she found Kent waiting for her, and her heart forgot its worries and joy flooded her face.

But a few minutes later he looked at her keenly.

"What has happened today?" he asked. "You look pale. Are you not feeling well?"

"Oh, I'm perfectly all right," smiled Jane.

"No, something is the matter! Now tell me everything. Anything disagreeable happen in the store?"

She looked at him startled and then grinned.

"Yes," she said, "I've been accused of carrying off a girl's sweetheart! What do you think of that? Perhaps you won't want to have anything to do with me any more."

"Darling!" he murmured in a low tone. "Tell me. What was it?"

"I've told you. Just that. A girl came into the store and openly accused me before everybody of stealing her fiancé."

"Who was it?" There was a hard set look about Kent's mouth.

"I'd rather not tell you, if you don't mind."

"But I must know. Was I that fiancé?"

"Yes."

"I thought so. And the girl was Evadne Laverock?"

"How did you know?"

"Because that's just the kind of thing she would do. Oh, if only I had never seen her! It's my foolishness that brought this on you. I should have the public shame, not you. Anyway, I should have guarded you against this, by telling you all about her, in the first place, though I didn't realize there was anything much to tell. Not yet, anyway. We had more important things to say. Well, here's the truth in a nutshell. I pretty well lost my head over her last summer, and thought I was in love for a few weeks, though we were never engaged. She had too many lovers, and when I protested she only laughed, and we had a disagreement. When I told her I wished she would stop drinking and swearing and smoking and live a quiet respectable life she got very angry and ran off to Europe for six months with never a word to me, thank God, all that time. By the time she came back I had begun to get my eyes open, and I knew I did not love her and never would. So that's the story. I am not her fiancé and never was, though one night when she looked particularly charming I almost told her I loved her. *Almost,* not quite, for somebody else came along and interrupted, and was I glad afterwards that they did! But oh, I'm ashamed that I ever had anything to do with her. You should have known it at once when I told you of my love, only it didn't seem at all important to me then. I know I never really loved her at all, and I thank God that she's out of my life forever!"

Jane smiled at him.

"Thank you for telling me. I knew it must be something like that or you never would have told me you loved me," she said, giving him a trusting look.

He crushed her hand softly in his.

"I knew you'd be like that," he said. "That's one of the reasons why I love you so. And now, let's forget her for awhile, and then by and by I want you to tell me all about it, where I can be sorry and comfort you in a proper way. I have my car near here and I thought maybe you'd like to take a ride, then we'll have dinner together somewhere. Will you go?"

"Oh, yes!" said Jane. "How lovely!"

So he put her into his car, and they drove out along a sunlit way into the near country, where the long shadows were beginning to fall across road and grass, and the night seemed wide in its preparation for the sunset which was coming soon. At last they drew up before the old Scarlett mansion!

Jane, who had been watching the houses along the other side of the road, suddenly looked up and saw it, recognized its likeness at once and exclaimed in wonder:

"Why, there is a house just like my grandfather's old home! Isn't that wonderful? And why are we stopping here? Do you know the owner?"

"Yes, I know the owner fairly well," said Kent, "though I haven't known her long. But I thought perhaps you would like to look at the house, it seemed so lovely, and so like the picture you showed us of your grandfather's."

"Yes indeed!" said Jane eagerly, not suspecting in the least. "How very nice of her to let us see it. Do you mean we may go inside?"

"Oh, yes. That's what she said."

"But I've just my working clothes on!" protested Jane looking down at herself.

"Oh, that won't matter," said Kent. "She won't be noticing your clothes."

They started up the brick walk and suddenly Jane stopped abruptly, looking off at the little rustic teahouse on the far side of the lawn.

"Oh!" she said excitedly, "it *is* my grandfather's house! It must be! There is the teahouse I remember, and isn't that a swing beyond it? But how could it be? Grandfather's house wasn't anywhere near here, was it? It was in a town called Hawthorne, near some city, I can't remember the name."

Kent was smiling and watching her with delight.

"This is Hawthorne," he said, "or used to be called that until it was incorporated into the city. And this was your grandfather's house, but isn't any more, because now it is yours! That is, if you want to keep it. It was not sold as you supposed. It passed to your Uncle Harold, and he in turn left it to his brother's child, evidently not knowing exactly where you were. The man who wants to buy it has friends living out here and he wants to pull it down and build it over into a modern house. He wants to begin at once!"

"How dreadful!" said Jane. "May I go inside?"

"That is what we came for," said Kent, slipping his arm inside hers and falling into step by her side.

He took out a key and unlocked the door and Jane stepped within the wide beautiful hall of her ancestral home.

An hour later they came slowly down the stairs, after having gone from room to room examining everything, and arrived back in the big living room, Jane sitting down in an old handsome chair opposite an oil painting of her grandmother when she was a bride.

"Oh, it is all so lovely!" she said plaintively. "I wish I could keep it. It is just as it used to be when I was little, and it would be wonderful to have it. But of course I never could."

"But why not?" asked Kent tenderly. "There seems to be no reason in the world why you shouldn't. Just because a man wants to buy it is no reason why you should sell something you want to keep."

"But," she said sadly, her eyes wide and earnest, "it costs a lot of money to keep a house, I've always heard. Just taxes are a big item, I know. I've heard people talk about them. Mrs. Forbes is worried now about the taxes on her little house, and what would this be? Something awful! I could never hope to make money enough to pay even a tithe of the taxes. And there would likely be repairs some day! No, it wouldn't be right for me to keep it!"

"Young lady, have you forgotten," said Kent watching her amusedly, "that you've taken me on for life? Do you count it nothing that I would be your husband, and as that I might naturally be counted on to help you out with your taxes now and then if it ever became necessary?"

"Oh!" she gasped, her cheeks turning pink. "I hadn't thought that far. But, of course, you are a young man and just beginning. It wouldn't be right for you to be hampered by a burden of debt and taxes and things. No, I'm sure it wouldn't be right. I must not be so selfish!"

"Well, bless your heart, you darling unselfish child! There's nothing like that to be in your scheme of things. The inheritance will carry the house many times over. Neither you nor I will have a cent to pay. The house was not all that was left to you in the will. There is quite a large fortune that was left you besides. There will be plenty to cover all expenses the house could make, and not be noticed out of what is left. I did not know until this morning how much it would be. I thought perhaps there was only a few thousand beside the house. But now I know, I am ashamed that I am daring to marry a rich wife. Of course I have a nice little sum put away myself, enough to start on, but not as much as you have. And so, in the face of this knowledge I could not do less than offer to let you off if you want to be let."

Jane looked at him aghast. Then suddenly when she saw the look in his own eyes, the hunger, the longing, the delight in her, she sprang from her chair and dashed across the room.

"Kent!" she cried as her arms went around his neck and she laid her lips on his lips, his forehead, his eyes. "This from you! To think I should have to endure such a ghastly thought twice in one day. First from the

Laverock woman demanding that I give you up, and next from you, suggesting that you don't want me!"

"Jane! Did I say that? Oh Jane, can I ever forgive myself that I let you in for such an awful experience!" His arms were around her now, and his head bowed with shame. But Jane was at peace, with her face nestled in his breast, and his lips on her hair.

"Oh, joy, joy, joy!" she breathed at last when they finally went reluctantly toward the door, in the gathering dusk, his arm still about her. "I never dreamed that there was joy in the world like this! Much less that I should ever have it!"

"Nor I either!" he said tenderly. "I never dreamed there was such a girl in this world as you, not in these days! Oh what a fool I was ever to think I could be satisfied with anything less!"

"And now," said Kent as they started back to the city, "Will you go to a nice quiet hotel somewhere and stay till we get married? Or do you want to go back to that pestiferous rooming house tonight?"

Jane thought for a minute and then she shook her head.

"No. No hotel!" she said decidedly. "I'll go back to the rooming house, for now anyway. I want to lie on the hard little bed and think there is a softer one coming. I want to look around that bare little room and know I've a whole home all beautiful and ready! I've been so used to telling myself my home was over in another world, in my Father's house, that I didn't think I'd ever have any other nice one down here. I thought maybe I could some day get a more comfortable room, when I was older and needed to save myself, but I didn't see how I could get it for a long, long time, if ever. So I'll enjoy anticipating it for a little while before I go anywhere, and get used to the idea before I change. It's been rather a long hard way, and I might not bear such a sudden change."

She laughed as she said it, but Kent looked at her tenderly and said, "You dear!"

Yet as they drew nearer the rooming house he looked up at its looming gloomy windows and sighed.

"I can't bear to think of you in that gloomy place, even for a night. I wish you'd let me take you home to the shore, to mother."

Jane shook her head decidedly.

"Not tonight!" she said. "And not to your mother, yet, either! Oh, I haven't had a chance yet to stop and think what your mother will say, or what your sister will think! I'm not the kind of girl they would want for you!"

"They'll be happy as two clams!" said Kent. "Trust me. Don't I know? And so will dad! I could see he liked you wonderfully well. They'll all be so glad I'm off Evadne for life they won't know how to stop rejoicing. They hated her. But that brings back my shame. I should never have gone with a girl like that, even for a day, and somehow back in my mind, I knew it all the time. I'm so glad God took hold of me and opened my eyes in time. But don't you worry about my family. They like you all right already, and wait till they really know you. They'll take you right into their hearts."

"I don't know," said Jane a little sadly, shaking her head. "They may not have liked Miss Laverock, but you know I'm a still different kind of a girl. You should have a well-educated girl who is used to the ways of the world. Your mother will feel so, I'm sure."

"No, she won't!" said Kent vehemently. "She recognizes your exquisite culture. As for the ways of the world, have you forgotten that you and I are not of this world any more?"

She gave him a sudden bright smile and nestled her hand in his, and he stooped over and kissed her tenderly.

"All right," he said resignedly, "go on up to your desolate little cubby hole if you must for tonight, but believe me I'm going to take you home to mother just as soon as possible. And I'm going right home and tell the folks now so that bugaboo will be out of the way forever, and you won't need to worry any more about your position with them. Good night. I'll see you tomorrow!"

24

"BUT I thought she told me she had no home and never had had one," said Audrey as they were discussing plans for the wedding.

Kent had come home and gathered his family together and broken the news to them that night, his face shining, his eyes full of a glad humility.

"Dad, mother, Audrey," he said standing in their midst and looking around on them, "I'm going to marry Jane, do you mind? I've been an awful fool and driven you nearly crazy, I know, going after the wrong girl, and I'm ashamed as I can be about it. I wish I could go back and wipe it all out somehow, out of your memories and mine, and out of Jane's. But she's terribly sweet and she's forgiven me, and I hope you'll love her. She's worried sick because she's afraid you're going to hate having a button salesgirl for a daughter. But I told her you had lots more sense than she thought you had and I'd tell you about it right away tonight. What do you say, folks, do you like my choice or not?"

"Like it fine, son," said his father heartily. "Ask mother. I guess you'll find she agrees with me."

"I'm sure I shall love her, my dear boy!" said Mrs. Havenner.

"Cheerio!" shouted Audrey gaily. "Hallelujah! I think it's the grandest thing you ever did. And I claim the honor of having discovered her."

"Yes, sister, and that was the grandest thing you ever did! But don't you dare take anyone less fine for yourself."

"All right with me, brother!" grinned Audrey. "I get you. I won't. And maybe I'll let you be a picker for me. You noticed I began to take your advice several days ago!"

And by such devious means had the family come to an early discussion of the wedding, which had scarcely been much discussed between the principle participants, save that Kent had urged that it be soon.

"Because I want to begin to take care of her," he explained to his family when they came to broach the question.

It was then that Kent's mother suggested in her large-heartedness that perhaps Jane would like to be married at their home, or perhaps quietly down at the shore. And Kent had explained that Jane had another plan, she had a place of her own where she thought it was most fitting she should be married, which brought about Audrey's astonished exclamation.

"Well, she hasn't ever had a home, Audrey," explained Kent as if he'd known her history always. "Her father and mother died sometime ago. But this is a place that belonged to her grandfather. It is very old. It has just come into her hands. She has a fancy she would like to be married from it! I think it's right she should have things as she wants them."

"Why, yes, of course," said Kent's mother thoughtfully. "But have you seen it? Is it all right? Of course I don't suppose you'll want a very large assembly, but then we have friends who would be hurt if they weren't invited. You could have the ceremony at our church, I suppose, and then have a little private reception at our house or hers."

"Yes, I've seen it, mother, and it's quite all right. You won't be ashamed. I think we'd better let Jane manage the way she wants to. You can offer anything you wish of course, but don't urge."

Dubiously the mother and daughter turned the matter over together and tried to plan ways they could help Jane out, but Kent went on his way rejoicing.

"We'll want to see her right away, of course," said Kent's mother. "Shall I call her up in the morning and get her to come right down to us?"

"She can't," said Kent grinning. "She can't leave the store right away. She insists she must stay through the month. It's one of the rules of the store that an employee does not leave without at least two weeks' notice, and she's going right on working till we're married."

"Why, how will she have any time to get ready?"

"Oh, she'll get ready afterward," laughed Kent. "You watch."

"But, my dear, of course we'll help her out. I wonder where we ought to begin?"

"Begin by loving her, mother, that's the most important thing. When she's convinced of that everything else will fall into line."

"Why, of course we'll love her! If she only knew how I looked at her in longing that first night she came here, and especially after that other painted girl came, if she could have known how I wished in my heart that it was Jane instead of the other that my boy fancied! Oh, we'll love her all right, Kent. She's our kind."

"Okay, mother, then everything else is all right!" and Kent went off to his bed well satisfied.

Jane went to work blithely all those days between.

Especially was she light-hearted after receiving the two lovely notes of welcome into the family, that Kent brought her the next morning after his talk with them all. He passed through the store quietly like any customer and merely stopped to hand them to her unobtrusively with a low-spoken promise: "See you at the door at five."

Not even sharp-eyed Nellie had noticed, for he had chosen the right moment, when all the others were busy and Jane's customer had just left.

And that night he told her all about the family conclave, and the hearty words of his father.

"But they can't understand why I won't let them give you a wedding at our house," he said with a grin.

"Oh," said Jane, looking troubled, "Why, I wouldn't want to disappoint them, they've been so lovely!" And then she added wistfully, "but it did seem nice to have a house that belonged. It's sort of like having a real family of my own, you know."

"Yes, of course," said Kent with quick sympathy, "I understand. And so will they after they have time to think it over."

"Why can't we take them out to the house pretty soon?" suggested Jane. "If they see it perhaps they will understand why I love it so."

"Of course," said Kent, "only I didn't know but you might want to surprise them at the wedding."

"No," said Jane, "they are family. They have a right to know. And then if they still think it would be better for me to go to them why—it will be all right! They are *my* family now, you know!"

"You dear!" breathed Kent softly. "Well, all right. Suppose we make it tomorrow after closing?"

"Lovely!" said Jane, her eyes sparkling. "I told the gardener's wife to wash the windows, and dust and take off the chair covers. Maybe Audrey would like to help us put up the curtains. Then it will look really livable."

"Of course she will, dear little housewife! I didn't know you were wise to those things."

But Jane only laughed.

"Perhaps you'd better get wise too," she said. "You might do something about getting the gas and electricity turned on."

"I'll attend to that, lady, right away today," he said humbly.

So the Havenner family, including the father, because he utterly refused to be left out of such an important occasion, arrived at the old Scarlett home in state, a few minutes after Jane and Kent got there, on Saturday afternoon.

They stared in wide-eyed amazement at the beautiful old house and grounds, and there was utmost approval and wonder in their eyes as they came up the brick walk to the porch.

"Why, Jane, dear!" said mother Havenner. "Such a wonderful old place! Of course you would want to be married here! How marvelous that you have it!"

Then they went inside.

Jane had had time to put flowers from the garden in most of the rooms, and it looked so homey they all exclaimed.

It was almost like a gathering of the two families, as they sat down in the big living room and looked up at the great oil-paintings while Jane explained who they all were, and then got out the old album which included her mother's wedding pictures.

And while they put up the living room curtains of delicate old yellowed lace, and admired everything, they settled all the plans for the wedding.

It was agreed that it should be a quiet wedding, no fuss and show. Just the dearest, most intimate friends, invited by note or called up on the telephone, and then the Havenners would give a small reception in their city house afterward to introduce their new daughter a trifle more formally to their acquaintances.

"Oh, it's lovely, *lovely,* Jane!" said Audrey, patting the filmy folds of the last curtain. "And how I do *love* my new sister!" and she caught Jane in a warm embrace and whirled her around the room gaily. "What a grand time you and I are going to have! I never supposed my brother would have the sense to pick out such a wonderful girl as you are!"

They would all have spoiled her if Jane hadn't been through so many hard things that she was impervious to spoiling.

And just before they turned out the lights and left for the night Audrey looked around the lovely room and said:

"Say, Jane, this would be a grand place to have a Bible class sometime! I just know Pat would enjoy teaching in a place like this!"

"Wouldn't it?" said Jane with a sparkle in her eyes. Audrey had been to the Thursday night Bible class with them this week and Jane had been longing to know how she liked it. "I have been thinking about that. When we get acquainted with the people around here perhaps we can get a group together. Wouldn't that be wonderful?"

"It certainly would," said Audrey.

As the days went by Jane flitted here and there in the store, picking out a few pretty clothes. The green coat she had wanted so long she could now buy outright, and not have to arrange for it by installments. She made it the basis of her fall outfit. A lovely green wool dress, and another of crepe. A brown wool, a lighter brown silk, some bright blouses, and then a couple of gay prints for morning around the house. How she enjoyed getting them together, and all the little accessories of her modest trousseau, and realizing that she could pay for them and not need to worry lest there wouldn't be enough over to pay her board for another week. Her heart was continually singing at the great things the Lord had done for her.

It was a pretty wedding, no ostentation, no fuss.

There were about fifty guests present, most of them relatives and intimate friends of the Havenner family. A few from the store, Miss Leech, Mr. Windle, Mr. Clark and his little girl, Hilda and the two other girls from the button counter.

Pat Whitney married them, and Audrey was the maid of honor. The rest of the wedding procession they skipped.

Jane wore her mother's wedding dress and veil and looked very sweet and quaint in the rich satin and real lace, a trifle yellowed from the years.

As the bride stood beneath her grandmother's portrait, some people thought they saw a resemblance between the two.

Mr. Havenner went about beaming, almost as if he were getting married himself. Hilda and the two girls from the button counter sat around adoringly and watched their erstwhile co-laborer going about these sweet old rooms, mistress of it all, wife of that "perfectly swell" looking young lawyer. They thought of Jane going untiringly about her work behind the counter, and wondered wistfully if a like change could ever come to them.

And when it was all over, and the wedding supper eaten, the bridal cake cut and distributed, Jane went upstairs throwing down her bouquet straight into the arms of her new sister-in-law, who stood at the foot of the stairs with Pat looking up.

Jane went into the room where she had stayed when she was a little girl visiting in that house so long ago, and changed to her new lovely green suit. Then she and Kent slipped down the back stairs and out through a basement door to Kent's car, which was hidden in a back street. The wedding guests, waiting to see them off with old shoes and rice in the decked-up car that stood before the door, were unaware that they were gone.

As they rounded the corner and caught another glimpse of the lighted windows Jane turned to look.

"It's a dear house," she breathed.

"Yes!" said Kent. "I love it too, you know."

She nestled toward him and slipped her arm inside his.

"I'm glad!" she said softly. And then after a minute added: "It will always make me think of my Heavenly mansion. It seems just as if it was sent me at a time when I had nothing, as a sort of picture-promise of our home in Heaven. It's just a place where God wants us to be happy and work for Him while we are waiting for the Heavenly home."

Then softly she began to sing, and Kent chanted with her, as they drove out into their new life:

> *"Oh Lord, you know,*
> *We have no friend like you,*
> *If Heaven is not our Home,*
> *Oh Lord, what shall we do?*

The angels beckon us
To Heaven's open door,
We can't feel at home
In this world any more."

About the Author

Grace Livingston Hill is well known as one of the most prolific writers of romantic fiction. Her personal life was fraught with joys and sorrows not unlike those experienced by many of her fictional heroines.

Born in Wellsville, New York, Grace nearly died during the first hours of life. But her loving parents and friends turned to God in prayer. She survived miraculously, thus her thankful father named her Grace.

Grace was always close to her father, a Presbyterian minister, and her mother, a published writer. It was from them that she learned the art of storytelling. When Grace was twelve, a close aunt surprised her with a hardbound, illustrated copy of one of Grace's stories. This was the beginning of Grace's journey into being a published author.

In 1892 Grace married Fred Hill, a young minister, and they soon had two lovely young daughters. Then came 1901, a difficult year for Grace—the year when, within months of each other, both her father and husband died. Suddenly Grace had to find a new place to live (her home was owned by the church where her husband had been pastor). It was a struggle for Grace to raise her young daughters alone, but through everything she kept writing. In 1902 she produced *The Angel of His Presence, The Story of a Whim,* and *An Unwilling Guest.* In 1903 her two books *According to the Pattern* and *Because of Stephen* were published.

It wasn't long before Grace was a well-known author, but she wanted to go beyond just entertaining her readers. She soon included the message of God's salvation through Jesus Christ in each of her books. For Grace, the most important thing she did was not write books but share the message of salvation, a message she felt God wanted her to share through the abilities he had given her.

In all, Grace Livingston Hill wrote more than one hundred books, all of which have sold thousands of copies and have touched the lives of readers around the world with their message of "enduring love" and the true way to lasting happiness: a relationship with God through his Son, Jesus Christ.

In an interview shortly before her death, Grace's devotion to her Lord still shone clear. She commented that whatever she had accomplished had been God's doing. She was only his servant, one who had tried to follow his teaching in all her thoughts and writing.

Don't miss these Grace Livingston Hill romance novels!

Mail your order with check or money order for the price of the book(s) plus $2.00 for postage and handling to: **Tyndale Family Products, P.O. Box 448, Wheaton, IL 60189-0448.** Allow 4-6 weeks for delivery. Prices subject to change.

The Grace Livingston Hill romance novels are available at your local bookstore, or you may order by mail (U.S. and territories only). For your convenience, use this page to place your order or write the information on a separate sheet of paper, including the order number for each book.